BARBARIAN BEAST BITCHES OF THE BADLANDS

Also by Carlton Mellick III

Satan Burger
Electric Jesus Corpse
Sunset With a Beard (stories)
Razor Wire Pubic Hair
Teeth and Tongue Landscape
The Steel Breakfast Era
The Baby Jesus Butt Plug
Fishy-fleshed
The Menstruating Mall
Ocean of Lard (with Kevin L. Donihe)
Punk Land
Sex and Death in Television Town
Sea of the Patchwork Cats
The Haunted Vagina
Cancer-cute (Avant Punk Army Exclusive)
War Slut
Sausagey Santa
Ugly Heaven, Beautiful Hell (with Jeffrey Thomas)
Adolf in Wonderland
Ultra Fuckers
Cybernetrix
The Egg Man
Apeshit
The Faggiest Vampire
The Cannibals of Candyland
Warrior Wolf Women of the Wasteland
The Kobold Wizard's Dildo of Enlightenment +2
Zombies and Shit
Crab Town
The Morbidly Obese Ninja

BARBARIAN BEAST BITCHES OF THE BADLANDS

CARLTON MELLICK III

Eraserhead Press
Portland, OR

ERASERHEAD PRESS
205 NE BRYANT
PORTLAND, OR 97211

WWW.ERASERHEADPRESS.COM

ISBN: 1-936383-65-9

Copyright © 2011 by Carlton Mellick III

Cover art copyright © 2011 by Ed Mironiuk
www.edmironiuk.com

Printed in the USA.

AUTHOR'S NOTE

So I was in the Eraserhead office a year and a half ago sitting next to Cameron Pierce, trying to come up with the title for a story I was going to write for a werewolf-themed anthology. I was thinking it would be good to return to the world I created in my werewolf novel *Warrior Wolf Women of the Wasteland*, but I wasn't going to do it unless I could come up with a similar title with a similarly cheesy alliteration. Cameron heard me laughing as I came up with one.

I turned to him and said, "How about *Barbarian Beast Babes of the Badlands?*"

I wasn't serious. It sounded like the title a stupid trashy USA Up All Night kind of T and A sci-fi movie staring softcore porn actresses, something like *Slave Girls from Beyond Infinity* or *Cannibal Women in the Avocado Jungle of Death*. But Cameron turned to me and said, "You *have* to go with that title."

So I decided to go with it. Most of my books usually start out as jokes. *The Faggiest Vampire, Cybernetrix, Zombies and Shit, Kobold Wizard's Dildo of Enlightenment +2*. All of these books were ideas I tossed out to friends as jokes. On every occasion somebody said "You *have* to write that book." And I usually do.

My intention was to write Barbarian Beast Babes of the Badlands in the vein of a comic from Heavy Metal magazine, full of sex and violence and scantily clad warrior women with huge bouncing breasts. It was just supposed to be a fun side story for fans of the Warrior Wolf Women universe. Nothing serious.

But I really got in to writing Barbarian Beast Babes and the short story ended up too long for the anthology. It was a novella. So I decided to write two more novellas and get them published together as a sequel.

Because Barbarian Beast Babes centered on Apple, a background character in Warrior Wolf Women of the Wasteland, I decided all three of the stories would focus on characters I didn't fully explore in the first book.

The second novella in this collection mostly revolves around The Hamburglar, who was one of my favorite characters in Warrior Wolf Women yet wasn't in the book much. I had an idea for a book called *Hamburglar of the Dead* about Hamburglar fighting zombies. This is basically what I decided to do for the second novella, *Horrendous Horror of the Hateful Hamburglar*, though the mutant creatures aren't exactly zombies.

The third novella takes up the bulk of this book. While the other two novellas are prequels to Warrior Wolf Women of the Wasteland, this novella is a direct sequel. It revolves around Hyena, who was one of my favorite minor characters in Warrior Wolf Women. I always regretted not doing anything with her character, so I put her in the foreground.

The three novellas all fit together into one story. Although they take place at three different times and feature different characters, they all revolve around the same conflict.

I decided to call the collection Barbarian Beast *Bitches* of the Badlands instead of Barbarian Beast *Babes* of the Badlands, to differentiate the title of the book with the title of the novella. Plus, I have a real problem with the word *babe*. I don't know why. Maybe it's because only douchebags use the word *babe*. But bitch works for me. A girl who prefers to be called a bitch over being called a babe is the kind of girl I'd rather hang out with.

So here it is. I hope you enjoy my return to the wasteland. If this book is successful I might return to it again with *Pippi of the Apocalypse* and/or *Dog Destroyers of the Deadlands*.

—Carlton Mellick III *6/22/2011*

CONTENTS

BARBARIAN BEAST BABES
OF THE BADLANDS

CHAPTER ONE

The wolf girl held her boyfriend's face in the palm of her hand, gazing into his gentle human eyes, curling her furry ears back into the locks of her licorice-black hair, hoping that he doesn't realize the lower half of his body is missing.

"You're going to become one of them someday," he said, tears running down his cheeks.

He wanted to look away, but the wolf girl's claw dug deep into his chin to keep his head in place. She didn't want him to see his severed legs dangling from the wrecked vehicle beside them; the feet still kicking back and forth like an impatient toddler at the dinner table.

"I'll never be like them," she whimpered. "Those things weren't human at all anymore. I won't allow myself to lose all of my humanity as they did."

Brown gore oozed out of his lips as he said, "But you become more and more like them every day. Every time we have sex you turn more and more into an animal . . ."

The wolf girl put a finger to his bloody mouth and hushed him while flicking away a strip of his intestines with her black fluffy tail.

"It doesn't matter what happens to me," she said, crying. "All I care about is you, Sam. I love you."

She smiled, flashing her long wolf fangs through black lips.

"I'm scared of you . . ." he told her.

Her ears lowered in shame. Then his body went limp in her arms as his eyes rolled into the back of his head. The wolf girl cried into his ripped-open torso, digging her black nose into his guts to snuggle her face within his wet fading warmth.

"I'm not that much of a monster, am I?" she asked his internal organs. "I've hardly turned into a wolf at all." Then she grabbed her tail to stop it from wagging.

The wolf girl stood and wiped her boyfriend's blood from her mini-skirt and frilly corset. She removed her yellow coat and draped it over her boyfriend's face.

"Oh, Sam . . ." she said, her eyes tearing up again.

The vehicles were in pieces all around her. Dead bodies littered the road. Smoke filled the air. She went from vehicle to vehicle, inspecting the large claw and teeth marks in the metal. There wasn't anyone else left alive. Several bodies were missing from the scene of the crash, most likely dragged away by the giant beasts that had attacked them.

The wolf girl didn't know what to do all on her own. She meandered through the smoking wreckage and picked a yellow apple from a fallen tree, where one of the vehicles had crashed. She bit into it and relished the sweet flavor. They didn't have apples like this back in the walled city from where she came. The apples there were pre-packaged and didn't have as much flavor. This yellow apple made her fuzzy ears perk up with joy.

She scratched her round itchy breasts through a mesh tank top. The see-through mesh shirt was worn so that her breasts would be completely visible, in order to seduce her boyfriend into having more sex with her. He was always timid when it came to sex, always worried they were going to get caught. So she always made sure to wear seductive clothing. Unfortunately, when the mesh shirt rubbed against the peach fuzz growing on her chest it caused her breasts to itch. This was problematic to her, because she knew her boyfriend wasn't attracted to her scratching her breasts all the time.

The wolf girl liked to have sex as much as possible, even though the act of having an orgasm was permanently turning her into a werewolf. Sex was the main reason she left the walled city with her boyfriend, since sex in the city was considered an illegal act by the oppressive government. Out in the wasteland, it might be complete chaos and hardship, but at least they could be together and be free to make love whenever they wanted. But she never would have forced them to leave had she known her boyfriend was going to be torn in half by a wolf the size of fifty nu-cows.

She heard the sound of motorcycles roaring down the road toward her and darted behind an overturned van. The engine roars stopped near the wreckage. The wolf girl peeked out from behind the van to see three motorcycles and two metal-plated vehicles armed with heavy machine guns. Six wasteland raiders emerged from the vehicles and went straight for the dead bodies, digging for ammunition and supplies.

"Dirty scavengers," the wolf girl grumbled to herself.

She then noticed that all six of the raiders were women and all of them were even further along in their transformation into beasts than she was. Many of them were coated in hair, with full muzzles and elongated claw-like hands. They wore armor that was a combination of leather clothing and plates of rusted metal taken from old cars. They were armed with shotguns, swords, and axes. The wolf girl squinted her eyes and saw each and every one of them as savage barbarians who wouldn't hesitate killing her if she made her presence known.

"Which way did they go?" one of the raiders said. She was the largest of them and the most wolf-like. She looked to be the alpha of the group.

"North, through the woods," said another wolf woman. This one was hairier than the alpha, but she was very petite. Her body was not that of a warrior. This one seemed to be some kind of engineer. She had a rumbling clockwork helmet on her head and some kind of black metal engine strapped to her back.

Not all of the beast women seemed to be wolves. There was also a rabbit girl, a skunk girl, and a hyena girl. In the walled city, nobody had ever heard of women turning into animals other than werewolves. These women must have been something different, something special.

The wolf girl bit into her apple and examined the hyena girl as she broke from the others and headed toward the overturned van. The hyena was not wearing armor like the other beast women, but she was covered with fur so it wasn't as if she needed to wear any clothes. Perhaps she preferred to travel light.

The wolf girl peeped out from behind the van with the apple sticking out of her mouth like a pig on a platter, examining the hyena girl as she removed food and weapons from the back of the van. Before the wolf girl could duck her head, the hyena looked over and saw her staring back. They locked eyes for a moment.

"Hey, Apple," the hyena girl said. "Come help me with this."

The girl with the apple in her mouth didn't realize it was she who was addressed as Apple. She pointed at herself questioningly.

"Yeah, you," said Hyena.

Apple pulled the fruit from her mouth and came out from behind the vehicle to see that Hyena needed assistance removing a crate from the back of the van. She held the apple in her armpit as she helped pull the crate into the street. Hyena cracked it open to reveal an arsenal of weaponry.

"Now that's what I call loot," Hyena said.

Machine guns, grenades, knives, and handguns. All of them were manufactured in the walled city. It was a great score for these bandits. Apple bit into the apple and nodded her head.

"Here," Hyena said, handing Apple a submachine gun. "You're

going to need this."

"Okay . . ." Apple held the gun like a scorpion by its tail.

"Who's this?" the alpha wolf growled as Hyena and Apple approached.

"Apple," Hyena said, nodding her head.

Hyena didn't think she needed to explain any more than that and walked away to load the new weapons into one of the raider vehicles.

The alpha wolf, the petite wolf in the helmet, and the rabbit girl circled Apple with their weapons aimed at her face.

"Were you part of this caravan?" the alpha wolf asked.

Apple nodded her head.

"Are you the only survivor?" she asked.

"Yeah, those giant wolves attacked us and killed everyone. Even my boyfriend."

"How long ago?"

"About twenty, maybe thirty minutes ago."

"Damn." The alpha kicked a clawed-up car bumper across the street. "They're further ahead than I thought."

The alpha yelled at the other barbarian girls. "Hurry it up, Warriors. We need to pick up the pace if we're ever going to catch up to those rogues."

Then she turned to the young girl. "Apple is it?"

"No, actually . . ." the wolf girl began.

"You're coming with us," the alpha said. "My name is Talon."

The alpha then pointed to the rabbit girl. "That's Bunny." The rabbit girl snarled at her.

Talon then pointed to the petite wolf girl with the engine on her back. "That's Kockwick." Kockwick removed goggles from her face and saluted Apple.

Then she pointed to a scraggly-looking wolf girl with an eyepatch standing over by the vehicles, assisting Hyena. "Wax is over there, and you've already met Hyena next to her."

Talon pointed to the last girl, the one who looked like a skunk, who was across the street just above Apple's dead boyfriend. "That's Skunky, but she prefers to be called Bat Girl."

Skunky jumped up and down, waving excitedly at Apple. Her cartoonishly large breasts bounced like jello as she jumped. "Hiya!" she said. While jumping, the skunk girl stomped clumsily down on Sam's spilled guts and slipped, landing right on his torso, causing gore to explode out of him like a popped balloon.

Apple nearly collapsed at the sight of her boyfriend's guts spraying into the air, but then something caught her by surprise. After Skunky landed on him, Sam moaned loudly. At first Apple thought it was just air being released from his lungs, but he moaned a second time. Then a third.

"What's going on?" Sam cried.

The skunk girl's mouth widened with joy as if she had just found a bag full of candy. She pulled the coat from his face, giggled, then looked up at Talon.

"This one's still alive!" Skunky said.

The others rushed over, Apple leading the pack. When they came to him, he didn't look very alive outside of his moaning. Most of the raiders seemed confused that he was still alive even though he had been cut in half with most of his guts spilled out all over the road.

"Why the fuck is he still alive?" Bunny said.

Talon elbowed the rabbit girl. Apple kneeled down and held her boyfriend's hand. Then looked up at the others.

"Is there anything you can do?" she asked.

The wolf women looked at each other.

"Yeah, we can put him out of his misery," Bunny said.

Talon elbowed her again.

Kockwick kneeled down and examined him. "There might be something I can do," she said. "I need my tools."

"Are you a doctor?" Apple said.

Kockwick looked up at her with her furry smiling face. "No, I'm a mechanic."

While Kockwick tried to fix up the mangled man, Talon took Apple aside so she wouldn't have to see the procedure.

"If anyone can help him, Kockwick can," Talon said.

Apple nodded.

"So is it true what they say?" Apple asked Talon. "Did those giant wolves that attacked our caravan used to be normal women like us?"

"Yes," Talon said. "You're new to the wasteland, so you probably don't know. The more you have orgasms the larger and more wolf-like you'll become. If you don't stop, eventually you'll no longer be human. You'll turn completely into an animal, a great beautiful creature of the wild, and you'll only get larger from there."

"Great beautiful creatures? But those things tried to kill me."

"The pack that attacked your caravan were rogues. Our big sisters have never attacked us in the past. They attack our enemies of the walled city, but they have never attacked us before. We are tracking down this pack to learn why they have developed this violent abnormal behavior. If we can't correct it then we must kill them."

Apple clenched her fists. "If Sam doesn't survive, I'll kill them either way."

"We could use your help," Talon said. "You might not be a warrior yet, but we need all the help we can get. Our hunting party started with fourteen. Now there are only six of us. If you join our tribe and fight with us we'll be seven."

"You want me to join your tribe?"

"Yes."

"Save Sam and I'll join."

Talon nodded her head. "I guess we'll have to wait and see then . . ."

Kockwick did save Sam, but not in the way Apple had imagined. Kockwick was at one time an engineer and inventor in the walled city. She was considered a rare genius, who designed machines that could replace organs and prolong human life. She could also design vehicles that would run on sunlight. Even though she was such an important asset to their society, they didn't make an exception of her after she began having sex illegally. She was exiled, just like all the other deviants.

When Apple saw her boyfriend walking toward her on two mechanical frog-shaped legs, she nearly screamed. She ran to him but was afraid to touch him. His insides were missing and replaced by pumps and gears. The lower half of his body was all machine. A black metal engine similar to the one strapped on Kockwick's back was connected to his waist, rumbling against his belly.

"Hey, look at me," Sam said. "I'm going to be okay."

Apple frowned at him.

"What's wrong?" he asked.

She blinked a couple of times. "You look . . . kind of . . . scary."

"Scary!" he cried. "But I would have died without these changes!"

"Yeah, I know," she said. "Still scary."

There was an awkward moment between them, then it was broken by Talon calling out. "Okay, Warriors, let's move out."

Apple and Sam wandered toward the vehicles. Sam's machine legs made a whir-chunk sound with every step. Whir-chunk, whir-chunk. Whir-chunk, whir-chunk. Apple found the noise irritating and rather creepy.

There were two cars for them to choose from. One was Kockwick's, the other was Skunky's. Both of the vehicles were once small dune-buggies that had been modified with more powerful engines, reinforced with steel plating and heavy artillery. They decided to go for Skunky's vehicle because the skunk girl was waving them over.

"Ride with me!" she said.

But before they could enter the vehicle, Bunny shoved herself between them.

"Where do you think you're going?" Bunny asked. She wasn't looking at both of them, just Sam. "You're not allowed to ride with Bat Girl."

"What?" Apple cried. "But there's more room in this vehicle?"

Bunny turned to Apple. "You can ride in here with Bat, but the Meat rides with the mechanic."

Skunky snuggled against Bunny and kissed her on the neck. "He's not your Meat, Bun-hop. You can't order him around."

The rabbit girl growled at Sam and Apple, but her temper was quickly subdued by the skunk girl's affection as she nuzzled her head against her shoulder. Bunny gave her a quick peck against the cheek, as if embarrassed to give her a real kiss when others were watching, and then got onto one of the motorcycles and revved the engine. Skunky blew her a kiss before she rode on ahead. Apple could tell they were a couple who were very much in love, but judging by their interaction she couldn't tell whether they had been together for several years or only several days.

"Apple, right?" Skunky asked

"Yeah. And you're Bat Girl?"

Skunky's eyes lit up to hear somebody besides Bunny call her Bat Girl. "Yeah! That's right!"

The skunk girl embraced Apple and licked her ear. Then smiled. "Come on!" Skunky said to Apple, big white teeth smiling behind black fur. "You ride with me!"

Apple looked at Sam, then looked back at Skunky. She got into the car without saying a word to her boyfriend. Sam sadly whir-chunked away from them, toward Kockwick's vehicle.

"Don't mind my Bunny," Skunky said to Apple inside of the car. "She doesn't like Meat . . . Er, I mean men. Unless she's eating them . . ." She giggled when she said that, but Apple could tell she wasn't joking. "Most of the Warriors don't like men. They don't have any rights in our tribe and are more like our personal property."

"So Sam is now kind of like my slave?" Apple asked.

"Yep, you own him."

Apple's eyes widened with excitement at the idea.

Wax jumped onto the back of the skunk girl's buggy, standing on the gunner's platform to man the heavy machinegun. Wax was very wolf-like, but she didn't have any hair on her body, not even her head.

Apple quietly asked Skunky what was wrong with Wax, and Skunky told her about how Wax was allergic to her own fur. Her wolf dander caused her to break out in horrible hives, afflicting her with rashes and swelling, her sinuses would clog with thick wolf snot and her eyes burned red. As long as she still had human DNA she would continue to be allergic to herself. Once the wolf DNA took over completely she would be fine, but Wax wasn't ready to lose her humanity. She had decided to shave off all of her hair and burn her skin one patch at a time to create scar tissue where no hair could ever grow again. Skunky explained that it was a horrendous, painful procedure, but it was the only way she could relieve her allergies.

Apple contemplated how ugly it had made the woman, with her scarred flesh and bald wolf features. She looked like some kind of goblin and was perhaps the most horrific person she had ever seen. Yet even with the deformities, Wax seemed to have a gracefulness that the other wolf girls did not possess, as if she had once been a wealthy upper-class dancer with celebrity status back when she lived in the walled city.

When Wax looked down to see Apple staring up at her, she just coldly glared. Apple could see a truly miserable soul behind those pale blue eyes. The soul of somebody who had once had everything and now lived a painful, ugly, cruel existence.

CHAPTER TWO

While the beast women drove their vehicles slowly through the forest, Apple examined Bunny as she led them between the trees.

Bunny's fur was dark brown. She had a short fluffy tail and floppy rabbit ears made of chainmail. Her clothing was sparse; spiked metal plates held together with leather straps.

"How come some of you are transforming into different animals? You're turning into rabbits and hyenas. I thought all women only turned into werewolves. Is Bunny a were-rabbit?"

Skunky laughed with her mouth wide open.

"No!" she said, her breasts jiggling as the car hit bumps in their path. "We're turning into wolves, too."

Apple was confused.

"We just think wolves are boring, so we try to make ourselves look like different kinds of animals through body modification. We want to be unique."

Skunky went on to explain how the wolf girls cut and styled their hair to look like the animals they would have preferred to transform into:

Skunky dyed a white stripe from her forehead down her back, clipped her ears, and added extensions of hair to her tail to make it twice as fluffy.

Hyena tattooed black spots onto her skin below her blonde fur coat, and dyed the hair on her face black, she also clipped her tail and styled it similar to that of a hyena's.

Bunny chopped off most of her tail and puffed out the fur into a fluffy ball. Then she attached floppy chainmail rabbit ears by weaving the chainmail into her natural wolf ears.

"Did it hurt to do all that stuff?" Apple asked.

"Oh, yeah, but it was totally worth it."

Skunky gave her the thumbs-up with her black furry hand.

21

Late in the evening, the Warriors arrived at a camp in the woods. The camp belonged to the enemies of the wolf women, a group who called themselves the Outlanders.

"Be on guard," Talon yelled to Skunky and Apple through the car window. The women armed themselves as they exited their vehicles, leaving Sam in the back seat but taking Apple with them. They stalked into the camp, hunched over, almost on all fours as they crept. They didn't see anybody around. The fire was smoldering, there were three vehicles parked nearby, but not a soul could be seen.

Talon drew two long-handled axes from her back and pulled open a flap on one of the tents. It was empty, except for a trail of blood on the floor leading to a large tear in the back of the tent. It looked as if a body had been dragged away. The blood trail stopped four feet outside the tent.

"Nobody's here," Talon said. "They're either all dead or they ran away."

"Did our big sisters do this?" Skunky asked.

Talon looked around. "Not sure. I can smell them. They've definitely been in the area recently. But there's no sign of an attack."

Hyena came out from behind one of the Outlander vehicles and yelled at Talon, "Over here."

The wolf girls followed Hyena into the woods. She led them to what at first appeared to Apple to be a large fallen tree trunk. But upon closer inspection, and judging by the smell, Apple realized that it was an enormous piece of feces left by one of the giant wolves.

"That's one big poop," Skunky said, pointing at the poop with a long black finger like nobody else had noticed.

Skunky looked at the others to see if anybody else was as excited about the size of the poop as she was, but they paid no attention to her.

"They've definitely been through here," Kockwick said.

Apple noticed something white sticking out of the feces. She leaned in to take a look. Then said, "What's inside of it?"

Talon rubbed away a layer of feces with her bare hand, revealing a human skeleton. Apple jumped back.

"It's a person?" Apple said.

Talon nodded at her.

"But why is it still in one piece?"

"This must be Baal's shit," Talon said. "She's the alpha of the rogue pack. She's big enough to swallow men whole."

"She's that big?"

"Bigger," Talon said. "For Baal, this poor piece of meat was as easy as slurping down a worm. If we continued digging we'd probably find a few more of them in there."

"There's something else in there as well," Kockwick said as they examined the skeleton. Kockwick inserted her gloved hand into the feces and pulled out a long snake-like creature. The thing shrieked and whipped around. It seemed to be made of some kind of metal. Its eyes glowed red.

"What is that?" Apple asked.

The wolf women all stared at it with perplexed expressions.

"No clue," Kockwick said as the creature snapped at her face with piranha-like teeth.

"Do you think these things have something to do with what's causing their strange behavior as of late?"

"Could be . . ." Kockwick said, placing the creature in a bag and twisting it up until the thing could no longer move. "I'll have to examine it better when we're in a safer place. It could just be some kind of strange new parasite."

While they spoke more about the possibilities of what the creature could be, Apple zoned out. She was just overwhelmed by how big the piece of shit was. The skeleton sticking out of it was so small in comparison. It made her feel tiny herself. The mass of feces was more than double the mass of all seven of the wolf girls combined. And they were supposed to be hunting the beast that shit it out? Apple wondered if joining these wolf women was such a good idea.

23

When they emerged from the forest, they encountered a group of armed men standing in the middle of the camp. They looked to be Outlander survivors who had fled from the wolf attack, and were now regrouping. They looked just as surprised to see the wolf girls as they were to see them.

There was a moment where both groups just stared at each other, as if they were both so caught off guard that they had forgotten they were enemy tribes. During this time, Apple noticed that there was something wrong with these men. They were not completely human. They were mutated. Many of the men had multiple limbs. Five arms, three legs. Some of them had enormously large heads that their small bodies could hardly hold upright. Others were coated in sores and blisters.

The pause was broken when Talon leapt off of the ground at them, driving the blade of one of her axes into the skull of the nearest bighead. Then Hyena opened fire on them, shredding two mutants before they could even raise their weapons. The others scattered, running in different directions for cover.

Bunny pulled a long deadly weapon from her back. It was boomerang-shaped, but the blades were like chainsaws. She held it by the handle, which allowed her to grip it safely, and then pulled a chord to rev up the miniature engine inside. There was a smile on her face as she watched the dual blades roar in her hand. Apple could tell that she was somebody who was happiest while she was killing.

As one of the mutants ran away, Bunny tossed the chainsaw boomerang at him. It whirred through the air and then sawed right through the man's midsection, cutting him into two pieces that fell in opposite directions. Then the boomerang curved in the air, decapitating another mutant as he tried climbing into a jeep. The boomerang continued through the air until it returned to Bunny, who caught it by the handle above her head. The blood dripping from the chainsaw blades created a wild sparkle in her eyes.

Apple didn't fire a single shot. She held her submachine gun in her hands, but was too overwhelmed by the battle to get herself to do anything. This mostly came from watching Talon fight, who killed with the precision of a falcon.

Talon was in the middle of a crowd of five men armed with guns. She was only armed with axes, but that's all she needed to tear them apart. She hacked one through the chest, dodged another's bullets, and then decapitated a third. Then she struck one of them in the back of the head and pulled him with the axe handle into the way of gun fire, to act as her human shield. Once the mutant shooter needed to reload, she tossed one of the axes into his face.

And when the last of the mutants came at her, firing, and screaming, she just twisted around to dodge the bullets and knocked his legs out from under him with the back of the axe head. He fell into her arms and she put him in a headlock.

The young mutant immediately gave up, dropped his weapon and began to cry. Talon hushed him, held him gently in her arms to calm him down. Once the man stopped crying, she snapped his neck.

The only mutant left had gotten into one of the vehicles and started it up. He hit the gas and the engine roared into the forest. Kockwick stepped forward and pointed her weapon at the fleeing man. Her weapon looked strange, homemade. It was like a cross between a grenade launcher, a crossbow, and a large telescope. When Kockwick fired, a black, eye-sized ball covered in spikes shot out of the barrel. It was launched up into the air like an arrow and came down on the mutant. The ball stuck into the back of his ribcage and the jeep crashed into a tree. The mutant, still alive, tried to get the spiked ball out of him, but before it could be removed it exploded, taking out the mutant and his vehicle together.

Bunny watched the flames as they rose into the twilit sky. It was so beautiful to her that it inspired her to grab Skunky and kiss her deeply, wrapping her claws around her furry black ass and squeezing hard.

"Now that was fun," Bunny said, but the skunk girl wanted her to stop talking and keep kissing.

25

With the mutants all dead, the wolf women decided to take over their camp for the night. Bunny and Skunky wandered off together for some alone time, Hyena and Wax kept watch along the perimeter of the camp, Sam went to find a tree to use as a bathroom somewhere, and Kockwick sat by the fire examining the metal snake creature which was now docile and weak.

"Is it natural?" Talon asked about the creature. "It looks like somebody constructed it."

Kockwick raised her goggles. "It sure doesn't seem like anybody created this, but I have no idea how it can be natural for an animal to grow a metal exoskeleton."

"Let me know if you figure anything out," Talon said, then she turned to Apple. "Where's your man?"

Apple replied, "Going to the bathroom somewhere."

Talon kneeled down. "If you want to be with us, you'll have to learn to follow the rules of our tribe. For starters, your man isn't allowed to wander by himself."

"He's not?"

"Your man is not an equal to you anymore. You own him. He is more like your pet, so you need to put a leash on him and make sure he doesn't wander."

"Oh . . ." Apple said. "Okay, I guess."

Kockwick said, "Plus, his battery is about to die. Almost any minute."

"Battery?" Apple asked.

"His engine is not as efficient as mine," she said, patting the machine on her back. "It is solar-powered so it really only works well during the day. He has power reserves, but they don't last very long in the dark. He'll survive until morning, but he won't be able to walk for long at night."

"His legs won't work?"

"No, so you might want to go find him before he collapses."

"I don't even know where he went," Apple stood up and looked around. Then charged off into the woods in the most logical direction possible.

"Oh, and don't feed him anything either," Kockwick yelled at her. "His digestive system doesn't function at night."

Apple found her boyfriend collapsed by a tree in the forest. He was moaning, but nobody could hear him until Apple came nearby.

"My machine broke," Sam said.

"It's not broken," Apple said. "It's solar-powered, so it doesn't work at night."

"I won't be able to walk at night ever again?"

She nodded. "Your digestive system doesn't work at night either."

A look of panic crossed Sam's face.

"I wish we never would have left," Sam said.

"All I wanted was to have sex more often . . ." Apple said.

Sam fell in lust with her because he thought she had the most beautiful Asian eyes. Most guys were attracted to plump girls with freckles and red hair, but Sam liked Asian-eyed girls. It was probably due to the fact that they were so rare in the walled city. Apple noticed him looking at her all the time when they were working in the recycling plant. Every chance he got, he just had to see her eyes again. He just couldn't stop himself from looking at her, even when she caught him staring.

She quickly became attracted to him because the guys she found most attractive were the ones who couldn't keep their eyes off of her. The more attracted they were to her, the more attracted she was to them . . . as long as they were not remarkably ugly. She didn't want a man who was going to be her equal, she wanted a man who would look up to her, worship her as a goddess and do everything she wanted him to do.

After they started dating, she realized that it was quite sexually frustrating to be around a man who found her irresistible when it was illegal to have sex without a permit. If you had sex illegally it was easy to prove because a woman's wolf features would begin to show. If this happened it meant banishment.

The first time they had sex, Apple wasn't thinking straight. Her desires were too strong and she just couldn't resist anymore. She seduced him into doing it, convinced him that it was what he wanted to do. As she reached orgasm, her eyes squeezed tightly shut. When she opened them, Sam saw two yellow wolf eyes glowing in the dark at him. The next day, Apple ditched work and stayed at his house. He tried to figure out ways for her to cover up her new wolf features, such as wearing sunglasses or hats that could cover her eyes. But, instead, she convinced him that they should just stay indoors and have more sex.

Eventually, the wolf features were too prominent to cover up. She had a full tail, pointy furry ears, wolf's teeth and lips, the tip of her nose was turning black, and her tongue was getting longer and wider. She convinced Sam that they should voluntarily exile themselves so that they could live in the wasteland and be together. Sam didn't like that idea at all, but Apple had her ways of making him change his mind.

"I never should have let you convince me to leave with you," said the remaining half of Sam as he fingered the hard metal parts of his body.

"Yeah, I don't know. . ." Apple said, lying down on the ground next to him to rub a long-nailed finger across his new body. "I'm glad we left, but I wish you didn't get all mechanical. I just wanted to be able to have sex with you more often. Do you even have a penis anymore?"

"Kockwick was able to re-attach it. I'm not sure if it works though."

"Let me see. . ." Apple opened a small hatch on the lower half of his body. "I hope your penis isn't solar-powered as well. I'd hate

28

to never be able to have sex at night again."

Sam covered the opening of the hatch before she could look into it. "I don't think you should be messing around with it. It was only just reattached."

"Don't worry so much." She pried his fingers away. Although he was larger than Apple, her wolf genes gave her the strength of three men his size, so he couldn't keep her hands away from him.

She reached into the compartment and grabbed his penis, then stroked it until it was erect. It was only able to stick halfway out of the compartment.

"This is going to be problematic," she said.

"No, it's fine," he said. "You shouldn't be having sex anymore anyway. You're already too wolf-like."

"I'm far less wolf-like than all the other girls out there," she said. "I still have a long way to go before I need to stop."

"You need to stop now," he said. "I think you're addicted to sex."

"I'm not addicted," she said. "I don't need to have sex every single day."

"Then let's not have sex today."

"But I want to have sex today."

"See what I mean?"

"But we have to have celebratory sex for finally leaving the walled city," she said, rubbing her hip against him. "And to celebrate you coming back to life after I thought you were dead."

"I don't want to."

This behavior angered Apple. It wasn't the way it used to be. She realized that because of her wolf features, Sam must have been getting less attracted to her. The Asian-eyes that originally attracted him were now yellow and beast-like. He no longer worshipped her like a goddess; she could no longer manipulate him into doing whatever she wanted him to do.

But then she remembered that he was now her property. He had to do whatever she wanted him to do. It was illegal for him to refuse.

Apple continued to stimulate him. It was a tight squeeze fitting her hand inside of the crotch compartment, but she was able to keep him hard.

"I said no," Sam said.

"What are you going to do?" she said. "You don't have any legs anymore. It's not like you can run away."

She smiled. It was supposed to be flirtatious and sexy, but the idea of being helpless was not erotic to Sam. He squirmed on the ground as she stroked the shaft down to the stitches.

"Don't break it off," he said.

Apple took that as an acknowledgement of submission and removed her underwear. She lifted her skirt and squatted down on top of him. The head of his penis slipped inside, but Apple found it incredibly uncomfortable to have his metal frame against her pelvic bone. Not only that, but the engine on his waist made it very difficult for her to move around on top of him.

"I don't like it," he said, his face cringing as if being inside of her was agony.

"Shut up." Apple was frustrated with the bad sex she was having. Not only did it hurt, but it was annoying that his penis wouldn't go inside of her very far and that every time she moved it slipped out and she had to figure out how to get it back in. The last straw came when his penis became flaccid, due to the discomfort, and shrank back into the crotch compartment.

"Damn it," Apple yelled.

She wasn't just pissed that they couldn't have sex, she was pissed that she might never be able to have sex with him ever again. She wondered if it would have just been better had he died on the road back there.

Sam tried to lift himself up, but Apple pushed him back on the ground and then pulled her crotch up his torso until his chin was between her thighs.

"You'll have to use your tongue," she said.

This shocked Sam. They had never had oral sex before, because it was incredibly taboo in the walled city. Since you could only get a permit to have sex for procreation, all other ways of giving a female an orgasm were completely unthinkable.

Before he could say anything, Apple put his face under her skirt and caressed his mouth with her soft vaginal lips until he gave into what she wanted. He opened his mouth and let her inside. Apple could tell he didn't know what to do, because he just kissed it as if the slippery folds were just another mouth. At first she thought it was awkward, but once he got into it his lips and tongue moved deeply and passionately against her. It was a romantic kind of kiss, like the kisses he would give her when they first fell in love.

But once she was getting close to orgasm, Apple could hear him whimpering under her skirt. Her legs were constricting tighter and tighter against the sides of his head. When she came, her thighs squeezed together so hard that it was as if she was trying to pop his skull. Her body changed around him: her thigh muscles flexing, growing against his face; her fur grew thicker on her arms and shoulders; her teeth and claws extended. Then she leaned her forehead against the tree in front of them.

She kept him under her skirt while she regained her breath, holding his mouth closed with her weight. She could tell he didn't find the experience very enjoyable, and she didn't want to hear him complain about it.

Apple carried Sam back to camp. On the way, she ran into Bunny and Skunky. They were in a tree, groping each other, and sniffing each other's necks. From the angle at which they were sitting, Apple could tell that the two wolf girls were watching her as she forced Sam to give her oral sex. Embarrassed by knowing this fact, Apple decided not to make eye contact with them, even though they were watching her, giggling.

"I thought Kockwick told you not to feed him," Bunny said.

Skunky laughed and pulled her girlfriend closer.

Apple kept walking.

When they got back to camp, Apple noticed Kockwick reclined against a rock rubbing her eyes. Talon was resting beside her. The metal creature was now dead, dissected, lying in a pan by the fire.

After putting Sam to bed in one of the less bloody tents, Apple asked, "Did you learn anything about it?"

Kockwick fidgeted with the gears on her helmet. "A little. I don't know if the creature is what has modified the behavior of our big sisters, but I have learned that it was born in salt water. Our big sisters must have been at the coast when they became infected by the creatures, so that's where we're going next."

"The coast?"

"The ocean."

"I've never been to the ocean before," Apple said.

"Neither have any of us."

By the tone of Kockwick's voice, it sounded like she did not like the idea of going to the coast one single bit.

CHAPTER THREE

The wolf girls decided to get out of camp early, once they heard the sound of engines in the forest. Talon could tell they were Outlanders, most likely checking in with their missing party. Based on the trail they had been following, the Warriors concluded that the giant wolves were headed back to the coast. Since they knew this was the case, they had decided to travel by road rather than trekking through the woods. It would take less time and they might even be able to catch up to them.

Apple was riding with Skunky and Wax again, the submachinegun in her lap. Skunky kept giving her a weird look as they drove down the bumpy street. It was almost as if the skunk girl had just realized that she found Apple rather attractive.

"I liked how you treated your man last night," Skunky said. "You really showed him whose property he is."

"Thanks. . ." Apple didn't know what else to say.

"I once owned a man but then he stabbed me and got away."

Apple thought she was joking until she spread her black fur to show off the scar.

Then Skunky said, "Since then I've been off of guys."

"That's why you're with Bunny now?"

Skunky's face lit up. It took her a bit to get the dumb smile off of her face so she could talk about it.

"I love her so much."

"She seems to love you, too."

"She didn't always love me. When we first met, she hated me. She used to pick on me and beat me up."

"Why'd she do that?"

"Because she hates weak people."

Skunky went on to tell Apple about how she fell in love with Bunny. It was the day she was exiled from the walled city and accepted as a member of the Warriors. Skunky was called Aya then. She was hardly a wolf girl, she only had the eyes and teeth. She was a large breasted pretty girl who wasn't used to the harsh, laborious lifestyle of a Warrior. She would stay back with the sick and pregnant women when the tribe went on raids. She would wear dresses and complain about the dirty living conditions.

Bunny, who was known as Malice at the time, teased her mercilessly. The first day they met, Aya was instantly attracted to Malice, even after she called her worthless for not being able to fire a weapon, then tripped her into the mud. From that moment on, Aya wanted to earn her respect. She tried to be one of Talon's motorcycle knights, but failed the test. For failing, Malice held her down and clawed deep gashes into her palms so that she couldn't ride motorcycles anymore. If Aya would have told anyone what she had done, Malice would have been punished, but Aya kept it a secret. She believed the punishment was fair.

Then Aya wanted to impress Malice by capturing a man and keeping him as her property, because Malice had four male slaves and judged the worth of other Warriors by the number of slaves they kept. Although Malice showed her a bit of respect for capturing a man, she quickly took that respect back once the male stabbed Aya in the side and escaped. Malice laughed at her when it happened, not the least bit surprised that she couldn't control her property.

Aya then decided that it was her lack of wolf DNA that caused her to be so weak, so she began giving herself orgasms to become more animalistic and fierce. But all it did was give Malice some extra hair to pull on when she was in a bullying mood.

One day, the mutants attacked their camp. The entire tribe was caught off guard as they slept. The mutants came in with nets and clubs, capturing women and clubbing them unconscious. When Malice ran out of her tent, she slammed into Aya and tripped. Aya tried to help her up, but the fallen wolf girl was pissed off and punched her as hard as she could in the stomach. Aya toppled over, curled up on the ground, watching as Malice ran off into battle.

Revving up her chainsaw boomerang, Malice was in ecstasy for another fight. Although most of the wolf women were shocked to be attacked in the night, Malice was pleasantly surprised. She used her boomerang as a sword and slashed through multi-armed men, decapitating them, cutting off their legs and leaving them crippled on the ground. A disease-skinned mutant flung a net over her, but she just cut through it and sliced him in half.

Then Malice saw the leader of the mutants. He was a tall muscled man with an enormous hamburger-shaped head. He carried a shotgun in each hand, two bullet belts across his chest. When Malice threw her boomerang at him, the mutant leader casually shot it out of the air, knocking it back into the trees. Three nets came down on her from different directions, then five large mutants dropped on her to hold her down. Malice spit and hissed at the mutant leader. He walked away from her, as if she wasn't even worth killing by his hand.

When Aya saw the cruel bully whom she loved being dragged away by the mutant men, she panicked. She couldn't allow Malice to be taken from her life before she was able to prove her worth. Aya picked up a machine gun from a mutant's severed arm and chased after them. Since she knew she was a lousy shot, she decided to get so close to them that there was no way she could possibly miss. She ran up behind them and emptied the rifle into their backs. All five of the men fell before they could turn around.

Tangled in the netting, Malice looked up at her in shock. She had no idea Aya had it in her. She never would have guessed that the woman she bullied so much would risk her life to come to her rescue. Aya smiled at her and Malice found herself smiling back.

Then a mutant on a motorcycle rode by, sweeping Aya up in a net and dragging her away. By that time, Talon had entered the fight and mutants were dropping by the dozens. The mutant leader sounded the retreat and his men quickly fled, taking the women they had captured with them. Although the Warriors were ordered not to follow, Malice didn't care. She had to save the woman who had saved her, mostly so that she could ask her why she had bothered to save her life. She grabbed her boomerang from the trees and ran toward the sound of the motorcycle.

Malice tried revving the boomerang, but the chainsaw mechanism wasn't working. When she got the mutant motorcycle rider in her sights, she tossed it at him. The boomerang hit him hard, but didn't cut him, bouncing off the back of his head. The force was enough to throw him from his bike.

Once on the ground, Malice pounced on top of him, clawing at his face and chest until he rolled over, covering his face with his hands. Then Malice got off of him, picked up the boomerang from where it had landed, and slammed it down into his head repeatedly until she bludgeoned him to death. Then hit him a few more times.

When she pulled Aya—all scrapped and bloody from being dragged through the ground—out of the net, she opened her mouth to ask her why she had saved her life. But before any words could come out, Aya wrapped her arms around her and passionately kissed her open lips.

Malice found herself kissing her back, and at that moment she realized that one of the main reasons she used to pick on Aya so mercilessly was because she was also attracted to her. Before, Malice hated the fact that she was attracted to somebody who was so weak. She didn't realize that bravery and determination was another kind of strength.

From that moment on, they were a couple. They loved each other more intensely than any of the other wolf girls could possibly understand. When they saw Hyena make her modifications to become a hyena, they decided they wanted to do the same. Malice became Bunny, because Aya thought that she should express her cuddly loveable side more. And Aya became Bat Girl, because she thought being a bat would make her seem more fearsome and tough. Unfortunately, her modifications didn't make her look like a bat, they made her look exactly like a skunk. So Bat Girl became Skunky.

And, from that day on, Skunky and Bunny were known throughout the tribe as an inseparable pair.

Ahead of them, coming head-on, five Outlander vehicles barreled toward them. The Warriors, never willing to back down from a fight, charged forward with weapons blazing.

Once they came closer to the attackers, Apple could see that the vehicles were not fully intact. They were ripped apart with claw marks down their hoods. They had missing doors and torn-open roofs. Some trucks were covered in blood; others were smoking and ready to break down.

Talon noticed it, too.

"They're not attacking," she yelled. "They're retreating."

"Retreating from what?" Skunky asked.

The Outlanders fired as they charged forward, as if they were hoping to fire a hole through the pack in order to drive through. Then Apple could see what they were running from: a mammoth red wolf. It was so large that it could barely fit on the road, as large as two semi-trucks side-by-side. It was like a red tidal wave crashing toward them, knocking down trees and crushing asphalt as it went.

"That's her," Skunky said. "That's Baal."

The beast had flaming red eyes and teeth as large as people. It had squirming silver hairs standing up along its back as it ran. The wolf snagged one of the Outlander's vehicles, thrashed it around in its mouth like a chew-toy, tossed it over its head, and then continued on after the next one.

"Into the forest," Talon yelled.

The three motorcycles roared off into the woods. Skunky was about to follow them until she noticed the bullets shattering Kockwick's windshield and piercing her torso. Kockwick's head fell to the steering wheel, landing on the horn. The horn blared as Skunky looked into the safety of the woods, then back at Kockwick's vehicle.

On the roof, Wax continued firing at all the vehicles getting closer and closer to them. Apple saw Sam's face in the next dune-buggy, staring at her with a look of panic as he tried to revive Kockwick. The mechanic was still alive, her head rolling against her shoulders, just barely conscious.

"Do something," Apple yelled at Skunky.

"Get us the hell out of here!" Wax yelled down at them, trying to do the best she could to take out the oncoming vehicles.

Skunky looked back to the woods one more time before she decided to help Kockwick. She slammed on the gas and rammed the back of her dune buggy into the front of the other. She held the gas down, slowly shoving the other car off the road. The oncoming vehicles were getting closer. Apple heard a yelp from above as a bullet pierced Wax's shoulder. The vehicles came closer. Blood leaked down the front windshield from the gunner's seat, but Wax kept on firing.

Only a few yards away from impact, Skunky drove both buggies into the dirt. The Outlander vehicles passed, missing them by mere inches. Then Baal passed them. The great red beast encompassed their entire field of vision as it went by. It was so large that all Apple could really make out was a furry mass with car-sized paws. Both Skunky and Apple held their breath as it passed by. It didn't stop for them, continuing after the larger, more appealing meal.

Apple looked off the side of the road and realized they had just nearly backed both dune buggies over a cliff.

"Oh crap," Apple said. "You nearly killed us."

Skunky's mouth dropped wide open as she looked at the steepness of the hill. "Yeah, that would have been bad!"

Then she looked at Apple and laughed with a wide open

mouth. "Instead of saving Kockwick and your boyfriend I would have pushed them off a cliff!" Skunky laughed even harder.

As she laughed, Apple looked through the window over the skunk girl's shoulder. A large black figure was speeding toward them. Skunky stopped laughing when she saw the fear in Apple's eyes. By the time she turned around, it was too late. A large black beta wolf rammed into Skunky's vehicle, knocking it away from the other car, right over the side of the cliff.

The dune buggy rolled down the hill, end over end. Wax held tightly to her weapon, but was crushed beneath the back bumper. Her lifeless body was hooked through the handles of the heavy machinegun, tossing her around like a rag doll as the car tumbled to the bottom of the hill.

They landed upside-down against the side of a tree. Apple hit her head hard, but was quickly awakened by Skunky.

"You okay? You okay?" Skunky said.

Apple nodded.

"We're still alive," the skunk girl said. "We're going to be fine."

Then the black wolf skulked down the hill toward them. When Skunky saw the wolf, she froze.

"Don't move," she whispered.

As the wolf arrived, it sniffed at the vehicle. Neither Apple nor Skunky moved or made a sound. They noticed something very wrong with the creature. It had long wires sticking straight out of its face, whipping around like they were full of electricity. The wires were the same creatures as the snake that was pulled out of the feces, only the heads were buried inside of the beast's flesh like long metal ticks.

The monstrous wolf continued to sniff the overturned dune buggy, but it wasn't the blood of Apple or Skunky that it smelled. It was Wax's blood.

The wolf followed the trail of blood away from the vehicle until it found Wax's body six yards away. Apple watched as the wolf stepped onto the corpse and then bit into it, ripping the upper torso into its mouth. The muscled flesh was flexible, and stretched like jerky.

"Okay, let's get out and sneak away very slowly," Skunky whispered.

Apple crawled out of the wrecked car first, sticking close to the ground. Skunky came out second, her automatic rifle getting caught on the door for moment until Apple helped her out. Once they got to their feet, the black wolf looked back at them, one of Wax's severed legs dangled from its mouth.

Both of the women opened fire on the wolf. Apple couldn't keep her gun steady as she fired, spreading the bullets everywhere else but on her target.

"Separate," Skunky yelled. "Run!"

Apple ran back up the hill where they came from. Skunky didn't go anywhere. She held her ground, firing her AK-47 at the beast as it charged toward her. As Apple continued up, she was passed by Talon and Bunny roaring down the hill on their motorcycles. Apple stopped running and turned around.

As the beast charged her, Skunky fired at it until the very last moment. Then she turned to run away. Bunny skid her bike to a halt as she saw the wolf coming down on her lover.

"No!" Bunny yelled, as she revved up her chainsaw boomerang.

Skunky looked back at Bunny. Their eyes met. The skunk girl just stared at the woman she loved for one last moment as the black beast chomped down into her.

Bunny screamed as she saw her girlfriend thrashing inside of the wolf's mouth. Talon jumped from her bike and ran toward the beast with her axes raised. Impaled on one of its fangs, Skunky cried out for help, blood gushing from black fur.

Bunny threw the chainsaw boomerang into the air as the skunk girl slid down the wolf's throat. The chainsaw blade grazed one of its eyeballs and severed an ear. Just before Talon could leap at the wolf's legs, it ran away, whimpering. Bunny caught her boomerang as it returned, then roared forward on her motorcycle.

"Wait," Talon yelled at Bunny, as she ran back for her own motorcycle.

Apple jumped on the back of Talon's bike, and together they chased after Bunny and the wolf. They flew through the forest, dodging trees, going as fast as they could. Ahead, they saw the black mass running through the woods, with Bunny following close behind. The enraged wolf girl was screaming at the wolf, tossing her boomerang at it, missing, catching it, and then throwing it again.

"Fire," Talon yelled at Apple.

Apple aimed her sub-machinegun over Talon's shoulder and fired at the wolf. The bullets sprayed in the wrong direction.

"We're going to have to teach you how to actually shoot that thing," Talon said.

Apple didn't bother using the gun after that.

Bunny went up a slope in the grass and hit a jump. In midair, she was level with the beast's face. She just had to toss her boomerang sideways for the chainsaw blades to slice right through its skull. The beast went down.

When Apple and Talon arrived, they found Bunny frantically cutting open the beast's belly with one side of the chainsaw blade.

"Batty?" she yelled at its stomach. "Bat Girl?"

When the stomach contents emptied onto the forest floor, Bunny tossed her boomerang and dove into its foul-smelling guts.

"Bunny," Talon yelled, worried about the state of her hysterical soldier. "Cut it out."

The rabbit girl pulled a wet black body out of the opened belly and cradled it in her arms. Apple couldn't tell if she had been chewed to death or suffocated in the creature's stomach, but the skunk girl was dead.

Bunny however couldn't accept that fact. She cradled her lover's body in her arms. "It'll be okay, Bat Girl," Bunny cried. "Your Bun-hop is here. I saved you again, just like the time you saved me."

Then the rabbit girl bawled. She cried louder than Apple had ever heard anyone cry. Seeing such a strong, tough woman as Bunny cry like that was something Apple would not have expected.

"Bunny, get out of there," Talon said.

Then Talon saw metal worms slithering through the guts toward the rabbit girl.

"Bunny," Talon screamed. "Get out of there!"

But it was too late, the worms darted out of the muck and bit into Bunny. The rabbit girl jumped to her feet, screaming, still holding Skunky's body as if trying to also protect it from the creatures. The worms burrowed beneath Bunny's skin, a dozen wiry snakes whipping through the air like a dozen kite tails.

Talon hacked through the metal worms with her axes, then dropped the weapons and began ripping them out with her bare hands. Some of them had gotten most of their bodies inside of her, but Talon managed to pull them all the way out.

She took Bunny away from the dead wolf, not sure if she had gotten them all.

"Are you okay?" Talon said.

Bunny was obviously not okay. She was weak. She couldn't even hold Skunky's body up anymore and let it go, plopping in the mud next to her.

"They injected me with something . . . some kind of poison," Bunny said.

Then Bunny fell into Talon's arms and the alpha wolf lifted her off of the ground. She left Skunky's corpse where it lay.

"Let's get her back to the others," Talon told Apple.

Apple nodded her head.

CHAPTER FOUR

They met up with the others and set up a camp further down the road, in the woods. They knew the other wolves were in the area, probably relaxing somewhere after eating a meal of mutant men, so they didn't plan to stay long. Just long enough to check on the conditions of Bunny and Kockwick. Plus, they knew the coast wasn't very far away and they wanted to get there long before dark.

Bunny was shivering and coated with so much sweat that her fur was flat to her muscles. She was still crying, her face buried in her hands.

Kockwick had lost so much blood that it didn't look like it was possible for her to pull through. Talon was at her side, inspecting her wounds. Talon wasn't the best at first aid, but she knew enough to stop the bleeding.

"I'm not worried about those," Kockwick said, her voice rough. "What I'm worried about is my life support."

Talon looked at the engine on Kockwick's back. It was making an odd rumbling noise. The bullets that had hit Kockwick passed through her body and pierced the machine on her back. If the machine were to break down, she would die. It wasn't functioning at full capacity anymore.

"Can you repair it?" Talon asked.

"I would need to use my spare to fix it," she said. "Unfortunately, I gave my spare to the boy over there."

They looked at Sam.

"If I removed it I'd kill him."

Apple and Sam looked at each other, then back at Talon. Talon looked at them, as if debating what should be done. They all lowered their eyes, contemplating their situation.

"What's to think about?" Bunny said through her fingers, a delirious voice. "Trading the life of a crippled piece of meat for one of our most essential sisters? It's an easy decision."

Kockwick shook her head. "No, I couldn't do that." She pointed at Apple and Sam. "Look at them. They're in love. I can't take that away."

"Warriors can't love Meat," Bunny said. "They are just for using and throwing away. The only true love is the love between two sisters."

Bunny started crying again.

Talon looked back at Kockwick. "It's your call. If you want me to take his life to save yours I will, but if you don't, I'll respect your decision."

"I don't," Kockwick said.

"Bullshit." Bunny pulled a handgun from the holster on her thigh. "I'll kill him myself. Then you won't have a choice but to use his machine."

Before she could aim it at Sam's head, Talon brought the back of an axe head down on her hand, slamming the gun into the dirt.

"Bunny, it's not your call," Talon said.

Bunny looked up at her leader, her eyes red and wet, shaking her head. "I'm really messed up, Talon."

Apple couldn't tell if she meant the poison in her system had messed her up, or if it was Skunky's death, or both.

"I can hear a voice in my head." Bunny poked at her temple. "It hurts when I try to block it out."

Talon kneeled down, recognizing Bunny's condition was worse than she thought.

"What is it saying?" Talon asked.

"Not exactly words," Bunny explained. "More like emotional sensations, attacking my brain."

"Relax, Bunny," Talon said. "You're just in shock."

"It could be some kind of mind control," Kockwick said.

Bunny began to cry again, covering her face. "It's trying to make me forget my Bat Girl, my Skunky. Don't let it take my precious little skunk girl away."

Hyena, standing on the other side of her motorcycle, shook

her head at the condition of her two wounded sisters. She motioned to Talon to follow her away from the group. When Talon went to her, they didn't walk far enough away to prevent Apple from hearing.

"What are we going to do?" Hyena asked Talon. "I don't think we have a chance of pulling this off with just the two of us."

"Not two." Talon looked over at Apple. "Three."

"She's not going to be of any use," Hyena said.

"You have to have faith in your sisters," Talon said.

"You know me," Hyena told Talon. "I never do." Then Hyena walked away.

Apple noticed Kockwick was watching her as she eavesdropped on Hyena's conversation.

"Pay no attention to Hyena," Kockwick said. "She's a lone wolf. . . I mean lone hyena." Kockwick chuckled a little until she gagged on the blood in her lungs.

"Kind of like Bunny?" Apple asked.

Kockwick looked over at the rabbit girl, who was so wrapped up in her tears that she didn't know they were talking about her.

"Bunny's no lone wolf," Kockwick said. "She's a gamma wolf who needs a lot of attention. She might act like a toughy, but she's actually the most sensitive of us all."

Bunny stood up and staggered drunkenly to the woods, then began wildly slashing at the bark of a tree with her claws. When she was done, she howled angrily at the sun.

"Just don't get on her bad side," Kockwick said. "People that sensitive are easy to piss off, and slow to forgive."

Bunny jumped to attention as a red blur flew through the camp. Her eyes were wild with lust at the sight of it. Another brown blur came through the camp, a giant wolf running past them at top speed.

"That's them," Talon yelled.

A third wolf with blonde hair came through the camp and snatched Sam up with its jaws as it raced through. Apple's face dropped with shock as she saw her boyfriend dangling out of the creature's mouth. He grabbed tightly to its nostrils to keep from being sucked further into its maw.

"After him," Talon said to Hyena and Bunny, who hopped onto their bikes and took off after the blonde wolf. Bunny was moving much slower than Hyena, her head wobbled as she rode through the trees.

"Help me get her in," Talon said to Apple, as she lifted Kockwick to her feet. Apple looked around in a panic as she helped carry the wounded woman into the remaining buggy. She couldn't believe what had happened.

"Who's driving?" Apple asked.

"You are," Talon said, tossing her the keys.

Apple looked down at them as if they were something from another planet. But before she could protest, Talon was on her motorcycle heading after Hyena.

Apple took the wheel and breathed a deep breath before starting up the engine.

"I really don't have much time left," Kockwick told Apple, loading her homemade launching weapon. "Get me close enough to that blonde wolf and I'll be able to save your boyfriend before I die. I didn't choose his life over my own for nothing."

Apple nodded her head, confident that they could save her boyfriend . . . if only she knew how to drive. Once she figured out all of the controls, she floored it. They raced through the woods, avoiding trees and rocks. Apple hit a jump and the buggy flew through the air over a ditch.

"Have you ever driven one of these before?" Kockwick asked.

"No, never. Am I doing it okay?"

"Well," Kockwick tried to smile. "You haven't killed us yet. That's a good sign."

Apple caught up to the others, trailing closely behind the blonde wolf. Sam was still alive in its mouth, his lower metal frame preventing the creature's jaws from biting through him. He was assaulted by a dozen metal worms curling out of the beast's muzzle at him like electric whiskers.

Hyena fired into the wolf's backside, but that only made it run faster. Bunny was too focused on keeping herself on her motorcycle to even contemplate an attack. Ahead, the other two wolves in the pack could be seen. Apple knew if they turned around to assist their blonde sister, she would never be able to rescue Sam.

Apple looked in her rearview mirror to see another brown blur behind the buggy.

"How many wolves are in this pack?" Apple asked Kockwick.

"Six, originally, including Baal and the two we killed."

"So that's four left?"

"Yeah."

"Okay, because I think I've found the fourth. Behind us."

Kockwick turned her head and then turned back calmly. "Well, whatever you do, don't slow down."

Apple ran over a large rock with one tire, tossing the vehicle to one side for a moment.

"Or crash into anything . . ." Kockwick continued.

Ahead of them, Bunny was beginning to act funny on her motorcycle. Her body was jerking and spasming. Then three tendrils emerged from her shoulders, long metal worms whipping through the wind.

"What's happening to her?" Apple asked.

"She's infected," Kockwick said. "Like our big sisters."

Bunny straightened her body as if she had just snapped out of the delirium, her body went stiff and she rode in a perfectly straight line. She sped up, flying past the blonde wolf toward the alpha, Baal. Talon and Hyena both could tell what was wrong with her. They sped past the blonde wolf to catch up with Bunny, leaving Apple to save her boyfriend by herself.

"It's just up to us now," Kockwick said.

47

When they got up alongside the blonde wolf, Apple found Sam still alive in its jaws. He was in shock, looking at her with a frozen gaze of terror. For some reason, he waved at Apple. For some reason, she waved back.

"I'll get him," Kockwick said.

She pointed her launcher out of the window and fired a spiky black ball at the creature. Blood splashed into blonde fur, as the ball stuck into its neck. There were three beeps, then the ball exploded.

The wolf's entire neck burst into hundreds of tiny bloody chunks, launching its head through the air. The giant blonde head rolled in circles, then landed on top of Apple's dune buggy.

Apple continued to drive, now with a giant wolf head on her roof, which contained her struggling boyfriend within its jaws. The brown wolf behind them was gaining ground due to the extra weight, but Apple didn't know what else to do but to keep going with the head on her roof.

Ahead, Hyena and Talon continued chasing after Bunny. As they passed one of the brown wolves, Talon pulled out one of her axes and hacked through the tendon on the back of its ankle. The beast fell to the ground. Without the tendon, it could no longer walk on that leg. The thing attempted to continue on, but could hardly move. When Kockwick zoomed past, she had her launcher pointed at its face but she didn't fire.

"Why didn't you kill it?" Apple asked.

Kockwick looked back at her. "Because she's one of us. We only kill them if it's absolutely necessary."

Apple nodded her head and continued on her path.

The chase ended up back on the highway and then continued for another twenty miles, but not even Talon could catch up to Bunny or the alpha wolf, Baal. Then they came to the end of the highway and hit another forest. And on the other side of the forest, was the coast.

Hyena and Talon stopped as they hit the edge of the beach. Apple slammed on the brakes just in time to avoid smashing into them. The giant wolf in the back did not attack, but instead leapt over the vehicles to catch up with its leader.

Apple's eyes widened at the sight of the vast ocean. She had heard of it before, and had seen a couple pictures, but she had no idea it would look like this. The sight overwhelmed her and made her heart sink in her chest.

Talon and the other wolf girls did not seem overwhelmed by encountering the ocean for the first time. They seemed more focused on Bunny, who was riding her motorcycle on the beach alongside the giant wolves.

"She joined their pack," Hyena said to Talon.

Talon's eyes were locked on her lost soldier.

"Not if I can help it," she said.

Sam cried out on the roof of the dune buggy, still caught in the creature's death grip jaws. Apple left the dune buggy and pried the beast's mouth open. Her boyfriend slipped out, covered in blood and thick saliva. His eyes were wide and quivering, distressed over the situation. Once he got to his mechanical feet, he walked away from them toward the forest.

"Where are you going?" Apple cried.

"Away from you," he said.

She followed after him.

"What's the matter?" she asked. "You're okay now."

"Okay?" Sam said. He pointed at his metal legs. "Does this look okay? I only have half of a body now and a mechanical lower half that only works when the sun is out. And then I was nearly eaten by a giant wolf. Again. And my girlfriend now treats me like her personal property. How could I possibly be okay?"

Apple moved in closer to him but he stepped away.

"I don't want to be with you anymore," he said.

"Why?" Apple's face was now becoming distressed.

"I was in that thing's mouth," he said. "It could have eaten me like a bite of cheeseburger."

"But you're okay."

"You're not getting it. That thing used to be a human, just like you. Some day you are going to be like that. You're going to be a monster."

"But, Sam . . ."

"You're addicted to sex," he said. "You're going to be one of them in no time. And now that you think I'm your property, you think you can have sex with me any time you want. How long will it be before you grow into one of them? A year? A month? A week? I bet it would be much sooner than you're thinking. And I don't want to be a part of it."

Sam whir-chunked madly away from her.

"But Sam, I love you . . ."

He continued walking until he disappeared into the trees.

"I order you to come back," she yelled.

He kept going.

Talon came up behind Apple, and put her arm around her neck.

"Let him go," Talon said. "It would never work out between you anyway. Just let him go."

Apple looked down at her long black claws.

"Come on," Talon said. "We need your help. I think we've figured out your place in the tribe."

"Oh yeah?" Apple asked.

"You're not a gunner," she said. "You're a driver."

CHAPTER FIVE

The plan was: Talon and Hyena would go around through the woods and get ahead of them further down the shore, while Kockwick and Apple would follow behind at a distance. It was important to get on both sides of the rogue pack, so that Bunny couldn't get away.

"Whatever you do, don't let her get past you," Talon said, as if Apple's life—in addition to Bunny's—depended on it.

Apple watched as Hyena and Talon sped off through the forest. She bent down to the window, and said to Kockwick, "It's just you and me, now."

But Kockwick wasn't moving. Her engine no longer made that funny sound, or any sound at all. Her eyes were open, as if she were staring far into the distance, but she was no longer alive. Apple would have to do this all on her own.

She drove down the beach, far behind the wolves, Kockwick's body lying by her side for the illusion of support, the blonde wolf head still on the roof. If the wolves were to turn on her she would have no way of defending herself without a gunner.

"If only I had Sam with me," she said, squeezing the steering wheel, angry at herself for treating him so badly.

Apple couldn't see Hyena and Talon anywhere up ahead. She began to wonder if something had happened to them in the woods, maybe they were attacked and killed by more rogue wolves. Perhaps she was the only one of them left, stalking behind these great beasts for no reason other than to get herself killed. Either way, she pushed on. She had to try to help Bunny, even though she was a bitch to Sam, because Talon wanted her to.

The wolves ahead stopped at the shore, looking out to sea. They sat like obedient dogs; the red alpha wolf, the black gamma wolf, and the brown rabbit wolf girl sitting on her motorcycle. Apple still couldn't see Hyena and Talon anywhere. She looked in the forest and on the other side of the beach, but they weren't there.

The tide went out as a large black mass emerged from the sea. It crawled onto the beach with large shiny tentacles. The thing was a colossus, some kind of black octopus creature that was as large as an apartment building. It had eight eyes, six horns, and a goopy snail-like mouth. White waves crashed against its massive frame. It roared salt water into the air, glaring at the wolves bowing before it.

The creature rolled open its large mouth and presented it to its followers, a dark toothless cave of foul-smelling mucus and rot. The wolves got to their feet and stepped forward, toward the creature's mouth. One at a time, they voluntarily climbed within the beast's open maw. With each one, the creature oozed its greasy lips around the wolf, slurping its furry body, then all eight of its eyes would close for a satisfying gulp.

Apple could see Bunny was coming up next. She had to do something to stop the creature from swallowing her. Without considering a game plan, Apple took the launcher from Kockwick's hand and hit the gas. She zoomed down the beach toward Bunny, sand spraying into the air.

The creature turned its attention from Bunny to Apple. Tentacles whipped out of the water and slammed down at the dune buggy, but Apple swerved to avoid them, spinning in the sand. She pointed the gun out of the driver's side window and pulled the trigger, launching a spiky black ball at the tentacles. The ball missed and hit the sand, but upon explosion the creature's tentacles were blown backwards away from her path. Apple took the opening, speeding toward Bunny.

A tentacle with a sharp metal tip pierced through the side of the dune buggy, lifted it off the ground, then coiled it up like a snake. Crushing metal sounds reverberated around her as the tentacle constricted the vehicle. Apple draped the launcher over her shoulder and crawled out of the window. She jumped just in time, before the vehicle was pulled beneath the waves.

The beast's mouth opened up again for Bunny. The rabbit girl stepped forward, wiry snakes squirming out of her head like a medusa. Apple ran at her, ready to launch another exploding ball right into its mouth. But before she could get there, Talon came flying down the beach straight at Bunny. Her motorcycle screaming at top speed. With one axe, Talon hacked open one of the beast's eyeballs, with the other she hooked Bunny by her gun strap, knocking her off her feet, and dragging her across the sand to safety.

The colossus widened its black hole mouth and roared, spraying globs of mucus across the beach. Apple realized she was now the closest thing to the creature, close enough to be covered in foul-smelling chunks of goo. At first, Apple thought it was going to scoop her up with a tentacle to eat her. Then she thought it was going to spray metal worms at her, to infect her with the mind control parasites. But, instead, the creature puked a massive pile of rotten stench onto the beach. A giant mound of wet meat. Apple wondered what the heck had just happened, why did the creature puke. Then she noticed movement within the pile . . .

Half-digested wolves uncoiled themselves, and stood out of the creature's vomit. Their bodies crawled with metal worms. Much of their flesh was melted off, some revealing their skeletons or internal tissue. Apple wondered how they were still alive, how were they able to move with so much flesh lost. But then she realized it was the worms that kept them alive. Every animal that the colossus swallowed was kept alive through the entire digestion process, obediently lying in the stomach sack allowing itself to digest.

After several wolves emerged from the puke—dozens more than the rogue wolf pack—Apple also saw mutant men standing out of it, as well as other forest creatures such as deer and bears, all in different stages of digestion. Completely under the tentacled creature's control, the army marched forward. Then they attacked.

Apple launched spiked balls at the mob as they charged her, blowing their liquid guts and skeletal frames across the sand. But they kept coming. She turned to run, but the giant wolves seemed even faster with their lightened bodies. They closed the gap between them within seconds.

Hyena raced out of the woods on her bike, with other wormed

creatures chasing after her. These wormed creatures were not like the digested ones. They were another group of infected animals that were on their way to the beach to feed the colossus, when their parasites gave them orders to attack. With armies on both sides, Apple didn't know where else to run but toward Hyena.

The hyena girl had a severed antler of a worm-controlled deer sticking out of her arm. There were bloody claw marks across her face and chest. She had been battling them in the woods, holding them back to give Talon and Apple time to save Bunny. Hyena must have realized that now Apple was the one in need of saving.

Before an orange slime-covered wolf skeleton could bite down into Apple, Hyena scooped her up onto the back of her bike and rode off down the beach. The creatures closed in on them, racing beside them along the water and the forest, biting at their heels.

The chainsaw boomerang whizzed over their heads, cutting through a wolf at their rear. The boomerang killed some infected mutant men on its return to Bunny's hand. At first, Apple thought Bunny was trying to help them, but then she saw the metal worms squirming all over her body like she was an angry porcupine. She could tell Bunny was trying to kill them.

Talon was heading in the opposite direction of Bunny, heading straight for the colossus. She weaved in and out of the wolves, decapitating skeletal men when she passed them. Once she got close enough, the tentacles of the colossus attacked her, whipping through the air like curly swords. Talon stood up on her bike, heading straight at the colossus' face. She cut through tentacles as they whipped at her, ducking under the ones that tried to swipe her off the bike.

Two tentacles tangled together through the wheels of the motorcycle, flinging Talon into the air. But Talon used the propulsion to glide through the wind at the creature, both axes high over her head. The blades sunk deep into the creature's forehead. The colossus let out a quick shriek, then it tried to thrash the wolf girl off. When that failed, it used its tentacles to grab at her, but Talon chopped them back. She blocked some of the attacking tentacles, and hacked others wide open.

Apple turned away from Talon to see Bunny tossing the boomerang again. Hyena ducked, but it nicked Apple's forearm. Furious at the bunny bitch, Apple pointed the launcher at her and shot off a spiky grenade in her direction, but just as it was firing Hyena knocked the weapon upward.

"Don't kill her!" Hyena cried.

The black grenade hit a nearby wolf instead, but as the beast exploded the force was enough to knock down the infected rabbit girl in the process. While on the ground, Bunny wasn't able to catch the boomerang when it returned and the weapon flew further up the beach until it crashed into the sand a hundred yards away. Apple sighed with relief knowing that the rabbit girl was no longer armed.

Apple looked back at Talon. The wolf woman was hacking into the brain of the colossus with both axes, one after another, as rapidly as a jackhammer. When a tentacle came in, Talon

would hack at it. Three severed tentacles lay on the beach below them. Once she hacked down into the brain, the colossus roared and lunged backward into the water. Talon continued hacking at the brain, trying to kill it, but the creature's brain was massive and could take a lot more damage.

Apple saw Talon hacking and hacking at it as the beast descended into the water, bringing Talon down with it. But even after she went under, Talon didn't stop swinging her axes.

Apple was thrown from the motorcycle, her weapon dropped to the ground, as one of the wolves caught up to them. For a split second, she thought the wolf had slammed into her with its muzzle, knocking her off, but then she felt a wet tongue against her belly and noticed that she was suspended in midair. The wolf had her in its teeth, carrying her by the midsection. Apple screamed as the thing ran away with her in its mouth. She watched Hyena looking back, but there was no way her wolf sister could turn around to help. The skeletal beast went in the opposite direction of Hyena, against the pack.

Although the colossus was mostly submerged, many of its tentacles were above water. In the way that the tentacles thrashed and whipped through the waves, Apple could tell that Talon was still alive beneath the surface, attacking the beast with her breath held tight. The water filled with black and red, changing the color of the waves crashing on the beach to an inky red wine-like hue.

Apple tried to push herself out of the creature's rotten mouth with her free arms. Green goo oozed out onto her body as she struggled. She couldn't push herself free. The more she resisted, the tighter the beast's grip became. Metal worms slid out of its nose, and out of the side of its muzzle. They sprang at Apple, biting into her flesh. She pulled them off of her as fast as she could, trying to get them out before they burrowed into her skin. But there were a few she couldn't reach near her stomach, blocked by the wolf's teeth, that she could feel crawling into her body. She cried out as they squirmed inside of her, feeling their toxins released into her flesh.

Then she hit the ground. The beast tumbled over a dead bear, releasing her from its mouth. Apple rolled across the sand, and looked back at the beast. It was dead. The metal worms dropped from her body. She pulled out the ones that had gotten into her stomach. They were limp, motionless. All around her, she saw beasts dropping to the ground, lifeless.

Apple looked at the sea. The tentacles were no longer thrashing, they were dropping against the beach, descending into the sea. The colossus was dead.

Scattered across the beach were the bodies of the colossus' victims. Screams of agony filled the air as half-digested beasts and men woke from their spell to discover the state of their bodies. Many of the creatures were too digested to recover and died instantly. Other creatures were in good enough shape to run off, into the forest. But some of the beasts were still alive, unable to move, cringing in agony at their melted flesh.

A mutant man lying nearby screamed as he noticed that all of his skin was missing. He was just a mass of soggy muscle. He could see his vomit-coated internal organs pulsing at him. One of his arms was melted to the bone. He pulled a knife out of his belt that had been fused to his hips and began cutting himself, as if in his crazed state of mind he believed that removing the burning muscle from his legs and chest would relieve the pain.

Apple stood up and looked around. She saw Hyena helping Bunny to her feet. The rabbit girl rubbed her head, confused, trying to figure out what was going on as she pulled the dead metal worms from her skin. The hyena girl walked away from her and began shooting at the half-digested wolves around her. She wanted to put them out of their misery as quickly as possible, although she saved the men for last.

The sea was becoming darker and darker with the colossus' blood. Apple looked out at the water, scanning the surface for her missing leader. Then she saw a dog muzzle shoot out from the waves to gasp for breath. It was Talon. Even under the water, she was able to kill the massive creature. As the alpha wolf swam toward the shore, Apple waved to her. Talon stood out of the water like a female goddess of the sea, covered in her opponent's oily blood, axes crossed on her back, marching casually through the waves as though defeating a colossal sea creature was something she did on a daily basis. Apple realized how much she respected this woman. She was the toughest person she had ever met. A true warrior, a barbarian queen.

As Apple admired her new leader, smiling with pride, a scream filled her ear from behind. She turned around to the skinless mutant man raising his knife at her. Apple only had enough time to raise her hands in defense as the knife came forward.

Then the mutant's head disappeared from his neck as the chainsaw boomerang buzzed past. Blood sprayed from the headless neck and the mutant dropped into the sand. Apple turned to the person who had just rescued her, but it was not Bunny or Hyena as she would have expected.

It was Sam.

"Sam," she yelled at her boyfriend, as he stood a ways down the blood-filled beach, looking at her with a sigh of relief. "You saved me!"

"I don't care that you're becoming a wolf girl," Sam said, as he whir-chunked toward her on metal legs. "I don't care if I have no working legs at night. I don't care if some day you become one of those massive beasts. All I want is to be with you."

Apple smiled and ran toward him. "I love you, Sam!"

"I love you, too!" he said. "More than anything!"

They ran along the beach with their arms wide open, ready to embrace. But just before Apple reached him, the chainsaw boomerang returned to its thrower and cut him in two. Blood exploded between them as Sam's upper half dropped to the ground, his metal legs still standing upright.

Apple cried, "Sam! No!"

Apple dropped into the sand next to him, she lifted his half a body and hugged it to her chest. Her Asian wolf eyes became thin lines as tears washed down her cheeks. Talon, Hyena, and Bunny saw what had happened and ran toward them.

"Sam, you can't die now," Apple said. "I need you."

His plastic replacement intestines uncoiled out of his torso between her thighs.

"It's okay," Sam said in a fading voice. "You don't need me anymore."

"Don't give up. We can put you back together again like before."

"Don't bother," he said. "It would be a waste of time."

"But what am I going to do without you, Sam?"

The other wolf women gathered behind Apple, staring down with concern. Sam looked up at them and smiled.

"You'll become a Warrior," he told Apple. "You'll fight mutants, go on raids, and ride with giant wolves. You'll live wild and free. It is the life you always wanted."

"But I won't have you . . ."

"You don't need me. With me around you'll have sex too much, causing your transformation into giant wolf to happen too soon. You still have a long life to live as a human. Make the most of that."

Sam's eyes began to roll. Apple tried to snap him out of it. "Don't you dare die! I promised myself to you. I plan to never have sex with anyone, unless it's with you!"

"Okay," Sam said. "One more time before I die."

"What?"

"Have sex with me right now," he said. "Quickly, before I die. It'll be the last time."

"Really?" Apple asked.

"Hurry," he moaned, trying to pull his intestines back into his body.

"Okay," she said.

Talon and Hyena looked at each other with confused faces as Apple removed her clothes, then Sam's clothes.

"Where's your penis?" Apple asked.

Sam pointed up at the metal legs still standing on the beach nearby. Apple opened the crotch compartment on the metal legs and pulled his penis out. Then she ripped it out of its stitches.

She held his penis in the palm of her hand. "How do I reattach it?"

Talon and Hyena shook their heads and walked away, toward their motorcycles. Bunny crossed her arms with a big smile on her face, curious to see what they were going to do. She looked to her right to giggle with Skunky, but then she noticed Skunky wasn't there with her. She lowered her head and turned away.

Apple examined the penis in her hand, discovering that the inside was part machine. She caressed the side of it and was surprised when the severed penis became erect. She smiled wide at the penis and looked down at Sam. He smiled back.

Sam opened his mouth and Apple put the bottom of his dick inside. He bit down on it, to hold it tightly in place. Apple slid the penis into her mouth to moisten the shaft, bringing it all the way down until her lips pressed against his in a strange hybrid of a kiss and a blowjob. Then she used his face as a saddle and inserted him into her vagina.

As she fucked his head into the sand, Apple thought about how much she loved him. Even though their relationship pretty much revolved around sex, it was the little things that made her love him. It was the way he made her feel like the most beautiful woman in the world, the way he thought of himself as the luckiest man in the world just to be holding her hand, the way he held his own severed penis in his mouth so that she could have a way to fuck him one more time before he died. Those were the important things about being in love.

And as she orgasmed against his dead face, Apple realized she would never be able to find another lover quite as perfect as Sam.

HORRENDOUS HORROR
OF THE
HATEFUL
HAMBURGLAR

CHAPTER ONE

The Hamburglar unsheathed his samurai swords as the rabid bear attacked. He slashed it through the chest, but the beast did not even slow down, long silver snakes curling out of its mouth as it went for his neck.

Leaping into the air, the permanent smile on the Hamburglar's face widened with glee as he cut through the animal's jaw. Its nose and muzzle were torn in half, but the thing didn't back down. It didn't even cry out.

Captain Richards charged through the trees to come to the Hambuglar's aid. With his four arms, he drew four repeaters from holsters on his gray uniform and fired sloppily at the bear. The Hamburglar had to backflip away from the creature to dodge the gunfire.

"Robble robble!" cried the Hamburglar at the Captain, his googly eyes curling with anger.

The Captain lowered his pistols. Two more soldiers came in from the woods, but Richards ordered them to stay out of the fight.

The beast roared with its mutilated jawbone—blood spraying from its split tongue—and then swiped its claw at its opponent. The Hamburglar cut the paw off of the beast with his short sword, and then with his long blade he pierced the beast through the neck and out the top of its head. Before the creature's lifeless body could hit the ground, the Hamburglar whipped his blades into the air, cleaning off the blood against the bear's fur in one quick swipe, and then sheathing the weapons in the scabbards on his waist.

Captain Richards holstered his guns and approached the Hamburglar. "What the hell was wrong with that thing?"

The Hamburglar looked at him with his sinister grin, but he did not answer.

"Rabies?" asked one of the soldiers as he stepped forward.

His name was Horatio, a young man with a perfectly manicured beard and a third leg growing out of his back like a long lizard tail.

The Captain looked closer. "No. Something else."

Greggy, the second soldier, kept his distance. He took a step back and a step sideways and then a step back, rubbing the barrel of his submachine gun with his sweaty palms. His eyes locked on the metal worms. They were still squirming through the animal's brown fur, squealing and glaring at them with red glowing eyes.

"What are they?" Horatio asked, going in for a closer look.

As the young soldier leaned in, the metal creatures leapt out of the fur at him. The Hamburglar unsheathed his swords, and with three lightning-fast slices he decapitated all five of the worms in midair. Horatio watched as ten red glowing eyes faded out and fell to his feet.

"Robble robble," said the Hamburglar to the young soldier as he returned the blades to their scabbards.

Then he walked away from the carcass, back to the road. His men followed suit.

They met up with the other five soldiers at the bus. The others did not stand to attention as their superiors arrived. They were drinking beers and shooting at squirrels in the trees. Captain Richards was in charge of the mission, even though the Hamburglar was his superior. His two lieutenants were Horatio, who climbed the ranks due to his skills as a sharp-shooter, and Tomahawk, who climbed the ranks due to his ferocious bloodlust in battle. Unfortunately, Tomahawk was the most unruly soldier in the Outlander army. He disrespected authority, unless he felt the respect was earned.

"Who said you could bring this on the mission?" Captain Richards asked Tomahawk, holding a mason jar half full of beer at the soldier.

Tomahawk looked back at him with smiling beefy cheeks. His tall platinum blond afro shined in the sunlight. "What?"

"Alcohol usage is barred from missions," said the Captain,

pouring out the beer on the side of the road.

"What the fuck?" Tomahawk said, flexing his third arm, which happened to be six times as muscled as his two natural arms.

The other four men gathered behind the Lieutenant. Even though Captain Richards was the ranking officer, the troops were far more loyal to Tomahawk. Only Horatio and that coward Greggy recognized the Captain's authority.

Richards stood his ground. A soldier with a red beret gave him a gnarled look. Another, who had four yellow horns growing from his head instead of hair, took a long swig of beer from his mason jar.

"We need to get to the Outpost before sundown," Richards told them. "We don't have time for your shit."

Then Richards turned and walked toward the bus. On the way, he confiscated the rest of the mason jars of beer.

Tomahawk took a few steps at him, raising his assault rifle as if to hit him in the back of the head with the butt of his gun, but he stopped as he saw the Hamburglar looking down at him from the roof of the bus. Tomahawk nodded with respect, gathered the rest of his men and entered the vehicle. He shoved Greggy with his shoulder as he passed him down the aisle of the bus. Although Tomahawk never respected authority, he knew better than to fuck with Hamburglar.

The vehicle was an old city bus from McDonaldland that they reinforced with steel plating and razor wire. It had been painted with green camouflage, so that it could be hidden in the forest if necessary. A section of the bus had been converted into a kitchenette, another had been converted into barracks. The vehicle was designed for long distance missions into the badlands. This would be their home for at least a week.

There were two gunner stations on the roof. Greggy and Horatio were stationed up there. Because he was their sniper, Horatio was always stationed on the roof. Greggy was up there because it was his turn in one of the gunner turrets, but he decided not to take his post at the back of the bus. That's where the Hamburglar liked to sit, dangling his black and white striped legs off the side, and glaring at the woods with his creepy cartoon smile. Greggy was very frightened of the Hamburglar. He was very frightened of everything.

The two of them were not friends, but Greggy seemed to have latched onto Horatio since the mission began. Horatio didn't want to make friends with him. He knew Greggy wasn't going to be around for very long. He knew Greggy was only sent on this mission because he was disposable. Still, he felt sorry for the guy. Even though he was a few years older than Horatio, he reminded the Lieutenant of his younger brother who was killed by the Bitches during a raid earlier in the year. His brother always had the same look of helplessness on his face, that lost doe-eyed look.

But Horatio had to admit, he was nervous around the Hamburglar as well. The man was a monster, both physically and psychologically. Besides the Mayor, he was the one man he would never cross.

The two soldiers stayed at the front of the bus, by the other turret station. The gunner at this station was nicknamed Sandwich. Horatio didn't know why. Sandwich had been in the Outlanders for fifteen years, ever since he was a teenager. Besides the Hamburglar and Tomahawk, he had been an Outlander longer than anyone on the mission. Sandwich was a big guy. He had a shaved head, large brown mutton chops, wore a muddy black wife-beater shirt exposing tattooed arms, and his glasses were cracked, held together with a rubber strap.

Sandwich sipped on a beer that he had hidden under his extra limbs, leaning back with his feet up on the barrel of the gun. He didn't bother to conceal the beer as Horatio approached, even though he was a superior officer who had the right to take it away.

"What's up?" Sandwich said, stroking his sideburns with his fifth arm.

"I was just curious." Horatio motioned to the Hamburglar. "What's up with him?"

"Who? Hamburglar?"

"Yeah. What's his story? Why doesn't he ever speak?"

"He's not much of a talker," he said. "Not even before they mutated his flesh to look like the Hamburglar."

"What was he like before he was the Hamburglar?"

"Just a normal psychopath."

He was originally named Willem Van Jaarsveld, before he became the Hamburglar. As a child, he was a small, thin boy, with neat black hair and a burgundy-colored suit. He never said a word to anybody. He didn't think anybody was worthy of his words. Young Willem believed himself to be a genius and a poet. The greatest poet in human history. He decided that not a single citizen of McDonaldland could possibly understand his greatness, so he did not allow them the privilege of hearing him speak his genius words.

Instead, Willem expressed his genius through music. He was trained as a pianist by his upper class parents, and by the age of seven he had already learned the instrument to mechanical perfection. His parents gave him everything he could possibly want and encouraged his creative arts, even though the arts were not exactly legal in the walled city. But no matter how much his parents gave to him, Willem showed them nothing but revulsion. He hated his parents. He did not believe they deserved such a brilliant son. He hated their greasy fingers and rolls of pasty fat dangling from the bottom of their shirts. He hated that they were not the most wealthy and powerful people in McDonaldland, even though they were one of the top twenty richest families at the time.

He especially hated his mother who had become part animal after conceiving him. He hated the hair she left on the furniture. He refused to eat at the same table as she, and didn't even want to look at her. He didn't even give her the slightest glance when she hung herself in the doorway of their McMansion, right beside him. He just played his piano louder so that her choking sounds did not interfere with his flawless music.

The other kids at school didn't like Willem. They thought he was weird and picked on him mercilessly, pushing him to the ground and kicking him in his scrawny stomach. Willem believed they picked on him because they were jealous of his genius, but it was really because Willem was a vegetarian, perhaps the only vegetarian in McDonaldland at the time. He did not like the way meat would make his fingers greasy when he ate it. He did not like the smell or the texture of it in his mouth. So he only ate salads or meatless burgers. This made him quite weak and scrawny compared to his hefty classmates, who ate nothing but cheeseburgers and french fries all day.

In order to defend himself against the bullies, Willem decided to teach himself how to fight. Without much strength, he knew that his fighting techniques would have to rely on speed. He researched books in the private library that only the upper class citizens could access, searching for fighting methods of the ancient world. That is when he discovered the ways of the samurai. He immediately fell in love with these aristocratic warriors of the past. They focused on speed and efficiency. They had a code of honor and would continuously strive for perfection. These were the first people Willem could relate to. From that day on, Willem considered himself the embodiment of the samurai.

For days, Willem labored continuously to create his first sword. It had to be technically perfect in structure, as well as a beautiful work of art. He studied books on how to craft the weapon and examined photographs for hours at a time. His father's servants gave him all the assistance he required. Eventually, he had a short katana of his own, that he wore in a leather scabbard around his waist beneath his burgundy suit coat.

The next time he was hassled by a bully on the way home from school, he unsheathed his sword and cut the boy's throat open. Pretending to be a noble samurai, he did not even look at his victim as he slaughtered him in the street. He heard blood fountaining out of the boy's neck, and a gurgling whimper as he died. But when Willem went to re-sheath his sword, he realized that the blade was missing. He turned around. It was still in the bully's throat.

This upset Willem greatly. He couldn't believe that his weapon was flawed. It was not a true blade of the samurai. He ran home and cried in his yellow bed, scolding himself for not living up to the greatness he knew was within him, clawing the skin on his wrists, combing his hair until his scalp began to bleed.

Once his tears ran dry, he decided not to give up on his dream. He would master the art of sword construction, even if it took him years to perfect. Then he would master the art of fighting with a sword. He knew there was no way he could fail in this task. He knew that nothing was impossible for a boy with such unparalleled genius.

"He really killed that kid?" Horatio asked Sandwich.

"Cut his throat and left him there for his parents to find him," Sandwich said. "The broken blade still sticking out of his neck."

"And nothing ever happened?" Horatio asked. "They never knew it was him?"

"A few years later, once the kid was carrying swords around with him everywhere he went, people figured it out. But by then there was nothing anybody could do about it. You can't accuse the social elite of murder unless you've got absolute proof."

Horatio looked at the Hamburglar on the other side of the bus. He was glaring into space with a psychopath's smile and perfect posture. His fingers were tapping on his knees as if playing the piano in his head.

A few hours later, they saw the Outpost on the horizon. The Outpost was the midpoint for doing trade with the community down in Texas, which was the only other civilization they knew of outside of McDonaldland. The Outlanders would bring goods to this facility, drop off beer, wine, meat, and produce, and pick up gasoline, citrus, and other commodities they could not produce for themselves. The Texans would do the same. This station was run by the Outlanders, but a few ambassadors from Texas stayed there to represent their people's interests.

It had been two weeks since the Outlanders had heard anything from the army stationed at the Outpost. There were supposed to be two deliveries since then, and not one of them showed up. The Mayor had assumed they were having transportation problems so he sent a couple trucks their way, but the truck drivers were never heard from again. Even though the Mayor needed as many men as possible to take out the Bitches, he decided to send the Hamburglar and eight soldiers to investigate the problem.

Captain Richards had been trying to convince the men that it was surely all just a misunderstanding and their mission was just to assist the soldiers at the Outpost with whatever setbacks they'd been having, but not a single one of the men believed everything was okay out there.

The Outpost was a large gray concrete fortress in the middle of a ruined highway town. It was the only structure still standing, as if decades of tornados had slowly torn down all of the buildings around it. There were several dead trees and mountains surrounding them, but it was mostly hills of rubble and scrap metal like a junkyard stretching across three square miles. The air out here was hot and dry. The land was mostly covered in dead yellow weeds.

Horatio looked through the scope on his hunting rifle, but couldn't see any signs of life. There were vehicles surrounding the property, but no people.

"Could they all be inside?" Greggy asked.

Horatio took his eye from the scope. "I don't know."

There was a buzzing noise in the air. Sandwich and Greggy

looked around, wondering where the noise was coming from. Horatio peeked into his scope and it looked as if some kind of bug was flying across the rubble hills at them. The bug grew bigger and bigger as it came.

Once it was large enough to see with his naked eye, Horatio lowered the scope from his face. He squinted his eyes. He wasn't sure, but the thing flying at them looked kind of like a boomerang, with chainsaw blades attached to it.

"Down!" Horatio screamed, pulling Greggy flat against the roof of the bus.

Sandwich was not able to duck in time. The chainsaw boomerang cut through his midsection, through the back of the gunner seat, and flew off into the woods. His upper body hit the roof next to Horatio and Greggy. Blood gushed out of his mouth, coating his fluffy mutton chops.

The boomerang returned to its thrower in the distance. Horatio tried to pinpoint the attacker's position, but it was too far away to see with the naked eye. He tried to look through his sniper scope, but Sandwich coughed blood onto the lens, his last act before he bled out. Wiping the lens with his uniform as quickly as possible, Horatio returned the scope to his eye, but could no longer see the buzzing weapon.

The bus continued up the road, all of the men in combat positions. The Hamburglar ran to the front of the bus, and shoved Greggy into the blood-smeared gunner seat beside them. Greggy took the machinegun's handles and pointed them at the distance, clueless to where he needed to shoot.

Captain Richards climbed onto the roof to order Horatio to take the enemy out, but the sharp-shooter was already on it. Richards gave him the order anyway, so that it seemed as if he was being useful.

Horatio saw the attacker on the next throw. It was a wolf woman, standing on the roof of the Outpost. After throwing the chainsaw boomerang, she ducked down to keep her position hidden.

"It's one of the Bitches!" Horatio said.

Richards lowered himself flat to the roof when he heard the

word Bitches. "So that's what happened to the Outpost. It was overtaken out by those hairy whores."

The chainsaw boomerang came at them again, this time it went for the front of the bus. Hamburglar drew both of his swords to defend his men, but the bus was swerving to the right and the boomerang missed completely.

Down below, Poppy, the mutant with the red beret cheered behind the wheel of the bus. He took a swig of his beer to celebrate outmaneuvering the wolf girl's attack. While he was taking the chug and straightening out the vehicle, he didn't realize the buzzing weapon as it made its return back to its thrower. The boomerang cut through one of the bus's side windows, severed both of Poppy's right arms, crashed through the front windshield, and sawed across the hood of the bus.

Poppy was shrieking as the bus rumbled to a stop, his beer pouring out onto the floor from one of his severed hands. Lockjaw, the mutant with the yellow horns, jumped to his friend and tried to stop the bleeding, fountains of gore splashing him in the face.

Horatio was in the zone. He was steady, the leg on his back straightening out like the tail of a creeping iguana. His rifle pointed at the spot where the wolf woman had ducked. He waited for the boomerang to return to her. As it became smaller and smaller, buzzing up to the top of the roof, Horatio saw the woman poke up to catch it.

He fired, hitting her in the chest. She flew backward, her floppy ears dancing as she fell, blood spraying a line of droplets into the air. Her boomerang bounced off the edge of the building and dropped silently to the ground.

"Got her!" Horatio said.

Captain Richards felt safe enough to get up from his lying position. "Good work."

He brushed off his uniform.

"How many more do you think are there?" Greggy asked the Captain.

"Two more, at most," he said. "I heard that the soldiers out here had captured a few Bitches some time ago. We were supposed to bring them back to our headquarters, but that's when the Outpost went silent."

"You think they got free and overpowered all the men?" Greggy asked. "Just the three of them versus an entire army?"

"Never underestimate a single one of those bitches," Richards said. "Some of them are as strong as a hundred men."

Greggy shook his head in disbelief.

Tomahawk opened the hood of the bus to discover the top half of the engine had been shredded. Smoke sizzled into his face.

"Fuck," Tomahawk yelled, punching the grill of the vehicle with his enormous third arm.

Lockjaw and Sun—a mutant with spiked shoulder pads and dark black skin—pulled Poppy from the bus. The wounded man was barely conscious. His arms were wrapped tightly with leather tourniquets. The bleeding had stopped and the man would likely pull through, but he was still in shock. They had nothing to dull the pain.

"We have to walk the rest of the way," said Captain Richards to his men. "Take only your weapons and ammunition. Leave everything else behind."

The men obeyed. Tomahawk strapped dual one-handed sledgehammers to his waist and draped a belt of ammo for his rifle over his shoulder. Horatio filled his cargo pants with bullets. Lockjaw and Sun were armed with shotguns and knives. Greggy carried his submachine gun under his arm so that nobody would notice his hands were shaking.

"Shouldn't we bury him?" Greggy asked the Captain.

He pointed up at the blood leaking down from the roof of the bus.

Richards looked up. "We'll have to take care of Sandwich later."

Once he was ready, Richards said, "Move out!"

But Hamburglar, Horatio, and Tomahawk were already a dozen yards into the distance, on their way to the Outpost.

CHAPTER TWO

Down the road, Horatio could see a group of soldiers running toward them. They moved quickly, as if they were desperate to reach them for safety.

"Looks like those Bitches didn't get all of our boys," said Tomahawk, wiping crumbs from his crusty blond mustache.

As the men came closer, Horatio noticed something strange about them. They were ripped apart as if they had been wounded by gunfire or grazed by chainsaws.

"Are they okay?" Horatio asked.

Once Horatio saw the long metal worms coiling out of their flesh, he knew what was wrong. These men were rabid, like the bear. The three Outlanders stopped in their tracks. They watched carefully as the rabid mutants charged forward, carrying axes and two-by-fours.

"What are they doing?" Tomahawk said.

"Trying to kill us," Horatio said.

The sharp-shooter put his gun to his chest and aimed the barrel at the closest attacker. He fired. The man's left shoulder was tossed back a bit but he continued running at them.

"Call that a shot?" Tomahawk criticized.

"I hit him in the chest!" Horatio said. "He should have at least went down."

Horatio fired again. The mutant was hit but it hardly fazed him.

"That one was in his heart," Horatio said. "He should be dead."

Tomahawk saw it, too. The man should've been killed by that hit. Blood was gushing out of the crazed man's chest, but he kept moving.

Hamburglar raced forward at the infected mutants. He had given his men time to kill the attackers at a distance, but his patience had run out. He charged with his head pointing forward, his hands crossed on the handles of his katana. As he reached the first row of men, Hamburglar drew both swords and decapitated four of them. Two on his right, two on his left, two for each sword. He re-sheathed his swords as the bodies stood there, blood and metal worms shooting out of their necks. The other mutants tumbled into their backs as the Hamburglar walked sideways around the bodies, ready for another attack.

Once the four corpses finally hit the ground, two more mutants with mouths full of worms lunged at Hamburglar. With one swipe, they were missing the tops of their skulls. One of them went down, but the other was still standing, shrieking, worms coiling in his soup bowl of a head. He swiped at the Hamburglar with a hatchet, but the samurai cut his arm off, then his face off, then his legs off, before he could get within range.

The other infected mutants went after Tomahawk as he fired his rifle at them. He hit several of them in the midsection but they wouldn't go down, so he drew his two sledgehammers and lowered them through two of their skulls. Gore and chunks of bone exploded beneath the weight of the steel mallets.

Horatio looked back to see dozens of other infected mutants coming in from the mountains of rubble surrounding the road, swarming the other soldiers on all sides. Greggy and the two carrying Poppy ran as fast as they could to catch up, while Captain Richards fired at the mob with his four repeaters. Soon there were nearly a hundred infected men on the road, their heads squirming with metal worms like medusas.

Then there was gunfire coming from the top of the bus. Horatio peeked through his scope to see Sandwich was still alive. Although he was just half a man, he had climbed back up into the gun turret. Worms crawled through the dead man's flesh as he fired at his brother soldiers.

A storm of bullets hit Sun in the back of his legs and he went down. Lockjaw kept moving without his fallen friend, knowing that he couldn't possibly carry another wounded man. Sun cried out for help as he crawled across the ground, one of his legs dangling by a meaty thread. Not even Captain Richards attempted to help him. He leapt over the wounded man and ran forward to catch up to the others.

Horatio aimed the rifle at Sandwich's face and fired. The man's bald head exploded. He was still alive up there, but half of his face was gone. He couldn't see clearly and no longer had the motor skills to work the heavy machine gun.

Poppy had snapped out of his state of shock and was running with his own legs by the time they caught up with Horatio. Lockjaw looked back at his fallen brother, Sun, who screamed as the infected mutants came down on him. Horatio aimed his rifle and took out as many of them as he could, blowing off their heads as they came in. After seven of them were dead, Horatio ran toward the wounded man.

He passed Captain Richards on the way to Sun.

"We need to get to him," Horatio said.

"Leave him." Captain Richards didn't stop running for a second.

"But he's still alive," Horatio said.

He continued on by himself. When he got to Sun, there were worms crawling across the ground toward him. Horatio smashed the worms with the butt of his gun, one by one. Then he picked Sun off the ground and carried him in the direction of the Outpost.

The swarm of men was enormous now, hundreds of them like a tidal wave rolling down the street at them. Even the Hamburglar seemed unnerved by the sight of their mass.

The bottom floor of the Outpost was also infested with rabid mutants as Tomahawk entered the building. He punched one of them across the room with his enormous third fist, then crushed one of their skulls between two colliding sledgehammers. Captain Richards was the next inside. Even though he was originally in the back of the group, he had caught up to his men and raced past them as they defended themselves against the attacking horde. Richards shot down two of the infected men as they came at Tomahawk, but

Tomahawk was more annoyed than thankful.

When Horatio arrived at the gate that surrounded the building, he passed Sun off to Lockjaw, then shot down three of the mutants that were getting close. He closed the gate on the horde and chained it up, but he didn't have a lock for it. He had to just knot it up the best he could. The fence wasn't going to hold them for long, but at least it would slow them down.

On the way into the building, Horatio saw the chainsaw boomerang lying in the dirt a few yards away from the entrance. He picked it up by the handle and carried it into the Outpost, his fellow soldiers' blood dripping down the side of his uniform.

Hamburglar was the last to enter, killing off as many of the crazed men as he could. Once they were all inside, Tomahawk and Lockjaw barricaded the door with supply crates, most of them filled with drums of gasoline.

"You sure that's a wise idea?" Horatio asked Tomahawk, pointing at the gas in the crates.

"It's a great idea," Tomahawk responded, wiping blood out of his white afro. "They try to get in and they'll explode."

"And we'll burn with them?" Horatio asked.

Tomahawk shrugged.

The bottom floor of the facility was a large warehouse space. High ceilings, boxes of supplies stacked in rows along the walls, forklifts, cold concrete floor. There weren't any stairs leading to the upper levels. The wooden stairs were collapsed in a pile in the corner of the room. Somebody had cut them down with a chainsaw.

Horatio scoured the floor for long metal worms and crushed them with the butt of his gun. They were crawling out of the dead infected bodies and scattering in all directions across the room.

"Did any of them get into you?" Horatio asked Sun.

Sun shook his head as drool came out of his black rubbery lips. "Almost. They crawled into my wounds but I was able to pull them back out."

Then Sun screamed as Lockjaw amputated his mangled leg with the chainsaw boomerang. The other leg was next.

"You can't save either of them?" Captain Richards asked Lockjaw.

Lockjaw shrugged. "No idea. I'm not a fucking doctor."

"But you're our medic," said Captain Richards.

"Medic? Like hell." Lockjaw laughed, the yellow horns on his head bobbing up and down. "I have a few years experience as a veterinarian's assistant, from back when I lived in McDonaldland. That's why they made me a medic."

"A vet?"

"All I know is that we're not going to get him to a real doctor soon enough to save his legs. But with his mutation, maybe he'll grow some new ones someday."

Sitting next to Sun, Poppy began to laugh. "And maybe I'll grow back some new arms, eh?"

The three of them laughed. It was funny because it was true. The one upside to their limb-growing disease was that they could always grow more arms and legs.

Captain Richards turned to Horatio. "We need to get to the upper levels. The other two wolf women could be anywhere."

"You think they're infected as well?" Horatio asked.

"I sure as hell hope not," said the Captain. "Bitches are bad enough when they aren't undead killing machines."

Horatio nodded his head and looked out the window behind the Captain's shoulder. The swarm of infested mutants was climbing the fence outside, ripping themselves through the razorwire rim, and gathering around the outside of the building. The windows were barred, but that wouldn't stop them for long.

It was up to Tomahawk, Hamburglar, Greggy, and Horatio to figure out how to get to the upper floors. Richards decided he would stay behind, with Lockjaw and the wounded, because he was afraid of what might be lurking up there. Greggy wanted to stay behind as well, but Richards ordered him to go.

"We need to make a man out of you," Richards said to Greggy. "Cowards make me sick."

There was a freight elevator on the other side of the building, by the mountain of crates filled with rotting produce. It was the only way to the upper floors. Unfortunately, the control for the elevator had been disabled. A saw had cut the panel in half. The four of them looked up the elevator shaft, into the shadows.

"It can still be operated from the other floors," Horatio said. "But somebody's going to have to climb up there and bring it down."

Horatio suggested the Lieutenant go.

Tomahawk shook his head. "I don't do heights. Let's send the wimp up there."

Greggy stepped back. "But wolf women could be up there."

"Don't worry, we'll cover you," Tomahawk said.

"I don't even know how I would climb up there," Greggy cried. "There's no ladder."

The Hamburglar was sick of their whining and stepped forward to do it himself. He climbed the bricks, straight up toward the ceiling. The soldiers watched his black flowing cape as he disappeared into the darkness above.

During his teenage years, the Hamburglar always enjoyed the darkness. He liked to block out the ugly, hopeless real world to better see the magnificent imaginary world in his head. The world of art, music, and perfection. The world of the samurai.

For hours on end, the Hamburglar would sit in the darkness and explore his mind. He would imagine an army of noble warriors crossing green fields toward battle. He would imagine their perfectly crafted blades of iron and steel glimmering in the sunlight. He would imagine their fights as masterworks of art and dance, their opponent's blood as paintings across the landscape. This would inspire him to create. It would inspire him to write music on his piano.

His father recognized young Willem's potential as a pianist. He was more inclined to encourage his piano playing than his sword-crafting hobby, so he pushed his son in the direction of music. He hired a piano tutor, one of the only music instructors in all of McDonaldland. Willem did not understand why this was necessary. He saw his music as flawless. He couldn't possibly become any better than he already was.

The very first day he met with the piano instructor, the plump effeminate man had Willem play a song for him before even introducing himself. Willem wanted to play one of his own compositions, but the tutor urged him to play something classical. He played Franz Schubert's Piano Sonata in B Flat, which was a work he felt he had perfected, even though he believed the composition was flawed.

Willem hoped that after he witnessed his brilliance, the tutor would understand that there was nothing he could possibly teach him and would then leave him alone. But, halfway through the performance, Willem noticed the tutor shaking his head and groaning deeply. He stopped playing and stared at the instructor's cringing face, his eyebrows raised high on his pale forehead.

"You know the piece well," said the tutor, still shaking his head. "But I've never seen someone play it with such lack of passion."

Willem continued to stare at him.

"You're mechanical. You play like a robot."

Willem continued to stare at him.

"What you are doing is hitting keys on an instrument. You are not truly playing music."

Willem continued to stare at him.

"Here," the tutor moved into the seat next to him, "I'll show you how to play with your soul."

Willem stomped up out of the seat and left the room. When he returned, he raised a half-made samurai sword above his head and cut the tutor's fucking head off, then finished the rest of the song.

As he played, Willem listened to the music as he created it and realized that he couldn't help but agree with the tutor. His delivery was flawed. It was mechanical and lacked emotion. He couldn't fathom how a genius such as himself could not have recognized this sooner.

The soldiers heard the elevator vibrate into life, then a metallic squealing noise as it slowly descended toward them. They backed away from the shaft as it arrived. When the doors opened, a thick mildew smell filled the air. The elevator was made of rotting wood, covered in black mold. They were surprised to see it empty. The Hamburglar did not come down with it.

"Where is he?" Greggy asked.

They listened, but could not hear any noises from the floors above.

"He's got to be up there somewhere," Tomahawk said. "Let's catch up."

The three of them boarded and hit the button for the second floor. The light in the elevator flickered on and off, creating a loud humming noise. As the elevator made its ascent, Tomahawk looked down at Greggy.

"You better not get in my way," Tomahawk said to him.

Greggy stepped back.

"He's a coward," Horatio said, getting between them. "But he's not completely useless. At least we have another man to back us up."

Tomahawk spit. "Lockjaw and Poppy are the only two I trust to back me up. Otherwise, I'd rather go solo."

"How far do you think you'd get without my help?" Horatio asked.

Tomahawk chuckled. "Far enough. I'll admit you're a good shot from a distance, but you're worthless in close combat."

"When you're a good shot from a distance, you don't need to worry about close combat."

Tomahawk smiled, then nodded. "We'll see how long you can keep that up in the corridors up there. Not all fights are from afar. Eventually, relying on long-range weapons is going to get you killed."

Horatio laughed. "Relying on short-range weapons is going to get you killed."

"We'll see."

"Yeah, we'll see."

When they arrived on the second floor, they could hardly see anything in the dim lighting. The hallways were lit by only a few light bulbs hanging from the ceiling spread nearly thirty feet apart, and the light was so faint it was as if the generator was working at half-power. All they could see was a pile of dead bodies littered across the floor and blood dripping from the walls.

"He's been through here," Tomahawk said, almost disappointed he didn't get to kill them himself.

They walked through the hall, following the Hamburglar's trail of bodies. As they passed the dead flesh, they saw metal worms squirming in the shadows. If he could see them clearly, Horatio would crush them with the butt of his rifle. Otherwise, he steered clear.

"Watch out for them," Horatio said to Greggy. "I believe those snake-things are what caused the psychotic behavior in these soldiers."

Tomahawk ignored the worms, too busy trying to catch up to the Hamburglar. One of the parasites was able to creep up to his ankle, but before it could attack, the large man crushed it under his boot without even realizing it.

"Be more careful," Horatio said, but Tomahawk wasn't paying attention to him either.

Around the corner, furry claws lunged out of the wall at Greggy and caught him by the throat. He cried out in a choking gasp as a claw squeezed his larynx. Tomahawk reached up and grabbed one of the light bulbs hanging from the ceiling, then pointed it at Greggy. Behind the bars of a jail cell were two wolf women. They shrieked out, grabbing at the struggling soldier, trying to pull him through the bars. Horatio tugged at his arm, trying to get him free but the wolf women were too strong.

"Get her off!" Greggy choked.

Tomahawk did nothing to help. He pointed the light at one wolf woman to get a better look, discovering metal worms crawling out of her mouth and forehead. Both women were infected. They were nude, their fur dread-locked with blood and urine. The beast shoved her muzzle through the bars to get closer to Greggy, drool leaking down his shoulder, his cries hit a higher octave.

Horatio let go of his arm and raised his rifle at the wolf woman's head. Then fired. Her skull popped like a balloon and she went down. Greggy tumbled away from the cell as the other woman clawed at his uniform. Horatio aimed at the second woman and shot her through the eye. She didn't go down, even with her eyeball blown out the back of her head, but her shrieks deepened into a drunken manly tone. With the next shot, Horatio aimed for her forehead. The bullet cracked her skull open and her corpse slid down the bars to the floor. When the only sound left was the trickling of their blood and the gasping of Greggy's breath, Tomahawk pointed the light bulb at Horatio.

"I guess we don't have to worry about the Bitches," Tomahawk said.

Greggy looked up at him and said, "Why did you just stand there?"

Tomahawk shrugged. "Saving you wasn't worth the bullets."

Before Greggy could further complain, Horatio changed the subject. "Where did Hamburglar go? These two were still alive, so he must not have gone this way."

"He's probably headed for the roof," Tomahawk said. "We should go after him."

Horatio shook his head. "We should clear this floor before going up. Hamburglar can take care of himself."

They went from room to room, but most of them were empty. The only living mutants were in a locked supply closet. They must have barricaded themselves within before they became infected. These men were so full of metal worms that their faces had mutated into scaly blobs. Horatio let Tomahawk take care of them, smashing in their skulls with his sledgehammers.

When the floor was clear, Tomahawk told Greggy to go downstairs and bring the others up. The frightened soldier just nodded and fled for the elevator without protest.

"It'll be safer for them up here," Tomahawk said.

Horatio was surprised to hear that. "It almost sounds like you're worried about them."

Tomahawk spit. "Well, I don't give a fuck about Richards, but I've been through a lot with Sun, Lockjaw, and Poppy. I'd hate to lose those assholes."

Horatio nodded. He said, "I hope Sun and Poppy pull through," but that was the wrong thing to say. Tomahawk's face became fuming, as if he was in denial about the condition of his two wounded friends. He looked at Horatio like he was considering breaking his skull between his two hammers.

"They'll be fine," Tomahawk said. "My men are nearly impossible to kill."

Then they went upstairs. The third floor was mostly barracks, with enough beds for three hundred men. It was important to keep the Outpost well-manned, because otherwise it would have been a prime target for wolf women raids. Without the supplies coming in from Texas, the Outlander army was at the mercy of McDonaldland, which was something the Mayor would not stand for.

The Hamburglar was just finishing off the last of the infected men, when Horatio and Tomahawk arrived. He was holding the head of the Captain of the Outpost, studying the fat worm dangling from its mouth.

"Robble-robble-robble," Hamburglar said, and tossed the head over his shoulder as he continued on his way.

They followed the Hamburglar to the roof access. The three of them looked up the stepladder to the hatch. It had been barricaded on both sides, but was now broken open.

"Think she's still alive up there?" Tomahawk asked.

"I shot her square in the chest," Horatio said. "She's dead."

"Well, you shot the one in the cage square in the face and she was still moving."

"But the one in the cage was infected," Horatio said. "The one on the roof could have still been alright."

"I'm sure she's just like the rest of them," Tomahawk said. "None of these poor bastards could have escaped infection."

"You don't know that for sure."

"Well, why don't I go find out for myself."

Tomahawk climbed the stepladder and crawled out onto the roof. "Wait here."

The Hamburglar ignored the Lieutenant and climbed up after him. Horatio stayed behind, pointing his rifle at the hatch, waiting for one of the infected to poke its head through. After a few minutes, he heard Tomahawk say, "There's no one up here. Just some empty cans of food."

Horatio called up, "She's got to still be up there somewhere."

A few more minutes of silence. Then Tomahawk's voice: "There's a trail of blood leading from the hatch to the edge of the roof. Maybe she fell off."

"From the hatch?" Horatio knew then that the trail wasn't leading from the hatch to the edge, but from the edge to the hatch. The wolf woman wasn't on the roof anymore, she was on the third floor, with him.

Before Horatio could turn around, something behind him grabbed onto his third leg and pulled him back. His feet fell out from under him as a furry woman pulled him into a back room, spun him around by his leg-tail and threw him against a blood-splattered wall. His face hit the bricks hard, bloody snot splashing from his nose, his gun sliding across the room. Then he crumbled to the floor.

"Hi there, Meat," she said as she closed and barricaded the door behind her.

Before Horatio could crawl to his rifle, the woman flipped him over and dropped her weight down in his lap, pinning him. She grabbed him by the throat and brought his face close to her eyes as if she was looking for something inside of him.

"Did any of those snakes bite you?" she asked.

Horatio shook his head, but while in her grip he could only move it centimeters. The woman didn't look much like a wolf. She was covered in scruffy dark brown fur, but her ears and tail were like that of a rabbit's.

"What's your name, Meat?" asked the rabbit/wolf woman, loosening her grip on his neck.

"Lieutenant Horatio Caras," he said.

"How many of you are there?"

"Eight of us, originally," he said. "But you killed one and severely wounded another. Oh, and one guy lost his legs trying to escape from those things out there, so there's really just five left standing."

The wolf woman squinted her eyes at him. She couldn't understand why he was being so cooperative.

"Are you lying?" she asked.

"No." He smiled.

"Why not?"

"Because it doesn't matter how many men are in our group," he said. "All you should concern yourself with is who we brought with us."

"Who's that?"

"The Hamburglar."

"Who?"

"You haven't heard of the Hamburglar? The assassin of the wasteland?"

She shook her head.

He chuckled. "Well, you'll meet him soon. By the time he's done with you I promise you'll fear his name."

"Bullshit," she said. "I fear no man. Men are just pieces of Meat to me. They are fat little piggies that I eat for dinner."

She licked her fangs as if to intimidate him, sniffing at his neck and growling, but her rabbit features looked more cute to him than frightening. After inhaling his scent, her eyes lit up with surprise, and then she sniffed some more.

"Wait a minute . . ." she said, then sniffed again.

She pulled a bullet out of her pocket and sniffed that, then him again. "Your scent is on this bullet." She squeezed his hips between her thighs and raised her voice. "You're the Meat who fucking shot me, aren't you?"

That's when Horatio noticed the wound on her chest, just below the shoulder. He could smell the burnt hair on her chest where she cauterized her own wound.

"Sorry about that," Horatio said.

She bared her teeth at him as if she was about to bite his face off, but then she said. "How the hell did you do that? I had to have been nearly seven hundred yards away from you."

"I'm good," Horatio said.

She squeezed his throat tightly. "Well, it fucking hurt like hell." She put her other hand around his neck and slowly crushed his esophagus.

"No piece of Meat shoots me and lives to talk about it," she said, enjoying the satisfaction of watching him struggle as she squeezed the life out of him.

But, before she could kill him, she felt something move. Between her legs, something hard was poking her in the crotch. She looked down, then back up at the man.

"Do you have a fucking erection?" she screamed.

Horatio blushed. "I'm sorry, but this kind of thing really turns me on."

Her mouth dropped and she jumped off of him.

"Men are so disgusting," she said, wiping his smell from her as she paced the room. "I fucking hate them all."

Horatio rubbed his neck and said, "What's your name?" Acting as if she hadn't just tried to kill him.

She stopped pacing and glared at him. "They call me Bunny."

"Cute name."

"Fuck you."

Horatio crossed his legs and casually said, "Tell me, Bunny, how the heck are you the only one here who's not full of those worms?"

She kneeled down near him. "I'm immune. I was infected with them before, about two years ago, but I was saved by my friends. All you have to do is kill the creature that controls the worms."

"What creature?"

"I don't know. We killed the one that infected me. I had no idea there were more of them out there."

"So we can still save all those men out there?"

"If you can find the creature and kill it, yeah. Unfortunately, the thing lives in the ocean. Good luck finding it."

"But your friends found it."

"A pack of Warriors would be able to track down such a creature, but not Meat like you. I plan to find the creature and kill it myself."

"I thought you hated men," he said. "Why would you kill that creature to save all those men outside?"

"I wouldn't do it for those men. I want to save my infected sisters that are locked up downstairs."

Horatio broke eye contact. Bunny knew something was wrong and her eyebrows curled with rage.

"You assholes didn't kill them did you?"

Horatio didn't move.

"Did you?"

He nodded. She screamed and punched him in the face so hard that the back of his head slammed against the wall behind him.

"I could have saved them!"

She stood up and kicked him in the stomach.

"Which one of you did it?" she yelled. Then she grabbed him by the throat and lifted him into the air. "If it was you I am going to rip your guts out."

Then the door broke open. Bunny turned around as the Hamburglar stepped inside, his fingers tapping on the handles of his sheathed katana.

"What the fuck are you?" she yelled, dropping the soldier from her claws.

As he hit the ground, Horatio rolled over, retrieved his rifle and pointed it up at the wolf woman.

"He's the fucking Hamburglar," Horatio said.

Bunny groaned and raised her hands in surrender, staring at the Hamburglar's gigantic cartoon-like head. The Hamburglar looked back at her. He took his hands off of the handles of his swords and wiggled his fingers in the air as if he was playing an invisible piano. Both Bunny and Horatio could almost hear the music that was going through the mutant's freakish head.

CHAPTER THREE

In order to fill his music with passion, young Hamburglar decided that he would need to fall in love. It was an emotion that he was unfamiliar with. The only thing he came close to loving was himself, but that was more of a deep respect than love.

As a teenager, Willem didn't interact with his classmates. He thought they were poor, immature, annoying, lazy fat asses. Some of the girls liked him, because of his class status in the community, so with his father's influence he was set up on a few dates.

The first girl he went on a date with was a very large blonde girl with green braces and a red dress. They went for burgers by the park. Because Willem wanted to walk rather than take the bus, the girl was exhausted by the time they arrived at the restaurant, even though it had only been five blocks. She needed to sit down at the table for over ten minutes to catch her breath, sweat pouring down her pasty yellow-freckled skin.

Willem went to get the food.

The girl said, "You're buying? Good. Get me three Big Macs."

Willem nodded and turned to go order.

"I'm not finished yet!" she yelled, pounding her fist against the table.

Then Willem waited a couple more minutes for her to catch her breath again. She said, "I also want a 10 piece chicken Mc-Nuggets with cran-peary dipping sauce, two apple pies, a premium bacon ranch salad with crispy chicken strips, large fries, and large Coke."

Willem didn't think she was serious at first, but the way she held her head as if she was having a mild stroke he could tell she wasn't in the joking mood. He ordered all of her food, writing it all down on paper for the cashier. He ordered for himself his usual meal: one Big N' Tasty, no meat.

After getting the food and sitting down, the fat girl, who

was actually only average weight for a McDonaldlandian, ripped the entire food tray out of his hand and started eating. Willem watched as orange secret sauce dribbled down her chin as she gorged on two Big Macs at once. Willem couldn't even look at her. Her saggy flesh, her greasy fingers, the corners of her mouth covered in mayo; he found her completely repulsive.

"So what's your deal?" the girl asked. "Why don't you ever talk?"

Hamburglar wanted to fall in love with a girl, but he didn't want to talk to one. He just nodded at her when she spoke.

"Jeri says you're like really rich and she's like the richest person I know so if she thinks you're rich then you must be like the richest kid in our class."

Willem just watched her swallowing the greasy food whole. He didn't bother grabbing his burger from the pile of food on the tray. He no longer had an appetite.

"You seem really skinny for such a rich kid and you dress like an idiot and you never talk and why aren't you eating?"

Then the girl grabbed Willem's meatless Big N' Tasty and took a bite.

"What the fuck is this?" she asked, staring at the empty space where a beef patty should have been. Then she tossed it over her shoulder.

Willem then realized that he really hated this girl. He hated her with all of his being. If the girls in McDonaldland were all like this, there was no way he could possibly fall in love with any of them.

"I think Big Macs are still the best thing you can get on the menu and Melanie thinks there should be more salad variety but who the heck cares about salads anyway?"

Willem wondered if she was ever going to shut up.

"When I get out of school I totally want to be in advertising design because I'm really good with colors and if you don't believe me just look at my fingernails . . ."

Willem really wanted her to shut up.

She wouldn't shut up.

"They're red and yellow striped," she said, holding out her nails, "and there's nobody with nails like mine in school because I'm the best at design because I'm like a genius with color."

Willem grabbed the plastic fork from the girl's premium bacon ranch salad with crispy chicken strips and stabbed her in the head with it. Even though the fork was plastic, he was able to pierce her skin at a downward angle, between her skull bone and forehead.

She sat there for a moment, confused by what had just happened until a tiny droplet of blood dropped onto the sesame seed bun of her Big Mac. Then she screamed, waving her hands like she was drying nail polish, not knowing what else to do. The plastic fork sticking out of her head made her look like some kind of retarded unicorn. Then he realized that she got ranch dressing on one of his fingers, so he got up and kicked the seat out from under her. She lay on the ground, covered in lettuce and pieces of burger, crying.

Willem walked away. He knew there was no way he was going to be able to find love with women such as these. He had to figure out another way to find his passion. There had to be something else he could love.

They locked Bunny in the cell with her dead sisters. She picked them up off the floor, kissed them on their foreheads, and covered them with a sheet caked in mud and hair. She sat there, in silence, like she was praying for their spirits. Horatio was ordered to guard her. He stood there, watching her through bars as tears dripped down her furry face.

There were steps coming from the darkened hallway. Captain Richards and Lockjaw appeared, their weapons drawn, Lockjaw holding the chainsaw boomerang out like a shield.

"So she's the only one left?" Richards asked Horatio.

"She's immune."

Richards looked into the cell at the angry, teary-eyed wolf

woman. "How'd all this happen?"

She glared at him.

"Did you Bitches have anything to do with it? Did you infect this army with your filthy rabies?"

Bunny stood up and wrapped her long fingers around the bars, her thick black fingernails pointing at the men. Richards stepped back.

"Those Zoners from Texas did this. Your trading partners."

Richards was surprised she knew about the Zoners. The Outlanders were supposed to keep them a secret, especially to their enemy, even when they were being kept prisoner. The Zoners were what they called the people from the Forbidden Zone, which was an area in the southern part of what used to be Texas. Even though they were trading partners and some Zoners lived at the Outpost, nobody knew anything about the Forbidden Zone. The Outlanders were not permitted to travel there or even speak to the Zoners about their culture or civilization. The Zoners didn't speak much. They kept to themselves and only spoke about trading procedure. The Mayor didn't mind that they kept secrets. All he wanted was their gasoline and supplies. He never thought of them as a threat.

"How did they do it?" the Captain asked. "Why?"

"You'll have to figure out why they did it yourself," Bunny said. "But I know how they did it. The food. I have no idea if they did it on purpose or not, but for some reason the food they delivered was infested with eggs. All of a sudden one day everyone at the Outpost was infected. The eggs hatched in their stomachs and those parasitic worms spread throughout their bodies. Then their minds were gone. That's when I started killing them off one at a time, but believe me that was the fun part."

"You didn't eat the food?"

"No, I ate the food. But I'm immune. For hours, I could feel them crawling around inside of me, but they weren't able to mess with my mind like they did two years ago."

Lockjaw, the vet/medic, stepped in and said, "It's a good thing the parasites knew you were an unsuitable host or they would probably still be inside of you, tearing your innards apart right now." Then he smiled, as if he was trying to freak her out.

Her eyes were locked on the chainsaw boomerang in the man's hand.

"Who said they're not still inside of me?" she said. "I've been cutting them out of my skin for the past week."

She showed him her belly and the medic could see movement beneath the skin, long snaking motions across her stomach. It was Lockjaw who became freaked out, taking a few steps back from her.

Richards said, "Did everyone eat the food? There wasn't a single man who wasn't infected?

"There were about a dozen who didn't eat the food because they were out on patrol during dinnertime. They didn't get infected. They were the ones who found the eggs in the food brought from the Forbidden Zone."

"What happened to them?"

"They only lasted a few days," she said. "One by one, they were killed off or infected. They wouldn't have lived even that long if they weren't smart enough to let me help them. If they would have actually listened to me they might have still been alive now."

"Bullshit," Richards said. "I bet you killed them as soon as they let you out of that cage."

"You know, that sounds exactly like something I would do." Bunny laughed and nodded her head. "But that's not what happened."

"Are you trying to convince us to let you out now?" Richards asked. "After you attacked us and killed one of our men? We're going to leave you to fucking rot."

"You'd survive much longer with my help," she said. "I'm the only one who's immune. If any of you try to fight them in close range you're eventually going to get bit by one of those worms. One bite and you're done for."

"Are you saying that the infection spreads by the bite of those snakes?" Lockjaw asked, his eyes widened.

She said, "That's how they lay their eggs in you."

"Fuck . . ." Lockjaw said.

"What?" Richards asked, but Horatio knew exactly what he was thinking.

"Sun was bit by several of them," Lockjaw said.

"You have to kill him," Bunny said through the bars. "He'll turn against you at any minute."

"Shut up," Lockjaw said to Bunny, waving her boomerang in her face.

"Let's go," Richards said.

The three men rushed down the hall, passing Tomahawk on the way. Richards yelled at him, "Watch the Bitch," as they passed.

"What's up?" he said, raising a sledgehammer in the air like a question mark.

"Just watch her!" Richards said.

He chuckled and continued on. "Yeah, I'll watch her alright."

Horatio looked back at him, wondering what the son of a bitch was planning to do to her.

As they approached the medical bay, they heard a series of gunshots.

"Fuck, he's already turned," Lockjaw yelled.

Then they saw Poppy running out of the medical bay, crossing the hall into another room, a trail of blood coming from his severed arms where the wounds had reopened. Horatio ran in first, aiming his gun at the legless man. He almost fired as Sun raised his arms at him.

"What are you doing?" Sun cried, dropping his pistol.

"The snakes bit you," Horatio said. "You're infected."

"They bit me in the legs, but you guys cut them off." Sun pointed at his bloody stumps. "I'm not the one who's infected, it's Poppy."

Horatio lowered his rifle and turned around to see Poppy charging them from behind.

"Look out," Horatio yelled at Captain Richards.

But before the Captain could turn around, the mutant grabbed him around the waist. Snakes curled out of his throat and bit him in the cheek. One of them slid down the front of his uniform.

The Captain shrieked and jerked himself free. Poppy ran for the elevator. Horatio turned and aimed his rifle at the fleeing man, but Richards was in his way. The Captain was in shock, ripping at his shirt to remove the creature burrowing into his chest. Lockjaw attempted to help him, but the Captain was thrashing around so much that he couldn't get close.

Horatio pushed his way through the men to get a clear shot at Poppy, but by then the infected man had already made it into the elevator. He hit a button and the elevator descended.

"Fuck, he got away," Horatio said.

He turned to the others. Richards ripped open his shirt. There was a hole in his chest, but no sign of the snake.

"Where'd it go?" Richards said.

"It went inside of you," said Lockjaw.

"No . . . no, it couldn't have." Richards felt around his torso for signs of movement. "It must have fallen out of the bottom of my shirt."

"I didn't see it fall."

"It's dark," said the Captain. "You can't see shit."

"It doesn't matter where it is," Horatio said. "One of them bit you in the face. You're definitely infected."

Captain Richards felt the wound on his face.

"I'm sorry, Captain," Horatio said. He looked at Lockjaw and they nodded at each other.

Lockjaw grabbed the string of the chainsaw boomerang to start it up, but before he got it running the Captain drew all four of his repeaters and pointed them at the two men.

"Drop it," he said to Lockjaw.

The medic dropped the weapon.

"Neither of you are to say a word about this to the others," Richards said.

"But you're infected," Horatio said. "There's nothing you can do. We've got to lock you up before you turn."

"Bullshit," Richards said. "All we know about what causes the infection is what the Bitch told us, and I don't believe her for one minute. How come Poppy was infected? He was never bit."

"Those worms are all over this place," Horatio said. "He could have been bit at any time when he was sitting on the ground downstairs. You know you've been infected. You know what has to be done."

He moved in closer to Horatio, jabbing the guns into his stomach. If the barrel of his rifle wasn't so long and the Captain wasn't so close, Horatio would have shot him right there.

"This doesn't concern you, Lieutenant," said the Captain. "I'll deal with this problem myself."

"You're putting us all at risk," said Horatio.

"Just follow my orders and keep your mouth shut." Then he looked at the medic. "Both of you. Besides, we've got a bigger issue right now."

"What?"

"Poppy is downstairs," Richards said. "I don't know how smart they are once they're infected, but if he's smart enough to work an elevator he's probably smart enough to break through our barricade. He could let the others in from outside."

Horatio looked over at the elevator shaft. "And then bring the lot of them back up here."

"We need to get ready for them." Richards kicked the wall. "Where the fuck is Hamburglar?"

The Hamburglar was outside of the Outpost, strolling through a field of white desert flowers between piles of rusted scrap metal. He sniffed at the flowers with his stubby nose. Stretching out his arms, he took a deep breath of the oily junkyard air and sighed.

He walked through the metal legs of a large rumbling machine shaped like a giant spider. It was as tall as a house and made snorting and squealing noises as the samurai walked through. He brushed his hand against one of its smooth metal legs and tapped his fingers against it as percussion to a self-composed melody that was going through his head.

An infected mutant came out from behind a collapsed tool shed and charged him, but it took Hamburglar a quick flick of his sword to behead his attacker. He didn't even have to open his eyes as he breathed deeply, the music dancing in his mind. Then he bent down, picked a flower and put it behind his ear.

The Hamburglar appreciated nature. Although it was very flawed, he could see patterns in nature that he found beautiful. When teenaged Hamburglar gave up on searching for love in human beings, he turned to other things that would inspire passion in him. The first thing he turned to was nature.

Willem spent much of his time gazing up at the sky and clouds, lying in the park. Once he felt full of life he would go to his piano and attempt to play with passion. His music was improving. He knew he was very close to perfection.

His father told him he could get another piano tutor as long as he didn't kill this one. Willem realized that he had learned something from the last tutor, just before he cut his head off, so it would be wise not to cut the next one's head off just for receiving criticism.

The new tutor also told him that he was not playing with enough passion. Willem tried playing again, summoning all of the

passion he had ever felt when surrounded by nature, but it still wasn't enough. The tutor just shook his head. Willem was pissed, but he refrained from killing the man. He relaxed, finished the lesson without incident, and the tutor left without a scratch on him.

But a few days later, Willem changed his mind and cut the asshole's throat out while he was taking a dump.

So, from then on, he put more of his focus into sword-fighting. He trained day and night, perfecting ancient techniques from the books he read. His sword-making skills were also increasing and he soon created a short katana that was in every way perfect. It was his first masterpiece. It was a katana he would use in battle for the rest of his life.

When he was an adult, he joined the Fry Guy police force and quickly worked his way up the ranks. He was the only officer allowed to carry a katana. It became his symbol. A symbol of peace and order. The citizens of McDonaldland feared him. Criminals feared him even more. When he walked by, people got out of his way. There was a rumor going around that every once in a while when Willem was walking through a crowd of people, he'd draw his sword and cut somebody's head off just for the heck of it.

The rumors were true, of course, but he didn't do it just for the heck of it. He did it to see if he could draw his sword, kill somebody, and re-sheath his weapon without anyone noticing. Although Willem was so fast with his blade that nobody could see him draw his sword, it was still pretty obvious who the murderer was. If Willem was in the vicinity when somebody got their head cut off it was a pretty safe bet that he was the one who did it. Still, nobody did anything about his vicious crimes. The other Fry Guys would never accuse him of the beheadings. There was nobody in McDonaldland more frightening than him.

CHAPTER FOUR

Sun was put into a chair and stationed in the hallway, within shooting range from the elevator. If anyone heard the gunfire they would come to his aid.

The others returned to Greggy and Tomahawk to find them inside of the cage with the wolf woman. They were trying to hold her down. Both men were bloody with claw-marks and the woman was bruised from being punched and kicked in the stomach several times. Her head was rolling against her shoulder, blood leaking through her fur, a wound from Tomahawk's club as he tried to knock her unconscious. But the wolf woman had a strong head and it didn't knock her out. She was still able to fight them off half-conscious.

"What the hell are you two doing?" Horatio asked.

"Just having some fun," Tomahawk said.

By just having some fun, he meant that he was trying to rape the woman. Horatio looked at Richards, but he had no problem with this. It was common for Outlanders to rape their female prisoners, even the hairier ones. Since there were no females in the Outlander army, this was the only way they were able to have sex.

Bunny kicked Tomahawk in the stomach and he fell back. He punched her with his massive third arm, but just as it landed in her chin she grabbed it with her claw and bent it back. His mutant appendage was powerful, but not as powerful as her werewolf strength.

"Get away from her," Horatio said.

"Don't worry, you can have your turn after me," Tomahawk said, arm wrestling with the woman.

"I don't want a turn."

Horatio was somebody who did not rape women. There were only a small percentage of Outlanders who did not. He didn't because he found nothing sexually enticing about rape and had no interest having sex with somebody who was disgusted by the idea of having sex with him. He was also morally opposed to it. Others, such as the Hamburglar, did not rape prisoners because they had no interest in sex in general, they saw lust as a weakness that they needed to bury deep down inside. Others, like Greggy, did not rape wolf women because they were scared of getting hurt or killed by them. It was not uncommon for a man to end up ripped to shreds in the attempt to rape the women. But still, Greggy would assist in holding down a prisoner if ordered to do so. Most of the Outlanders assumed those who didn't rape were just homosexual.

"What are you gay or something?" Tomahawk asked.

"She's infected, idiot," Horatio said. "She's immune, but she's still a carrier. Get the hell away from her, now."

Tomahawk laughed at him, but then he saw the movement beneath her skin. He stepped back. Greggy dropped her. They ran out of the cage before she could get to her feet.

"We've got a problem," Richards said to Tomahawk once the asshole composed himself. Horatio could see sweat leaking in large streams down the Captain's face and neck. He was definitely infected and already beginning to change. "Poppy's one of them."

"What?" Tomahawk yelled, pissed at Richards as if it were his fault. "Where is he?"

"Downstairs. Most likely tearing down our barricade and letting the horde in. He also has control of the elevator so I need you to help Sun keep guard by the shaft."

Tomahawk's third fist was squeezing, as if ready to break somebody's face open. Instead of releasing his aggression on his commanding officer, he turned and stomped down the hallway toward Sun.

Richards turned to Greg. "Find the Hamburglar and tell him to go after Poppy, then back up Tomahawk."

Greggy stood there, staring at the sweat pouring down the Captain's neck.

"Now!" Richards said. "Move it!"

Greggy nearly fell over trying to run away, up to the third

floor where he thought the Hamburglar was most likely to be hiding.

"You two are with me," Richards said to Lockjaw and Horatio, then he moved down the hall. His steps were somewhat off balance.

"Where we going?" Lockjaw asked.

"The roof."

Captain Richards stood at the edge of the roof, looking down at the mob below.

He turned to Horatio. "Lieutenant, I want you to take out as many of them as you can."

Horatio nodded, and stared down at the entrance of the Outpost through his scope. The door was still barricaded, so if Poppy was going to let the horde in, he had yet to accomplish it. There were about a dozen men trying to get into the Outpost, banging on the barred windows until their fists became bloody. The rest of the yard was filled with dozens more of them, and beyond the gate there were even more. They just wandered in a daze, looking around as if something was calling to them in the distance but they couldn't tell which direction it was coming from.

The Captain turned to Lockjaw. "Help him out all you can. If those things get through, come down and let us know. But, Horatio, you man this post until they're all dead or you're out of bullets."

They both nodded at him.

As he walked away, Horatio looked at Lockjaw and whispered, "We've got to keep an eye on him."

"Should I shoot him in the back now?" Lockjaw said. Then he smiled, his yellow horns bobbing back and forth.

Horatio shook his head. "We'll wait until he changes, but let's make sure we're there when it happens. Don't want anyone else infected because of him."

Then Horatio aimed his rifle at a mutant standing by the front entrance, clawing at the door. The mutant's head exploded as Horatio pulled the trigger and its body fell limp to the ground.

"This is going to be a while," Horatio said, chuckling.

Lockjaw laughed with him, but both of them fell silent when they noticed that the entire swarm of infected men were looking up at them. They were all frozen in place, staring up at the two men on the roof. Then, in unison, they all screamed and charged the building.

"What the fuck?" Lockjaw said.

Horatio aimed at another one and took him out. Mutants ripped at the windows and doors, looking up at them as if the only reason they wanted to get through was to get at the two on the roof. The mutants on the other side of the gate began scaling the fence to get into the yard. Other mutants tried scaling the side of the building to get to the two men. Some of them were able to make it halfway up before they slid back down with bloody palms and fingernails peeled back to the knuckles.

Then there was movement in the mountains of rubble. Dead trees growing out of rusted vehicles were thrashing in the air as if dinosaurs were barreling through the woods toward the Outpost. One tree broke from its roots and collapsed onto the fence, making it easier for the infected mutants to get into the yard.

Horatio took his aim away from the mutants at the gate and aimed at the junkyard forest. Through the scope, he could see some kind of machine. It was crashing through the trees, oozing smoke from black pipes.

"What the hell is that?" Lockjaw asked, pulling out his shotgun.

Then it appeared. A giant machine walking on four spider-like legs stepped out of the trees and lumbered toward them. Then another appeared, and another. Through the scope, Horatio could see that there were living animals in the center of each machine. Increasing the focus on his scope, Horatio recognized them as warthogs. Their limbs had been cut off and replaced by these large four-story tall mechanical ones. Like nu-cows, the tops of their skulls were missing and large neuro-implants were attached to their brains. They must have been engineered to act like sentinels for the Outpost. Normally they would be controlled via remote by Outlanders from a distance, but these creatures were no longer being controlled by men, they were under the influence of the metal worms that were squirming through their flesh.

Horatio aimed for one and fired, but it missed the target. They were protected by so much metal that only a small portion of their faces were showing. There were parts of their sides and back that were uncovered, but hitting them in these places would not kill the infected animals.

"I can't get a good shot," Horatio said.

"Forget about them," Lockjaw said, pointing down. "Focus on the ones at the entrance."

Horatio looked down and noticed movement through the windows of the warehouse. Somebody was inside, knocking over the crates filled with gasoline to get the doors open.

"It's Poppy," Horatio said.

Horatio aimed his gun through the window, but couldn't get a clear shot. He couldn't distinguish any human body parts due to the light reflecting off of the glass.

"I'll handle it," Lockjaw said, pumping his shotgun.

As Lockjaw aimed over the roof, Horatio yelled out, "No, don't!"

But Horatio didn't knock the barrel of Lockjaw's gun out of the way until it was too late. The shotgun pellets scattered in the air, breaking through the window, and hitting the gasoline leaking across the warehouse floor. The explosion caused the building to rumble. Infected mutants were thrown away from the building as a flame cloud filled the yard.

When the smoke cleared, Horatio saw a layer of fire across the ground surrounding the entrance to the Outpost. The infected mutants stood up, covered in flames. Even fire wouldn't stop them. They shrieked like metallic bats and then charged into the wide-open warehouse door.

"Oops," Lockjaw said.

Horatio wasn't amused. "Get down there and let the others know they've broken through."

Lockjaw ran for the hatch to the third floor.

"And keep an eye on Richards," Horatio said.

One of the mechanical warthogs stomped in front of the roof, close enough so that the Lieutenant could see dual Gatling guns positioned in the front of the machine just below the infected beast.

"Get down!" Horatio yelled.

The guns opened fire. Lockjaw didn't get down, instead he turned around and fired his shotgun at the pig. His bullets ricocheted off the metal exterior. He pumped his weapon and fired three more shots. Then his chest was torn apart by the storm of bullets. He fell to his knees and fired one more time, hitting the edge of the roof by Horatio, as he collapsed face first into a pool of his own blood. Dead.

The machine turned its Gatlings on the sharp-shooter, shredding the side of the roof Horatio was using for cover. He put his hands over his head as chunks of asphalt fell on him, crawling across the roof away from the storm of bullets.

Once he was clear, he raised his weapon over the ledge and aimed for the warthog's face. The metal worms snaked in and out of the animal's ears and eyes. Horatio fired, but missed the six inch space around the creature's head that was not blocked by steel casing. The bullet gave away the shooter's new position, and the machine moved its aim at Horatio. He got off another shot before ducking, just barely missing the bullet storm.

He crawled to another location. This time he relaxed, aimed right for the infected pig's head, then squeezed the trigger. The bullet bounced off the edge of a metal plate. Horatio grunted with frustration. Instead of ducking as the Gatlings shifted toward him, he fired continuously, not aiming for the pig anymore, but the engine.

Two bullets pierced the fuel tank, releasing streams of gasoline down the front of the engine. As Horatio ducked, the

Gatlings fired at him and the spark from the discharging bullets ignited the gas. A wave of heat pressed against Horatio's back as the machine exploded. Rotten pig guts and metal shrapnel rained down onto the rooftop.

Horatio stood and stepped back. The machine collapsed down through the edge of the roof, releasing burning metal worms at the lieutenant's boots.

Looking down at the mutants screaming up at him from the yard, he noticed something new running toward the Outpost. It was the Hamburglar, racing out of the woods, cutting through infected mutants as he jumped over the sheet of flames into the warehouse.

"How the fuck did he get down there?" Horatio asked.

Then he noticed the horde was coming toward the wall below him. They were using the collapsed machine as a ladder, climbing up the legs to the roof. The two remaining sentinel machines opened fire on him.

As he ducked down and scurried toward the hatch, an army of infected men leapt from the burning machine onto the rooftop and charged him.

"Fucking hell," Horatio said as he jumped down to the third floor.

He closed the hatch behind him and locked it. The mutants stomped and scratched at the other side. It wasn't going to hold long, but he didn't have time to reinforce the barrier. The others still didn't know the front entrance had been compromised.

Greggy couldn't find the Hamburglar anywhere. When he met up with Richards, the Captain said, "Where the fuck have you been?"

"I couldn't find him. Anywhere."

Tomahawk and Sun had their rifles aimed at the elevator shaft, prepared for the horde to ascend at any moment.

"You're fucking useless," Captain Richards said, blood dripping down the corners of his eyes. "Get in position."

Greggy stood next to Richards and raised his submachine gun at the shaft. A small metal worm tore through the skin on one of the Captain's wrists and crawled over the barrel of his repeater. He grabbed it with one of his extra limbs and pulled it out of his flesh, a spurt of blood splashing into his mouth.

"Where did that come from?" Greggy asked, staring at the worm in the Captain's hand.

Richards tossed it over his shoulder, rubbing blood from his lips.

"Nowhere . . ." he said. "It was nothing. Just hold your position."

Greggy didn't stop looking at him. He could see movement underneath the man's skin, on his neck just below his left ear.

"Captain . . ." Greggy said, pointing at the side of his head.

Then the sound of the elevator whirred into life. Greggy moved the barrel of his gun to the shaft, slowly backing away from the Captain, his rifle shaking in his hand.

Tomahawk opened fire on the elevator doors as it reached the second floor, but the doors didn't open. The elevator passed their floor and continued up the shaft.

"Fuck," Tomahawk yelled. "It's going to the third floor!"

Tomahawk ran in the other direction toward the stairs, leaving his crippled friend in his chair on the front line. Richards ran after him. Greggy went to help Sun when he heard the noise. There was shrieking coming up the shaft from below as mutants climbed up the brick walls below the elevator. Then, like a swarm of cockroaches, the infected men crawled out of the dark hole and attacked.

On the front line, Sun and Greggy opened fire. They didn't have time to aim for heads, so they just shot randomly at the crowd racing toward them. Some of them fell, others continued forward. Richards turned around to assist his men, but Tomahawk continued up the stairs to the third floor.

As the Captain fired, he could feel a worm crawling up his sinuses. It chewed its way through the back of his eyeball and peeled back his cornea as it emerged, coiling against the bridge of his nose. Richards screamed and ripped it out of him; his pupil suctioned around its body created a popping noise as it came out. He covered the eye with one hand and continued firing with the other three.

Greggy abandoned Sun as the infected arrived. The crazed men tore into Sun with knives, opening large gashes to allow the worms to crawl in. Sun screamed, firing his shotgun into their faces as they cut him. Behind the chair, Greggy sprayed them with bullets, but he couldn't stop them from cutting open Sun's throat and puking a stomach-full of parasites into the neck hole.

Then the infected men targeted Greg. They cornered him, reaching for his chest with worms twisting out of their finger tips. Greggy fired at them until his clip ran out, then he kicked them and pushed them away from him. He focused more on the snakes than the men, hitting them away from him with the side of his submachine gun.

Then Greggy saw something coming up the elevator shaft. It wasn't another infected mutant. It was Hamburglar. He flipped out of the shaft and decapitated three infected men before landing.

"Robble robble!" he said, then slashed his way through the crowd.

Limbs and blood flew through the air as he jerked his swords lightning-fast at the mutants. They barely got a chance to turn their heads before he cut the fronts of their faces off, brains leaking down their chests like runny eggs.

As the Hamburglar fought his way through the crowd, Greggy screamed "Yeah!" at the samurai, pushing back the men around him. "Just in time!"

Then the mutants in front of Greggy fell into halves as Hamburglar's long blade sliced through all of them at once. Greggy raised his fist and cheered as the Samurai continued past.

Then Greggy looked down to see blood leaking from his midsection. He lifted his shirt, a long gash in his stomach went all the way around his hips. Before he could feel the pain, Greggy's upper torso slid off of his lower half and his body split into two. As his blood and intestines oozed out of him, the last thing Greggy did before he died was curse himself for forgetting one of the most basics rules of being a soldier in the Outlander army:

When the Hamburglar's swords are drawn, you get the fuck out of his way.

On the third floor, Horatio ran into Tomahawk finishing off the last of the infected mutants coming off of the elevator. He watched Tomahawk struggle to pull a hammer out of a mutant's skull, pushing the dead man's shoulder back with the heel of his boot.

"There's a ton of them on the roof," Horatio said. "They'll break through the hatch at any minute."

An explosion of blood and dead worms splashed across the elevator floor as Tomahawk ripped his hammer free.

"We need to get out of here," Tomahawk said. "Now."

They went toward the stairs leading to the second floor. Horatio loaded his rifle with the last of his bullets.

"Running low?" Tomahawk said, examining the small quantity of rounds remaining in the sharp-shooter's hands.

"I'll be fine if we can find the armory," Horatio said.

Tomahawk shook his afro. "No time."

As they went down the stairs, the large man raised his hammer above his head.

"I bet you wish you knew how to fight with a hand weapon now," Tomahawk said. "My hammers never run out of bullets."

Horatio finished loading and cocked the gun, then aimed it over Tomahawk's shoulder and fired. Tomahawk looked up at Horatio, rubbing the ringing noise from his ear with a *what the fuck?* face. Horatio pointed to the dead mutant that was hiding in the shadows at the bottom of the stairs.

"You might be good with your hammers, but you have terrible eyes."

Tomahawk shook his head in disgust as Horatio smiled at him.

The Hamburglar cut through the backs of two infected men, severing their spines, and they fell to the floor. Then he spun around and cut a third through the brain down the center of its face. When this one fell, the Hamburglar realized it was the last of them and jerked his blades into the air to flick his enemy's blood across the dimly lit wall.

As he raised his swords to return them to their scabbards, stepping through the pile of corpses that stretched the entire length of hallway, Hamburglar heard a gunshot. He looked down to see a hole in his chest.

"Robble?" he said.

Hamburglar looked up to see Richards glaring at him across the hall, worms crawling in and out of his face. The infected Captain fired again and three more holes appeared on the Hamburglar's torso.

"Robble!" screamed the samurai as he threw his short katana at Richards.

The sword flew through the air like a glimmering harpoon and impaled the Captain's face, throwing him backward, nailing his head to the wall behind him.

Richards gurgled, grabbing at the sword pierced through the center of his nose, trying to pull himself from the wall, watching the Hamburglar as he approached.

Hamburglar looked at him up close, his little red tongue curling out of his cartoonish smile. Richards was still alive, his eyeballs rolling around in the sockets, worms crawling out of his wound across the blade.

Then Hamburglar flicked his long katana across the Captain's neck. The infected man's body fell to the floor, his head still nailed to the wall. When the samurai pulled out the sword, the severed head was still attached to the blade. He shook it but the head wouldn't come off.

Then a ball of worms slipped out of the Captain's neck and coated the Hamburglar's hand, biting into his flesh and burrowing into his wrist. Hamburglar stomped on the head and pulled it off of his blade, then sheathed both swords. He raised his hand to his eyes and watched as the worms crawled into him. Just gazing at them and moving his fingers slowly until they were all the way inside.

Then the Hamburglar squeezed a fist, flexing the muscles in his hand and upper arm. The worms inside of him were compressed by his muscles, crushing them tightly until they popped. Then with his other hand he squeezed them out the holes they entered through like toothpaste from a tube.

The Hamburglar was immune to all diseases and infections. His body was so full of chemicals and preservatives that it was not a hospitable place for viruses or parasites. The preservatives in his body made him practically immortal. He did not age. He did not require much food or sleep. He was very difficult to kill, even without his deadly samurai skills.

Soon after he became the chief of the Fry Guy police force in McDonaldland, he heard about a man who had reconstructive surgery to look like the Mayor McCheese character from the McDonald's Bible. The Mayor was the official spokesperson for the Blessed McDonald's Corporation and acted as the city's leader. It was Willem who proposed the idea to undergo the same operation. He wanted to become the Hamburglar who, in the McDonald's Bible, was the punisher of all sinners. The Blessed McDonald's Corporation was very enthusiastic about the idea and put him into surgery immediately.

From that day on, Willem was the Hamburglar. He turned the Fry Guy police force into the toughest, most ruthless army

McDonaldland had every known. With his second katana master-piece perfected, he was complete. He never required a gun to fight crime, he had his two swords. And with real criminals to fight, he was able to practice his samurai skills on an almost daily basis.

Mayor McCheese became fast friends with Hamburglar. At long last, Hamburglar had found himself a man he could call his equal. While the Mayor was not as skilled of a warrior as Hamburglar, he had impressive ambitions and ideas. The Mayor believed only the intelligent and the strong should have full rights as citizens. He believed in a powerful military force. He believed in order, in art, in perfection. Not only that, but he loved the Hamburglar's piano playing.

They would spend their weekends together, drinking the fin-est illegal wine that only the wealthiest of McDonaldland citizens were privy to, attempting not to spill every single drop while sip-ping with their oversized mutant heads. Hamburglar would listen to the Mayor's big plans for the future of their city and then the Mayor would listen to Hamburglar play piano long into the night.

"That was genius," the Mayor would say after every con-certo. "Absolute genius."

The Hamburglar adored hearing him say that.

But the Mayor knew how to stroke men's egos. He under-stood how to win their favor. It was quite obvious to him that all the Hamburglar needed was a little appreciation. He knew that the man was desperate to be admired, to have his brilliance recognized, to be treated not as a peer but as a better. Although the Mayor did enjoy the Hamburglar's music, he too knew it wasn't quite perfect, it wasn't passionate enough.

Although he had no idea the Mayor was exaggerating his appreciation for the music, Hamburglar himself could recog-nize that his music was lacking no matter how much it was praised. He had become the greatest warrior in all of McDon-aldland, a master of the sword, a new world samurai, but he would not be satisfied until he could also master music. It was his mission to finally experience the emotion of love, so that he could express his passion in his art.

CHAPTER FIVE

Tomahawk and Horatio ran into Hamburglar downstairs. They saw all the dead bodies surrounding them. They saw Richards' uniform on a headless corpse. They saw what was left of Greggy and Sun.

"So that's it?" Tomahawk said. "We're the only three left?"

Hamburglar ogled them with his sinister grin but said nothing.

"Looks that way," Horatio said, his rifle pointing at the ceiling.

"Fuck," Tomahawk said. "What now?"

"There's still hundreds of them downstairs," Horatio said. "And a ton more that will probably break in from the roof at any minute. Not to mention the sentinels patrolling the building."

"The what?"

"You'll have to see them for yourself."

Then three infected mutants came up from the elevator shaft and charged them, but Hamburglar cut them down before they had a chance to interrupt the conversation.

Tomahawk didn't even blink. "I say we just fight our way through the yard, find a vehicle that works and get the hell out of here."

"Think any of the vehicles run?"

"No time to worry about that now," Tomahawk said.

As they turned to move toward the shaft, they realized the Hamburglar was already on his way.

"Wait," Bunny yelled as they passed her cell. "You can't leave me here."

Tomahawk passed her by, but Horatio paused.

"Fuck her," Tomahawk said.

"I can help you," the woman said.

Horatio stared at her, contemplating whether he could trust her or not.

"She might be useful," Horatio said.

Tomahawk turned around. "You can't be serious. Let's go."

"Where's the key?" Horatio asked.

"How the fuck should I know?" Tomahawk said.

"Your Captain had it," Bunny said.

"Okay." Horatio went in the direction of Richards' body.

"If you're going to free that Bitch then I'm leaving without you," Tomahawk said.

"Wait for me. I'll just be a second."

Tomahawk shook his head and continued on. Before he got to the shaft, he turned around and said. "She's a Bitch. She'll turn on you. I promise."

But Horatio was already digging for keys in the headless Captain's uniform.

The infected came running downstairs from the roof as Horatio pulled the jail key out of the mouth of a large metal worm crawling out of Richards' anus. He fired one round at the leading mutant coming out of the stairwell, causing those behind him to trip and stumble, slowing the entire horde down.

Just before he unlocked the cell, he stared Bunny in the eyes, as if looking for a sign that she was not trustworthy. She understood the look he was giving her.

"I don't trust you either," she said. "But what choice do we have?"

Horatio unlocked the door and stepped back. He just waited with his weapon out to the side, giving her a chance to kill him if that's what she desired. But she stepped to him without the slightest sign of aggression.

"I'll trust you," he said, as an infected man came at him from behind.

Before it could reach him, Bunny grabbed the screaming mutant's neck and slammed his face between the bars of the cell, cracking his skull inwards in the process.

Then she said, "Where's my weapon?"

Horatio took her to the hallway outside the medical bay where Lockjaw had dropped her chainsaw boomerang. The floor was now littered with dead bodies. It was buried in there somewhere.

As Bunny searched through the corpses, Horatio fired at the mutants coming at them. He used his bullets conservatively, killing only the fast-moving ones.

"Hurry up," Horatio said.

Bunny kicked through the bodies. The mutants got closer.

"Hurry up," Horatio said.

They were too close and too many for him to shoot, so he raised his gun to use as a bat. Then the chainsaws roared as Bunny found her weapon. She lifted it over her head and revved the engine, drowning out the screams of their attackers.

Horatio ducked as she used her boomerang like a chainsaw sword, slashing the arriving mutants and emptying their stomach contents onto the floor.

"Let's go," Bunny said.

Horatio ran toward the elevator, but she called him back. "Not that way. The roof." And although he had no idea what she had planned, Horatio went along.

Bunny hacked through the mutants, killing all the ones near them, and then tossed her boomerang at the crowd at the end of the hall. They screamed as they fell into halves, the boomerang not slowing down a bit as it sliced through. It bounced off the back wall and returned, shredding through the last two standing mutants, and into her hand.

"Upstairs," Bunny said.

They went up to the roof, slashing through necks and bellies. Horatio stayed back, avoiding the metal worms that were spraying out of the flesh, conserving his bullets.

"Why are we going to the roof?" Horatio asked.

"My secret weapon is up there," Bunny said, as five men surrounded her.

Then she spun around in a circle with her chainsaw blades out, decapitating all five men at once.

After Tomahawk climbed down the elevator shaft, he noticed he was all alone in the warehouse with a dozen infected mutants coming after him, catching him off guard. Using his assault rifle, he emptied his clip into the crowd, their blood splashing into his eyes. He felt tiny maggot-sized worms squirming in his corneas and rubbed them out as quickly as he could. They weren't on his fingers when he pulled them away and he wondered if they had punctured his retinas and gotten inside. While stepping through the warehouse, he could feel tickling sensations in his eyes but he thought it might just be paranoia.

Outside, he fired his last clip into the crowd of mutants, and then moved onto his hammers. He held them out, one in each hand, his third hand pumping a fist, as he yelled the battle cry of a Viking warlord. Then he charged into the horde, aiming to crush some skulls.

Hamburglar was slicing his way through the army of worm-coated soldiers, cutting them down as easily as paper dolls. Music was playing in his head, beautiful passionate music.

In the search for love, Hamburglar made many bad decisions. He was desperate to bring passion into his music and was willing to try anything. He tried spending time with his father, hoping to figure out how to love the man who raised him, but his father had been completely terrified of him ever since he transformed his flesh into that of the Hamburglar. He represented the devil, after all, and his father would not spend much time with him.

Then the Hamburglar tried to experience the love for a pet. He bought a McPuppy and played with it, took care of it. But the little animal only lasted a week before he cut it in half for urinating on his pristine living room carpet.

Then he made the biggest mistake of all. When he was drunk with the Mayor one night, the Hamburglar was seduced into having sex with him. Although the Hamburglar considered himself asexual, that night he learned the Mayor was quite fond of the male gender. While drunk on illegal wine, the Mayor wondered what it would be like to sleep with the Hamburglar, and suggested the idea to him as if it were a business proposal. Wondering if he could find love with the Mayor, the only living person on the planet he truly respected, Hamburglar decided to give it a try.

The next morning, the two of them awoke naked in bed together, their giant heads dwarfing the pillows beneath them as they both stared at the ceiling, not saying a word to each other. They could hear each other's breaths, the Hamburglar's fingers fidgeting with the top of the silken sheet. The Mayor cleared his throat, looking over at the Hamburglar, and then back at the ceiling.

Neither of them knew what to say. Neither of them wanted to be the first to leave the bed. So they just lay there in an awkward silence, wishing they hadn't had so much to drink the night before.

"So," the Mayor began, after twenty more minutes of discomfort. "Let's pretend that never happened."

The Hamburglar nodded his bulbous head, then continued staring at the ceiling in awkward silence.

On the roof, Bunny went to a crate on the other side of the building. It was full of supplies.

"What's all this?" Horatio said.

Bunny tossed her boomerang at a couple mutants as they climbed off of the metal spider machine still collapsed against the side of the building.

"I had been living up here for the past week," she said. "This is what's left of my supplies."

Horatio could tell she had no food left. It was mostly a bunch of empty cans. She probably hadn't eaten in days.

"Here we go," Bunny said as she pulled a device out from a pile of fur-coated blankets.

She caught her boomerang as it returned and then took the device to the edge of the roof. Down below, Horatio could see the Hamburglar and Tomahawk fighting a crowd of mutants. Hamburglar with his two swords slicing bodies apart. Tomahawk with his two sledgehammers, crushing brains out of skulls and hearts out of ribcages.

Bunny put the device on the ledge of the roof, and Horatio could tell it was some kind of remote control.

"The last Meat left alive after this army became infected taught me how to use this," she said. "It's been quite useful."

When the rabbit/wolf girl moved the controls on the device, one of the spider sentinels stomped around the building toward them. As it arrived, Horatio ducked but Bunny just smiled at it.

"Are you controlling that thing?" Horatio asked.

Bunny smirked. "Mostly. The worms are also controlling the animal's brain, but this device has a stronger influence."

As Bunny moved a secondary joystick and held down a red button on its handle, the sentinel opened fire on the mutants below. The wolf girl laughed as the Gatlings shredded apart their jittering bodies.

"Now what?" Horatio said.

"What do you mean? We just try to kill them all until there's none left to stop us from walking out of here."

"That's it? We can't kill them all. We'll just run out of bullets."

"Well, what else can we do?" she asked.

"Well," Horatio pointed at the device, "when you showed me that control for the sentinel, I thought we were going to ride it out of here."

Bunny's lips curled into a smile. "Huh, I never thought about that. I wonder if it would work."

She controlled the sentinel toward the edge of the roof and jumped onto the top of the machine, just above the infected warthog.

Bunny held out her hand. "Come on, Meat. Let's get the hell

out of here."

Horatio took her furry claw and she pulled him into her arms. "Careful," she said, balancing him in an awkward embrace. Since she was over a foot taller than him, he found his chin pressed firmly between her breasts.

Then she sat down, her legs dangling off the front of the machine, the control in her lap. The roof of the sentinel was not very large, about a quarter the size of the roof of a car. Horatio had to squeeze in tight around Bunny, wrapping his arms around her hairy waist.

"Hold on tight," she said, and then they began to move, firing into the mutants underfoot.

Tomahawk's arms were beginning to get tired. He had swung his sledgehammers around so much that the muscles were pulled and twisted. One of his arms was so sore that he had to switch to using a handgun, and even the act of pulling the trigger sent a needle of pain up his arm. His large third arm was only slightly weakened and was able to crush skulls continually without tire. Unfortunately, this arm wasn't as fast and agile as his natural arms. It was like a lumbering tank, not able to crush more than one skull every other minute.

The Hamburglar didn't notice Tomahawk was weakening or else he might have come to his aid, but he was too absorbed in the music within his head, too absorbed in killing.

The Hamburglar never gave up trying to find love and passion, but the more he failed the more difficult it became to keep optimism. Eventually, he spent more and more time practicing his swordsmanship, and less and less time trying to find love. Fighting made him happy, failing at music did not. So he focused more on being a samurai.

Bunny's fluffy tail wiggled in the soft flesh below Horatio's belly-button as she fired the Gatling guns into the third sentinel. Her waist was warm against his hands, her ass tight against his crotch.

As the beast within the machine was shredded to bits and collapsing into the junkyard, Bunny felt something stiff growing beneath her tail.

"Do you have a fucking erection again?" Bunny yelled.

Horatio blushed. "Sorry. This is the closest I've been to a woman in an incredibly long time."

"Well, cut it out," she said.

"I wish I could."

He wagged his third leg like a tail.

She grumbled loudly, firing into the swarm of mutants below to release her aggression.

A mutant grabbed Tomahawk by his slowly moving third arm. This arm was strong enough to crush the mutant's head, but the infected man wouldn't let go of the wrist, dropping all of his weight to the ground. All of a sudden Tomahawk couldn't move very quickly, dragging this clingy mutant through the yard.

Tomahawk pointed his handgun at the man's head, but it only made a clicking noise when he pulled the trigger. Out of bullets. He tried smashing the man's skull with his free sledgehammer but couldn't break his head open at the awkward angle.

Dragging the clinging man all the way across the yard, Tomahawk arrived at a supply truck and attempted to turn it on. The engine wouldn't start. It seemed as if the battery were dead. He moved to another vehicle, still dragging the man who didn't try to bite or harm him, just holding on tightly.Another mutant came at him and he cracked its forehead with his free hammer, its dead body flipping backward as if he had just been clotheslined.

The car was small but could carry a couple of people. This one started up fine, but the engine made some glugging noise for a couple minutes before it died. It was out of gas.

"Fuck me," Tomahawk said.

The Hamburglar stabbed one mutant through each of his eyes, the blades poking out the back of his head, then he pulled them out and gutted two more mutants coming at him from each side.

The Hamburglar thought back to all the fun he used to have when he was the Chief of Police in McDonaldland. It was his job to escort criminals out of the city, but once they were brought out of the city walls he wouldn't just let them go. He would give them one of his swords, the long one, to fight him with. If they refused to pick up the sword after a few minutes, the criminal was beheaded on the spot. But if the criminal was willing to play his game, he gave the person a fair fight.

This was one way that Hamburglar was able to get his samurai practice in. He fought the most dirty, hardened criminals—sometimes blindfolded—trying to cut them down in as quickly and efficiently a manner as possible, only drawing his sword for a split second for a lethal attack. Then he would re-sheath his weapon as the blood-spraying body collapsed to the ground.

These were some of Hamburglar's favorite memories.

Horatio felt something crawling into his arm, and something else crawling into his stomach. He looked down and noticed that small metal worms were exiting Bunny's body and entering his. They crawled from her hips and asshole, burrowing deep into his flesh.

"Your worms," Horatio cried, watching his arms as the parasites disappeared inside of him. "You're infecting me!"

Tomahawk removed the battery from the car and was trying to bring it over to the supply truck. He hoped that all the truck needed was a new battery or else he'd be fucked.

Then he felt the mutant he was dragging bite down on one of his fingers. He slammed his free sledgehammer down on the little man's head, not caring about the awkward angle anymore, but as soon as it made contact Tomahawk's arm muscle tweaked and an intense pain shot up his limb.

He dropped to the ground and the mutant bit him again. Then a gang of infected men swarmed him, jumping on top of him and ripping through his uniform to cut open his flesh. He felt metal worms slide down his throat as he opened his mouth to scream.

Bunny saw the worms entering Horatio's wrists.

She turned around and stared him in the eyes. "Well, I guess this is where you get off."

Then she leaned forward to spin around and kicked him in the stomach, knocking him off the machine. He flipped over the side of the sentinel and hit the ground hard, breaking his arm out of the socket. The sentinel's back feet barely missed him as they stomped down near his head.

He heard the wolf girl laughing up there as she continued on without him.

She yelled down, "I guess that's what you get for shooting my sisters, Meat!"

Horatio rolled across the ground in pain, retrieving his rifle with his good arm.

"That fucking Bitch," he said as he cocked the gun.

Then he aimed up at the sentinel and fired, but missed. He fired again. Missed. With one arm out of socket it was nearly impossible to aim correctly. Before he could get off a third shot, a crowd of mutants were piling on top of him.

As their bodies were ripped open and filled with worms, Horatio and Tomahawk looked at each other across the yard. When their eyes locked, they chuckled at each other.

"Told you short-range weapons would get you killed," Horatio said, even though Tomahawk was too far away to hear.

"Told you long-range weapons would get you killed," Tomahawk said, at the exact same time.

They just laughed at each other as they bled out, their eyes rolling back, their limbs dropping limp.

The Hamburglar did eventually find love.

It happened one day outside the walls of McDonaldland. He was escorting six people from the city. Three wolf women and their three male lovers. He learned that all of them were skilled fighters. Two of them were fencing champions, three were experts in hand to hand combat. It was the most exciting fight he had ever had in his life. Six skilled fighters versus him. It was challenging, exhilarating.

But even with their skills and their number, the six of them didn't stand a chance. The Hamburglar was just too talented with a blade. They did last pretty long, though. Nearly ten minutes. They were incredibly fun to kill.

As he cut open their stomachs and slashed their throats, the Hamburglar realized he had found love. It wasn't a person he was in love with. It wasn't a family member, or a pet, or the beauty of nature. No, he realized he was in love with killing people.

He thought it was romantic the way their flesh ripped open and their entrails poured out. He found it sexual to stab his sword into another person's body. It made his heart melt to see his opponent's blood pouring out of them.

Yes, he was head over heels in love with killing people. Killing was his mistress, his best friend, his soul mate. Killing was what completed him. He didn't understand how he couldn't have realized it before. Of course he was in love with it. He had always been in love with it. For he was the Hamburglar, the champion of death.

So he began to channel his love for death into his music and it transformed his piano playing into powerful compositions of art made sound. His performances were filled with more passion than McDonaldland had ever seen before. He was finally perfect. A true genius.

And as he slaughtered the mutants two by two, the Hamburglar channeled his love for their deaths into a symphony that was playing inside of his head. His blades danced to the rhythm, decapitating heads and dismembering hands and feet.

He didn't notice Horatio and Tomahawk being torn to shreds behind him. He didn't realize the wolf woman escaping on a giant mechanical spider. He was too busy getting intimate with his lover. His body pressed tightly to hers, engulfed by her sweet juices, kissing her deeply, their hearts beating as one.

FEROCIOUS FEMALE FURRIES IN THE FORBIDDEN ZONE

Chapter 1

Hyena

Hyena rides her motorcycle ahead of the pack, all alone on the road, just as she likes it. There's something she finds romantic about being alone on the open road—the wind blowing through her spotted fur, the nipples on her naked fuzzy breasts chilling into stiffness, the rumbling of the machine between her thighs. It puts her mind at ease. And after yesterday's battle in McDonaldland, she desperately needs her mind at ease.

She doesn't want to look back at her sisters riding far behind her, because it would remind her that only seventeen of them are left. Although the Warriors had won the war, over ninety percent of her tribe had been killed in recent weeks. They are hardly a tribe anymore. They're now just a roaming gang of wolf bitches.

There is something on the road up ahead, moving toward her. It is not a vehicle. It is some kind of tall machine walking on metal legs. Hyena squints her eyes. The thing is shaped a bit like a spider, with somebody on top of it, riding it like a motorcycle.

Hyena readies her machine gun and slows down for her sisters to catch up. The new leader of the Warriors, Talon, speeds up to ride alongside her.

"What is it?" Talon asks.

Hyena shrugs. "It doesn't look friendly."

When they get closer, they notice the Gatling guns mounted on the sides of the machine. That's enough to tell them that the thing is hostile. Hyena aims her gun at the rider, speeding up to get into range.

"Wait," Talon calls.

Then she points up at the rider. When Hyena sees a fellow wolf woman up there, she lowers her weapon.

The mechanical spider comes to a halt when it meets the Warrior gang. Their sister riding it, Bunny, hops down to greet them.

"You're alive?" Hyena asks.

"Nice to see you, too, bitch," Bunny says with a toothy smile. Then she looks up at the sentinel she was riding. "Glad I ran into you guys. This thing moves so slow I thought it would take me all year trying to get back to you."

It had been several weeks since any of them had seen Bunny. She had been captured during a raid on an Outlander supply run, deep in the wasteland where Warriors rarely traveled. She wasn't there during the final battle against the Outlanders. She doesn't know what's happened yet.

The rest of the Warrior bikes and vehicles pull over around the spider machine. Bunny looks at them and waves at those she respects enough to acknowledge.

"So what are you doing way out here?" Bunny asks. "You surely didn't come to rescue me."

Hyena and Talon look at each other. They don't know how to break the news to her.

"Are you all on a raid or something?"

By the way Talon looks at her, Bunny can tell something is wrong.

"What happened?" Bunny asks. "Where is everyone?"

Talon glances over at her sisters watching from the vehicles around them. She takes Bunny aside.

"We're all that's left."

Bunny's eyes quiver. She exposes her fangs as if to laugh or say something, but her mouth just hangs open.

Talon continues, "Over the past few weeks, the Meat army was getting more and more aggressive. It escalated into full war. We won in the end, but not many of us survived."

"What about Grandma?" Bunny asks.

Talon shakes her head.

Bunny has to step away to take it all in.

"We decided to leave our woods, get as far away from Mc-Donaldland as possible. We're going to find somewhere else we can call home."

"You've taken Grandma's place as leader now?" Bunny asks.

Talon nods.

"Who will be second in command? Who will lead the knights?"

"Slayer," Talon says.

"Slayer?" Bunny says. "That kid? Hyena and I have been knights since she was still a citizen of McDonaldland. Why did you pick her?"

"She's grown up a lot in the past few weeks," Talon says. "Besides, deep down you know that neither you nor Hyena have what it takes to lead the knights."

"But Slayer?"

"It's already been decided."

Talon doesn't want to speak about it any further. She knows that complaining about Slayer's advancement is just Bunny's way of dodging the reality of the situation. But as a new leader, she can't have her decisions questioned. She turns to the others.

"Let's get off the road and set up camp," Talon says.

The women are eager to comply. They have not stopped to rest for more than five minutes since they left McDonaldland the day before. It's about time they got some food and sleep.

Hyena sets up her tent away from the others. Even though wolf women are pack animals, Hyena prefers to sleep away from the pack, even if it's considered dangerous to do so. When she lived in McDonaldland, she was the same way. But back then it was different. In the wasteland, her sisters usually respect the fact that she prefers to be alone. But privacy for her was nonexistent in McDonaldland.

She was a chubby, voluptuous girl weighing over 250 pounds, which was the perfect weight for a McDonaldland girl her age. All the boys were infatuated with her beauty, her curvy hips, her big ass, her bulbous breasts, and the numerous rolls in her soft white flesh. All the girls wanted to be just like her, all the boys wanted to date her. She was the most popular girl in school.

But she loathed all the attention. She didn't want to be popular. She wanted to be ignored. She wanted to be treated like an outcast. She started dressing differently, cutting her red and yellow clothing into unusual designs, inventing new makeup configurations which often made her look like a clown.

But instead of ostracizing her for her strange new looks, her classmates saw it as a cool new trend and copied her style. Everyone was going to school looking like clowns. Even though it was against dress code, the ultra conservative teachers and parents approved because they saw it as an homage to their savior from the McDonaldland Bible, Ronald McDonald.

Worse than the kids at school, Hyena couldn't handle the attention that her family gave her. She was their fat little angel. Most of her life, her parents put her into beauty pageants which she would often win. They wanted her to become a popular model after school, so that she could make them rich enough to retire early. They thought she would be the perfect pretty face to appear on billboard advertisements, holding Big Macs and triple cheeseburgers next to her cleavage. Nothing sounded worse to Hyena than that lifestyle. If she became a celebrity she would have even less privacy. Not a single person in McDonaldland would ever leave her alone. But her parents didn't give her any choice.

Not only did their dreams for her future annoy Hyena, but they also never allowed her any privacy. She wasn't allowed to lock her bedroom door, or even keep it closed. She wasn't even allowed to use the bathroom in private. After she had gone through puberty, her parents were paranoid that Hyena might give in to her sexual urges and experimental with masturbation. Then she would get kicked out of the city and they would lose their future meal ticket.

Hyena often fantasized about leaving McDonaldland and going off into the wilds of the wasteland, where she could be left alone. All she had to do was masturbate a single time and the government would kick her out. But she didn't want to get kicked out for masturbating. It seemed dishonorable to her. Like suicide, it was the coward's way out. Hyena was no coward.

As Hyena sits by her tent, struggling to start a fire with wet kindling, she hears someone creeping through the trees. Hyena smells the wind. She can't see her, but she can smell who it is. It's Nova, going off on her own again. Nova also seems to like to be alone, especially in recent weeks. But unlike Hyena, she doesn't go off on her own because she finds it more comfortable and relaxing. Nova's been going off on her own because she's depressed. She just wants to get away from her problems.

Talon comes to Hyena's tent and sits down next to her.

"How are they doing?" Hyena asks, trying to dry her kindling against her spotted furry hip.

Talon shakes her head. "It's going to be a long time before they recover from what's happened."

"Are you making a plan to boost morale?"

"Not yet," Talon says. "They need time to mourn. The only thing that's going to boost morale is to start going back on raids, and they're not ready for that yet."

With the kindling dry, Hyena puts it back in the fire pit and tries to light it again. "Not to mention there isn't anyone to raid way out here in the middle of nowhere."

Talon shakes her head. "There's other civilizations out here somewhere. We know of at least one, in Texas. I'm sure there's even more if we look hard enough."

Hyena gets a small flame to appear among the kindling. "I'm ready to go on raids whenever you give the order."

"I know you are, Hyena."

Talon pulls out one of her axes and hacks into a log, creating wood to feed the fire.

Talon smells something in the air.

"Who is that?" she says. "Is that Nova?"

"Yeah," Hyena says.

"She's . . ." Talon smells again. "She's masturbating."

"Yeah," Hyena says. "I can smell it, too."

Hyena wipes the wind away from her nose.

"She's going through a tough time," Talon says. "I think she wants to turn, so that she can forget about everything that's happened to her."

"She's taking the coward's way out," Hyena says.

"We all cope differently," Talon says. Then she takes a deep breath of the sexual aroma through her black, wet nostrils.

Nova was kicked out of McDonaldland because she had been raped. A lot of girls were kicked out of McDonaldland for getting raped. When Hyena lived there, she always wished that she was one of those girls. She wished she would have a reason to be kicked out of McDonaldland, other than masturbating. So Hyena did whatever she could in hopes that somebody would rape her. She used to go on dates with horny asshole jocks, hoping they would try to take advantage of her, but they were all wimps. Even when she got them in private and seduced them, grabbing at their cocks through their pants until they had raging hard-ons, they did nothing. They all seemed scared of sex, scared of what she would do to them if she transformed into a wolf after she climaxed. McDonaldland media was quite proficient in scaring the sex out of young people.

Then Hyena started going into the bad parts of town, walking the streets alone at night, hoping somebody would rape her. But she didn't have any luck. Whenever she saw a suspicious-looking man out in the streets, she would follow him, stalk him, hoping that he would turn around and grab her. But these men, even the ones that were obviously on the prowl, seemed more scared of her than she was of them. They were predators who were beginning to feel like prey.

Eventually, Hyena couldn't take it anymore. After a night of walking the streets, running into creepy-looking guy after creepy-looking guy, none of which tried to do anything, she had had enough. The next lone man she saw, she wasn't going to let him get away with not raping her.

As a sleazy low-class thug of man crossed her path, she grabbed him and pulled him into a secluded alley.

"Rape me," she told him, her eyes angry.

The man didn't know what to do. He was confused.

"I said rape me, you piece of shit!"

The man pushed her out of the way and tried to scurry out of the alley, but Hyena grabbed a yellow brick from the ground and swung it at the back of his head. He fell to the ground.

He waved his arms out at her. She sat down on his chest, pin-

ning him to the ground with her hefty butt cheeks, and hit him with
the brick again.

"Stop it!" he cried.

She hit him again.

"Are you going to rape me or not?" she said.

He didn't answer. She hit him again, hard, right in the center of
the face. Blood gushed out of his nostrils and right eye.

"You broke my nose," he cried.

She hit him again, breaking out three of his teeth.

"If you don't rape me I'm going to fucking crush your head
open."

She raised the brick high above her head, ready to murder him
right then and there.

"Okay," he said, holding out his hands in surrender. "I'll do it!

Just don't hit me again!"

The man was bleeding and shaking in fear as he lay on top of Hyena, raping her. She had the brick aimed directly at his head. If he stopped or tried to get away before he finished raping her, she promised she would beat him to death before he could get three feet.

She reported the rape the next morning, but discovered that her rapist had already been to the police station. He was in the hospital and had to get thirty-six stitches in his face. After admitting her guilt, the rumors started to fly. She was the first female in McDonaldland to ever be convicted of rape. Her parents were disgraced. They wouldn't even speak to her as she was exiled.

But Hyena couldn't have been happier. She was finally going to be rid of her family, her friends, and her life in McDonaldland. She would finally be left all alone, in a vast empty wasteland with no parents, no classmates, and no social responsibility.

"There's something I wanted to talk to you about," Talon says to Hyena. "It's about Slayer."

Hyena looks over at her while chewing a barbequed squirrel thigh.

Talon says, "With Slayer now leading the knights, she's going to need help. She won't be able to do it on her own, just as I wasn't able to do it when I first led the knights. I'm relying on you to guide her and help her become a strong leader. I want you to be her right hand."

Hyena shakes her head immediately.

"You should ask somebody else," Hyena says, choking down squirrel foot.

"There isn't anyone else," Talon says.

Hyena doesn't like the serious look in Talon's eyes.

"I'm sorry," Hyena says. "I'll fight beside her, but I won't be her babysitter. I won't be her right hand. I'm no beta wolf."

"Why not?"

"How long have you known me? I hate being responsible for other people. I certainly don't want to be responsible for *her*."

Talon can see there's something else. "You don't think I chose the right leader for the knights, do you?"

After a moment of silence, Hyena shakes her head. She decides to be honest.

"She has potential," Hyena says. "But I don't think she's ready to be a leader. She's young. She's going to make mistakes, even get people killed."

"But out of everyone who's left, she's the right person for the job. I know she is."

"Even so, I'm not the right person to guide her. She should be getting that from you. You're the one with the experience. You're the one with the advice she needs."

"But I'm not always going to be around when she needs help," Talon says. "You will."

"I prefer to stay in the background," Hyena says. "I keep quiet and follow orders. That's who I am."

"You're afraid of responsibility."

Hyena coughs on her meat.

Talon says, "Pippi left us. The other knights are dead. Aside from Slayer, you're the only one left. I'm sure I can convince Bunny to rejoin the knights, but she can't be Slayer's right hand. It's got to be you."

Hyena looks away and focuses on her food. "I'll think about it."

Talon stands up. "Another thing, I want you to move your tent closer into camp before it gets dark."

"Why?"

"Remember two years ago, when some of our big sisters were infected with those metal parasites?"

Hyena nods.

"Well, they're back. Bunny said the Outpost where she was imprisoned for the past week was overrun by the parasites. Hundreds of men were infected. She barely made it out of there alive."

Hyena looks at her food, searching for parasites in the meat.

"She said this whole region is likely crawling with the infected," Talon says. "We need to keep a strong guard overnight."

"I'm sure it will be fine," Hyena says. She has no intention of moving her tent into camp, no matter the danger.

"I hope so," Talon says.

Chapter 2

Slayer

The middle of the night. Hyena wakes to strange sounds coming from the woods, rubbing grit from the fur on her eyelids. They are moaning, bellowing sounds, like some kind of animal is dying out in the woods. She grabs her spear and machine gun, and creeps into camp.

When she arrives, she finds Talon and Slayer at the edge of the camp, staring off into the darkness beyond the trees. The other wolf girls are poking their heads out of their tents or sitting around the fire with weapons in their laps.

As she arrives, Slayer asks, "What is it?"

The young wolf woman's fur is so thick and black that Hyena can't make out any detail of her face in the dim firelight. Just a black fuzzy ball with two yellow glowing eyes.

Talon hushes her and listens more carefully. Then she says, "Some kind of animal."

"Only one?"

"It sounds that way."

There is the sound of branches breaking in the distance as the beast staggers through the brush.

"I want you to check it out," Talon says to Slayer. "Take Hyena and one other warrior with you. If you get into trouble call out and I'll come running. If you find anything that's got metal worms crawling on its flesh, you get the hell out of there."

Slayer nods and grabs her gun. Then she calls out to a small wolf girl sitting by the fire. "Vermin, you're with us."

Hyena is surprised by Slayer's choice in warrior to accompany them. Vermin is a small, scraggly girl who isn't much in a fight. An omega wolf.

Hyena has to ask. "Why Vermin?"

Slayer's fur puffs out at the question.

Hyena says, "Hunter, Marrow and Arsenic are the obvious choices. Or Bunny. They are the strongest warriors after Talon."

Slayer shakes her head. "They're too big and loud. I'm not looking for strong. I want stealthy."

Then she tosses Vermin a machete. The grungy wolf girl sheaths it through a muddy rotten leather belt around her waist. She has a big smile on her face, grit between her thin pointy teeth, as the three of them enter the woods. She's excited to finally be able to do something. Most of the time, she's ordered to stay back at camp and stay out of trouble.

Hyena doesn't like Vermin very much. The girl always has a skunky, vinegary smell to her. Her thick dark fur is always knotted and matted, with leaves and weeds tangled within. Sometimes she can be found cutting dried shit out of the fur on her ass. She's like the dirty stray dog that nobody ever wants to pet.

When Hyena first joined the Warriors, she ran into the same problem that she had in McDonaldland: people paid too much attention to her. After a few months alone in the wild, Hyena ran across the wolf women and decided to join them. She enjoyed her time alone, but knew her chances of survival were greater joining a pack. During her time alone, Hyena had dropped a hundred pounds without losing any of her curves, so when the other wolf women met her they all fell in love with her beauty. They all wanted to be her friend.

And just like in McDonaldland, Hyena tried to get everyone to hate her, so she came up with the idea of modifying her appearance. She turned herself into a Hyena, so that she wouldn't fit in. But many wolf girls, like Bunny and Skunky, only cheered her new look. They started copying her idea and modified their looks as well. She was cursed with being the trend-starting type. Eventually, she had to start treating the other wolf women like shit. It was the only way to give them the message that she preferred to be left alone.

Hyena met Vermin years later. The scraggly girl had been a part of the tribe since she was a little kid, long before Hyena joined, but Hyena had never noticed her before.

As Hyena looks like a Hyena, Vermin looks like a rat. At first, Hyena thought Vermin was just another trend-follower who modified her wolf features to look like another animal. She hated when new wolf women followed her trend. But then Hyena learned that Vermin did not modify herself to look rat-like. She wasn't modified at all. It's just a mere coincidence that her natural wolf features make her look exactly like a rat.

As they go deep into the woods, Slayer and Vermin become nearly invisible in the dark, disappearing into the shadows. Their steps are quiet, practically inaudible. If it wasn't for their smells, Hyena wouldn't be able to keep track of them. And they haven't even gone into stealth mode yet.

Slayer uses her long black fingers to give the women commands, ordering Vermin to flank left and Hyena to flank right. Her two subordinates go directly into action, sneaking through the brush toward the moaning animal cries.

Hyena knows Talon sent the three of them out there together on purpose. She's testing Slayer and Hyena both. She wants to see how quickly the young wolf woman takes to command, who she chooses to keep in her company, and she wants to see how Hyena takes to being Slayer's beta wolf. Hyena loves and admires Talon, but the dog-faced bitch really knows how to piss her off.

Alone and creeping through the brush along the right side of the animal, Hyena gets a better smell of what they are dealing with. She smells deer fur, open wounds, blood in the air. The aroma causes her to instinctually growl from the shadows, her muscles flexing, ready to pounce.

When she sees the deer, it is crawling through the trees, its stomach ripped open, its insides leaking out through the forest. As it struggles, Hyena can tell that it's stuck. Some of its intestines are tangled around a fallen tree branch, pinning it to the spot.

The breeze changes direction and Hyena can smell other animals in the forest coming closer. Their odor is very similar to that of her big sisters, but their movements aren't loud enough to be.

Her eyes widen when they come out of the trees and approach the wounded animal. They are wolves. Real wolves. Hyena had thought real wolves had gone extinct ages ago. She had only seen them previously as illustrations in books.

The wolves creep slowly to the animal, growls under their breath, then they attack. They go for the neck, finishing the animal off, then devour its meat with snarling ferocity. It's a beautiful sight. Real wolves on a real hunt, enjoying their bounty.

Hyena continues flanking the beasts until she runs into Vermin's vinegary stink. It takes her a while to figure out where the grimy woman is hiding, even when she knows she's only few feet away from her. Vermin gives her position away when she smiles widely at Hyena, her teeth reflecting the moonlight. The rat girl seems even more excited to see real wolves than she is.

A crashing noise in the woods startles the wolves. They stop eating and look into the dark, all in the same direction. Something else is coming toward them. As it speeds through the trees, the wolf pack disperses, fleeing in the other direction.

One of the smaller wolves isn't fast enough and the unseen predator takes it down, bites into it, holds it down by the scruff of its neck. The first thing Hyena notices are metal worms whipping out of its face and down its spine. An infected gray wolf.

As the crazed beast releases its parasites into the smaller wolf, Vermin slowly pulls two small cylinders out of her belt strap. She screws them together and forms a blowgun, her weapon of choice. Hyena grabs her arm and shakes her head at the wolf girl. Talon told them to get the hell out of there if they came in contact with anything infected. But as soon as Hyena releases her hand and wipes away the girl's foul-smelling grease and dander covering her palm, Vermin just loads up the blowgun and returns to her original goal.

Vermin blows a poison dart into the infected wolf. The creature barks and snarls at the pricking sensation, then turns to the two wolf women. It moves two feet in their direction and then collapses to the ground, paralyzed. Vermin whips out her machete, leaps like a jumping spider out of the bushes, and chops the creature's head off in one swing. Then she decapitates the other wolf, to put it out of its misery.

"Don't get any of those worms on you," Hyena yells, moving toward her.

But Vermin is already stepping away from it, shaking the blood and parasite larvae off the blade.

Slayer steps out of the woods and meets them. The way she looks at her, Hyena can tell she's proud of her decision to bring Vermin along with them. She doesn't say a word about it; no congratulating Vermin on killing the infected wolf single-handedly, no rubbing Hyena's nose in the fact that she was right about stealth over strength. She just stands there calmly, like a statuesque warrior, and nods her head at her two subordinates. The kid's confidence really pisses Hyena off.

"Let's get back to camp and tell the others," Slayer says. "There's bound to be more infected animals nearby."

But the second she finishes saying that, they hear screaming back at camp. Then gunfire. The wolf women are under attack.

The three wolf women race toward camp. As they run, they hear the chaos of combat; bullets ripping through the trees, growls and snarls of heated warriors, the cries of their sisters as they fall in battle.

A young wolf girl dashes through the woods toward them. A horrified look splayed across her face as she flees for her life, as if something monstrous is pursuing her.

"Run!" the girl yells as she charges, ready to plow through them if they don't get out of her way. "We have to get out of here!"

Then her body explodes into a rainbow of blood as an enormous beast barrels into her. Not from behind, but from her right side, coming out of nowhere. An infected moose. Its antlers tear her in half on impact, then it tramples her corpse, crushing her skull into the earth, as it continues running through the trees.

Hyena looks down at the girl's pulverized body. She no longer has a face and most of her guts are now spread across the ground, like a bloody trail left behind by the infected animal. She was new to the tribe, having joined only a few days ago, after being rescued from the Outlander facility prison with Talon and Nova. After enduring rape and torture at the hands of the Outlanders, escaping the fate of being turned into a food animal for the people of McDonaldland, and surviving the great war that took the lives of over ninety percent of the wolf women tribe, she ended up dying here, pathetically, like human roadkill.

As the moose circles back and heads in their direction, Slayer snaps Hyena out of it.

"Come on!" she says.

Hyena raises her rifle and they head into camp, losing the moose in a thicket of trees.

When the camp comes into view, the place is a war zone. Dozens of infected forest creatures are raging through the trees at their sisters, attacking wildly. They are mostly large animals—elk, deer, moose, and even a couple of wild bulls. At least one of their sisters is already dead, others are wounded. One wolf woman is on the ground screaming, wriggling as an elk chews open her stomach and pukes metal worms into her belly. Bunny is riding her metal sentinel, spider-walking through the camp, blasting at the rabid deer with Gatling guns. Talon hacks at the animals with her dual axes as they stampede at her subordinates.

The three wolf women open fire as they enter camp, painting the oncoming beasts with bullet holes. But the animals keep coming. Slayer is taken aback.

"The worms keep them moving," Hyena tells her. "You have to sever the spine or damage the brain to stop them."

Slayer nods in agreement, then formulates a strategy.

"Get up a tree," Slayer tells Vermin. "Get as many as you can with your darts. They'll be more effective than bullets."

Vermin nods her head and goes for the nearest tree, climbing up like a raggedy spider monkey.

Slayer turns to Hyena. "Watch my back."

A deer crosses their path, dragging a screaming wolf girl. It's got her by the ankle, biting down on it as if it were a wolf-like predator carrying away its prey. Blood and meat dribble from its teeth. The woman screeches wildly, worms entering the holes in her ankle, sheets of skin peeling off as her face is dragged across the dirt. Slayer fires at the deer. She shoots off its lower jaw and the wolf girl is let free. Slayer steps forward and fires three more bullets into its face as the wounded girl runs for cover. The deer escapes before Slayer can take it down.

They reach the main group of wolf women, standing back-to-back in the center of camp. Inside their circle, there are two wounded girls, quivering and curled into balls as metal worms crawl under their skin. Slayer immediately takes command of the five women still standing.

"Aim for the legs or faces," Slayer tells them, as the thrashing animals circle them like sharks.

With Slayer's guidance, the women take out three deer, all of them focusing on one at a time. From up above, Vermin's darts hit seven of the animals, stopping them in their tracks. Hyena begins to feel as if the worst is over.

But then something happens. The animals get smarter. Instead of attacking chaotically through the camp, they team up and combine forces. Two elk and a moose go for Bunny in the sentinel. All at the same time, they slam their weight into one of the machine's legs, bending it in half. The sentinel falls, crashing into one of the warrior vehicles, pinning Bunny down.

The deer gang up on Vermin, slamming their antlers into

the tree trunk, trying to shake her off. Vermin holds onto the trunk tightly like a tick in a wolf's armpit. The creatures aren't able to knock her off, but with all the shaking she is no longer able to aim her blowgun at them, not even for a split second.

Four of the elk try to split up the crowd in the center of camp, they charge right through them until a few women splinter off in different directions. Then the deer choose one of them, Arsenic, the largest warrior of the group. They crowd around her, keeping her from getting back to the others. She lowers her axe into an elk's forehead. The axe becomes lodged in the animal's skull, but it doesn't go down. The animal stands up on its hind legs and kicks Arsenic in the face with such force that the top half of her head pops off in a gob of messy pulp.

Slayer regroups the women and orders them not to separate again. There are only two women left standing in the camp outside of their group. One is Talon, standing back to back with a warrior named Marrow. Talon hacks through antlers and elk flesh as the animals come near her. Marrow blasts them with her shotgun. But

the unified elk quickly separate the two women and go after Marrow. They circle her, squeeze her into an awkward fighting stance.

Marrow aims her shotgun at the ground and blows out the knees of two of the elk, then blows off the face of another. Hyena thinks she might have a chance. The woman has always been a solid fighter. She takes out all four of the elk, blowing out their knees first, then targeting their faces with a close-range shotgun blast.

But Marrow isn't paying close enough attention to what's around her. Three more elk come in and knock her off her feet. As she lays on the ground, she blows one of their heads off in a shower of brain and gore. When she crawls away from the animals and goes back to Talon, she realizes the mistake she's made. Marrow's gunshot blast had coated Talon's back with the animal's insides, covering her with blood and dozens of tiny metal parasites.

"Talon!" Slayer cries, as the worms burrow into her leader's back.

As Marrow does her best to lay down cover fire to protect her leader, Talon swipes at the worms. She gets some of them off, but most of them make it into her skin. Then a deer plows into her, knocking her off her feet, throwing her axes from her hands, and tossing her up into the air. When Marrow sees Talon hit the ground, she abandons her fallen leader and crosses the camp, joining Slayer's group.

Talon gets up. There is a fire in her eyes that Hyena has never seen before. Her dog snout snarls fiercely. Like a fully transformed werewolf, she charges at the deer that had knocked her down, running on all fours after the animal. Fully embracing her predatory instincts, Talon leaps up on top of the deer and sinks her claws into its flesh. Then she rips its throat out with her teeth as it carries her off into the forest. It doesn't fall down even with its neck torn open, continuing to flee away from the camp into the darkness. Talon hangs on, feasting on the animal as it runs, worms biting her in the chest, squirming down her throat.

With Talon infected, Hyena realizes that it's up to Slayer now. She'll have to lead them through this battle. But just one look at the young black wolf and Hyena can tell that she's not troubled by this turn of events.

"Get to the vehicles," Slayer tells the women.

They follow her lead, leaping over dead animals and collapsed tents. Hyena helps the wounded girls to safety, careful not to get too close to their parasite-ridden flesh. Once at the vehicles, they find Apple and Nova inside one of the cars, shooting at deer through the windows.

"Turn this car around," Slayer yells at Apple. "We need a barricade."

Then she orders another wolf girl, Baretta, to get into the other vehicle and pull it in. As soon as the vehicles are in position, the wolf women come to a turning point in the battle. The eight women left standing fire at the crazed animals from above, behind, and within the vehicles, taking down deer after deer.

"Aim for the legs," Slayer yells.

The deer attempt to leap over the vehicles to get at them, but with machine guns spraying across their ankles they collapse before they get off the ground. After a dozen of them go down, the animals become timid and fall back. Even in their rabid state, they recognize their efforts are hopeless.

But one animal doesn't stand down. An eighteen-hundred-pound moose barrels toward them. Hyena knows that an animal that size could hit their vehicle barrier so hard that it would crush all of them against the car behind them. When she looks at Slayer, she can tell the black wolf is worried about the same thing.

High in the trees, Vermin blows a dart into the moose. It doesn't slow down. She blows another one. The animal's massive weight is just too much for the poison to have any effect. When Slayer realizes Vermin's darts aren't going to save them, she steps up.

"Cover me," Slayer says to Hyena, handing off her machine gun.

"What are you going to do?" Hyena asks.

Slayer licks her tongue at the beta wolf and puts the blade of a hunting knife between her teeth. Without saying a word, she hops over the hood of the car and races cheetah-like toward the infected moose. Racing on her front and back paws, grinding her teeth on the blade in her mouth, she leaps through the fire like a demon bat. And a second before the beast and the beast woman collide, Slayer grabs the knife out of her mouth, rolls out of the way, and plunges the blade into the moose's foot.

The blade goes deep enough into the ground that it nails the hoof to the spot, but the beast is moving with too much force to stop. As Slayer holds the knife down with all of her wolf-strength, the moose's leg rips from its body when its massive weight plows forward. Once it hits the ground, Slayer pulls the knife out, grabs the animal by one of its giant antlers, and stabs it in the head until it stops moving. Then she backs away before any of the parasites get to her.

Bear Slayer was Slayer's original tribe name. They gave it to her because she killed a large bear when she was only a child, with nothing but a sharpened stick. Hyena always thought those were just rumors. She figured it had to have been an exaggeration or just an all out lie. But after witnessing Slayer take down the rabid moose with a hunting knife, she begins to wonder if those rumors weren't actually completely true.

Hyena and a few of the wolf women come out of hiding to kill the other wounded deer in the camp, and Vermin slides out of the tree to finish off the animals she paralyzed with her darts.

The wolf girls stand in the middle of the destruction, looking around as if amazed any of them made it through alive at all. Before any of them get a chance to speak, Talon comes staggering out of the woods into the camp with deer blood leaking from her mouth down her chest. She goes for her misplaced axes and gives Slayer a nod of approval as she straps them to her back. Then she collapses onto the dead moose's back like she mistook it for a big comfortable bed.

After assessing the situation, Hyena returns to Slayer who is still leaning over Talon's unconscious body.

"Dice, Arsenic, and Spink are dead," Hyena tells her. "Kimmy, Hunter, Likki, and Celia are infected." Then she looks down at their leader below. "In addition to Talon."

Slayer nods.

"Are our infected sisters going to end up like these animals?" Slayer asks. "Will they attack us?"

"Yes," Hyena says. "Once the parasites take over their minds."

Slayer nods.

"Then we should kill them before that happens." Slayer's words are cold and detached. "Take care of it."

When she turns to walk away, Hyena stops her.

"Wait," Hyena says. "There's a way we can save them.

Slayer looks back.

"Bunny was infected before and we saved her," Hyena says. "We just have to kill the creature that controls the parasites."

"How do we find it?"

"It lives in the ocean. We'll probably be able to find it if we follow the coast."

"I don't want to give our sisters false hope," Slayer says.

"We have to try," Hyena says.

Slayer thinks about it for a quick moment.

"Do we still have any Meat cages?" Slayer asks.

"Yeah," Hyena says.

"Lock them up for now," Slayer says. "We're pulling out of here within the hour."

Then Slayer walks away. As she strides through camp with the confidence of a young Talon, Hyena realizes she was wrong about the young girl. Slayer does have what it takes to be a leader. A great one. And she's more than ready, no matter her age.

Hyena, on the other hand, still isn't sure if she's the right person to be Slayer's second in command.

Chapter 3

Talon

When Talon is conscious, metal worms crawling through her face, she asks to see Slayer, Hyena, and Bunny.

Bunny is the last to arrive, licking her wounds, walking with a slight limp. She was unconscious for half the battle and didn't even know what had happened to Talon until a minute beforehand. She had always thought the hard dog-faced bitch was indestructible. She had to see it to believe it.

"I want you to assemble your team of knights, find the sea beast, and kill it no matter the cost," Talon tells Slayer. "I don't care about my life, but our sisters must be cured."

151

She doesn't have to tell this to the three warriors. Even if she would have persuaded them not to go, they would still go.

"There should be eight knights just as there have always been," Talon tells Slayer. "Choose five more from whoever is left. Leave the others to guard the infected. Tell them to keep us locked in this cage no matter what happens."

Slayer nods. "We won't fail."

Hyena doesn't approve of Slayer's overconfidence.

"It's going to be more difficult than you think," Hyena tells her. "We were lucky to have defeated the ocean creature the last time."

"But you will be eight," Talon says. "We beat the creature and we were only three."

"But you were one of the three," Hyena says to Talon. "One of you is worth a hundred knights."

Talon snorts a worm up her black nostril like snot. "Don't underestimate yourselves. If you all fight together you will figure out a way to beat it."

"The tough part will be finding the creature," Slayer says.

Bunny steps in. "No, that should be the easy part. Any of the infected animals could lead us to the monster. All we have to do is find them and follow them, and with the number of infected animals in this area we shouldn't have a problem with that."

Slayer nods. "We can do this."

Talon smiles at the serious look on Slayer's face. She can tell the little wild girl has really grown up.

"I know you can," Talon says.

"Who do we have left to choose from?" Slayer asks Hyena and Bunny, as they discuss who Slayer should choose to join the knights.

"There's only eight left to choose from," Hyena says.

"Which eight?"

Hyena lists them off, "Marrow, Baretta, Zizzy, Vyra, Apple, Toy, Nova, and Vermin.

"We take five and leave three?" Slayer asks.

Then she ponders it over in her head. A few seconds later, she's already made a firm decision.

"Let's take Baretta, Zizzy, Vyra, Toy and Vermin. Let's leave Nova, Apple, and Marrow."

"What?" both Bunny and Hyena say at the same time.

"Apple should go with us," Hyena says. "She's fought these creatures before."

As she says this, Apple walks by chomping on an apple. "Huh?"

"She did hold up pretty good two years ago," Bunny says. "And that was before she actually knew how to fight."

"Wait a minute…" Apple interjects. "Don't sign me up for this thing. I barely survived last time."

"I don't want Apple," Slayer says.

"Yeah, she doesn't want me," Apple says.

Nobody is acknowledging her even though the conversation is about her.

"She's not a warrior," Slayer says. "She's just a driver."

"I'm just a driver," Apple says.

"But she's older and more experienced than the other girls," Hyena says.

Slayer shakes her head. "She'd be useless."

"Yeah, I'd be useless," Apple says.

Hyena says, "She's not my first choice either, but she's in the top five. Trust me, let's take her."

"No, don't trust her," Apple says, chewing a bite of apple. "Leave me."

"I think her experience with these parasites would be more useful here," Slayer says, "keeping an eye on Talon. She stays behind. That's final."

"Yay!" Apple says, lifting her arms victoriously into the air and walking away from them. They still don't acknowledge her.

"I think you should leave Toy, Zizzy, and Vermin," Hyena says.

"I need Toy and Vermin," Slayer says.

"Have you ever seen Toy in a fight?" Hyena says. "She's a mechanic. She's not knight material."

"But we could use a mechanic."

"Forget about Toy," Bunny says. "She's injured. We should leave her."

Slayer looks over at the wolf girl mechanic by the vehicles and sees her bandaged leg. Then she nods at Hyena in agreement.

Hyena continues her thought, "And Vermin might be useful when sneaking around in the shadows, but how is she on a bike? Has she even ridden a bike before?"

"I could always use someone like Vermin," Slayer says. "She's one of my top choices."

"But you cut my two top choices," Hyena says. "Marrow and Nova."

"I can't use Marrow and Nova."

"Marrow is the strongest of the bunch and Nova killed the Hamburglar."

"Are you serious?" Bunny says. "She actually *killed* the Hamburglar?"

"In single combat," Hyena says.

"I only thought Talon could defeat someone like that," Bunny says.

"She's knight material more than any of them."

"But Nova and Marrow are both suffering from personal issues," Slayer says. "Their heads just aren't in the game. Marrow hasn't even begun to recover from her sisters dying in the war. Talon is infected right now because of her. She's not thinking clearly."

"But they are the only two I would have definitely chosen of the eight," Hyena says. "You're choosing all the kids. Vyra, Zizzy, Vermin, Baretta? They have no idea what to do in a battle."

"That's what everyone told Pippi and I when we were their age. Then Talon gave us a chance. We quickly proved ourselves despite what everyone said about us."

"If you take Nova and Marrow, I don't care who you pick for the other three."

Slayer thinks about it for a minute.

"I'll take Nova if you can convince her to come with us," Slayer says. "But I don't think she'll go. I don't want her unless she's feeling up to it."

"I'll convince her," Hyena says. "But you should leave Zizzy and take Marrow. She's a solid fighter."

"I don't want to separate Zizzy, Baretta, and Vyra. They make a great team."

"I'm sorry," Hyena says. "But I won't be your beta wolf if you don't trust me on this. Marrow should go. Zizzy should stay."

"I want Zizzy."

"If Marrow isn't going then that's it, I'm out."

Slayer thinks for a minute. Her deep eyes staring off into the night sky.

"Fine," Slayer says. "For you, I'll compromise. We can take Nova and Marrow, but we don't leave Zizzy. We'll leave Baretta."

Bunny says, "Of those three girls, Baretta's the best shot. Why leave her?"

"She might be the better shot at target practice," Slayer says, "but she's the most nervous of the three during battle. The only way I'd feel confident in her is if she had her two friends backing her up, giving her support."

She points at the three girls sitting by the fire. Teenagers with bright, excited looks in their faces. She focuses on Zizzy, the scrawny albino girl with cold white eyes and long white hair that flows past her waist.

"Zizzy is the bravest of the three," Slayer says. "I'd rather have her than any of them."

"Then leave Vyra," Hyena says about the tall girl with the overly tan skin. "You can have the best shot and the bravest. Leave the mediocre soldier."

Slayer doesn't like that idea.

"I agree," Bunny says. "It's a good compromise."

"It's not the team I want," Slayer says. "Our chances of success will be much lower."

"You'll still get Zizzy and Vermin," Hyena says.

"I really wish we could just leave Marrow . . ." Slayer says.

"Marrow isn't debatable," Hyena says. "We take Marrow, Nova, Baretta, Vermin, and Zizzy. We leave Vyra, Apple, and Toy. Sound good?"

Slayer doesn't respond for a moment. Then she shakes her head. "I'll think about it. The final decision is up to me."

"It's the best decision," Hyena says. "Unless you want to leave Vermin and Zizzy in exchange for Apple and Vyra."

Slayer doesn't like Hyena's tone. "I'll think about it."

Then she walks off, toward the mechanic.

Bunny smiles at Hyena. "I've never seen you get so worked up over something."

"I really hate Talon for putting me in this position."

"As Slayer's second in command?" Bunny asks.

Hyena sighs loudly, ignoring the rabbit girl next to her.

"If she doesn't agree to the compromise, I'm breaking

Zizzy's legs so that she doesn't have a choice."

Bunny snickers under her breath and steps away.

"How many bikes are ready to go?" Hyena asks the mechanic, Toy.

Toy rubs grease onto her red fur. In the back of her truck, there are multiple motorcycle parts. It's her job to keep all of the vehicles running, especially the motorcycles for the knights of their gang. As an apprentice of the engineer, Kockwick, she is talented at reconstructing new vehicles out of old junk.

"Four," Toy says. "But I can get you a fifth if you wait until midday tomorrow."

"We want to get out of here as soon as possible," Hyena says. "Four will be fine. We'll just double-up."

"Is Slayer going to ride with you?" Toy asks. "The way Talon rode with her second in command, Mars?"

"Slayer is going to ride Talon's bike," Hyena says. "It's got the most muscle. And I'm riding my own bike."

"Are you sure?" Toy asks. "You should stick by her side, especially on her first time leading the knights."

"I don't ride anything but my own bike."

Marrow comes up to Toy's truck and picks out the bike she wants.

"That one," Marrow says, pointing at Slayer's old bike. She knows Slayer will be riding Talon's bike, so she wants the next best available.

Marrow has already assumed she would be riding with the knights, knowing that she's the toughest warrior of the eight candidates. She would have been shocked to learn how much Hyena had to fight Slayer to get her on the team.

"When do we pull out?" Marrow asks Hyena.

Hyena says, "Twenty minutes."

By the campfire, Slayer is telling the younger girls which ones are coming. Although none of them had ever been taken seriously by many of the warriors due to their age and lack of fighting experience, they knew at least one of them had to be able to join the knights due to lack of candidates.

Based on Baretta's animated reaction and the disappointed look on Vyra's face, it seems as if Slayer did decide to take Hyena's advice. Baretta, Zizzy, and Vermin will be joining the knights. Vyra stays. The spiky black-haired wolf girl is so devastated by the news she looks like she could rip somebody's face off.

"You know, I never really cared to join the knights before," Marrow says to Hyena, leaning on the side of the pickup truck with her round hip thrust to one side. "I always could have, you know. I've always been really good at riding and shooting. But I'm more of a leader than a follower, and you know how Talon is. She's the alpha wolf. She hates riding with really strong warriors like me who'd be too much competition."

Hyena knows Marrow has always been one of the better warriors, but she never knew Marrow thought of herself as good enough to be competition for Talon. None of the warriors but the old leader, Grandma, were in Talon's league.

"I probably should be leading the knights now," Marrow says. "But, you know, Slayer was always Talon's favorite. Everyone likes her. It's all just a popularity contest and has nothing to do with who is the best suited for the job. I'm suited for the job, of course, but I'm not the type who wins popularity contests. I don't care for that kind of bullshit."

Hyena wonders why Marrow is talking to her like this. Everyone knows she hates casual conversation. She wonders if people are going to always talk to her like this now that she's Slayer's right arm. Or maybe it's because there are just not many people in their tribe left to talk to.

"I notice you ride with a spear," Marrow says. "I'm a shotgun bitch, myself. I don't do melee weapons. They break too easy in a fight. There ain't no melee weapon that can outlast my shotgun."

As Marrow continues talking about her prowess with a shotgun, Toy rolls out Hyena's bike and gives her an *it's ready* nod.

"All gassed up?" Hyena asks, cutting Marrow off to speak to Toy.

"Yeah," Toy says. "Plus extra in the canisters."

"Thanks." Hyena heads off with the bike toward her camp to pack, leaving Marrow in mid-conversation.

Although Marrow's a competent fighter, Hyena is not going to enjoy riding with her if she's always going to be talking about herself like that. There's nothing Hyena hates more than a woman with an over-inflated ego.

The eight warrior knights ride out of the moonlit camp, two per bike. Apple, Vyra, and Toy wave goodbye, wishing them all luck and trying not to show any sign of doubt. Three of the infected wolf women have already gone rabid, thrashing at the bars of their cage as the motorcycles drive by. Talon looks like she's just barely hanging in there, trying with all her might to keep control of her senses as the metal worms crawl in and out of her snout.

Hyena ended up with Vermin riding on the back of her bike. She is not in a very good mood as she rides with the rat girl's body pressed against her naked back, drenching her fur and bike seat with vinegary oils. At least, while they're moving, the wind will blow her stink back away from Hyena's nose. But Vermin couldn't be happier to be riding with Hyena, her mouth permanently stuck in a wide open smile with her wolf tongue dangling out in the wind.

Slayer leads the pack with Zizzy holding tightly to her waist, followed by Hyena and Vermin, then Bunny and Baretta—who rides in a sidecar that Toy attached to Bunny's motorcycle, rather than on the back of her bike, since Bunny is still a carrier of the parasites and could easily infect anyone who gets too close to her.

Far behind the pack, Marrow and Nova ride, but Marrow has a difficult time keeping control of her bike as they get onto the cracked ancient highway.

When Slayer notices this, she falls back to check on the two stragglers.

"Any problems with the bike?" Slayer yells over their motors.

Even though Slayer is genuinely trying to find and solve a problem if one exists, Marrow only hears her leader's tone of voice as a condemning one and reacts defensively.

"It's because she's on my back," Marrow yells, pointing at Nova. "I'm used to riding solo and *she* moves around too much."

Slayer eyes the older warrior woman for a few yards.

"You can go back to camp and switch places with Vyra if you like," Slayer tells her. "She wouldn't have any problems riding with anyone on her back. Tomorrow afternoon Toy will have a fifth bike ready and you'll be able to catch up to us, riding solo."

Marrow takes it as a threat, but Slayer is actually serious. It is the best solution for Marrow's problem. That is, unless Marrow is just making up excuses for her poor riding skills.

"I'll be fine," Marrow says. She turns to Nova. "Just quit moving around so much, you wiggly bitch."

Then Marrow speeds up, to prove she knows what she's doing and nearly knocks Nova off when she hits a pothole. Nova wiggles twice as much after that.

Back at camp, when Hyena and Slayer asked Nova to join the knights, they found her masturbating out in the woods again. Hyena came up behind her, and even though they smelled each other, Nova wouldn't stop. She was naked, her spiked armor piled near the tree behind her.

By the look on her face, Nova was taking no pleasure from the act. It was almost as if the act of masturbating was frustrating and tedious to her. She just wanted to have an orgasm so she could take another step closer to becoming a full werewolf.

As she finished, Hyena asked her, "We want you to ride with us."

Nova leaned back against a tree trunk with her thin coffee-colored legs spread, her muscles tensed, convulsing slightly as her body transformed. She couldn't say anything for several minutes, but she seemed like she could listen.

"You're a good fighter," Hyena said. "You killed the Hamburglar in the war, escaped from the Outlander prison camp, and I even saw you take on Casper and her crew single-handedly. You were *made* to be a knight."

They waited until Nova could speak again.

"I don't even know how to ride a motorcycle," Nova said with the long bangs of her short black hair covering her eyes.

"You don't have to ride," Hyena said. "We don't have enough bikes for everyone yet anyway."

Nova took deep breaths, casually fidgeting with her pubic hair. "I'm done with fighting. You should count on somebody else. I'm not going to be around much longer."

Hyena growled with frustration.

Slayer put her hand on Hyena's shoulder to calm her down. "Let her stay. She's got a lot of masturbating to do."

As they turned to walk away, Slayer spoke to Hyena loud enough so that Nova could hear. "She's only had two or three orgasms in her entire life. She's practically still human. It's going to take her weeks, maybe months to fully turn, even if she masturbates nonstop."

Slayer looked back and squinted her eyes at the dark-skinned girl. "It's too bad. We could have really used her. *Talon* could have really used her. And if I were her, I would be begging to ride into battle. Nothing takes my mind off of my problems like riding into battle."

Then they returned to camp.

Hyena was surprised when Nova entered the camp five minutes later. She didn't say anything, nor did Slayer say anything to her. The depressed wolf girl just got ready to go, calmly packing up her things without even making eye contact with any of her fellow sisters.

Chapter 4

Baretta

The wolf girls follow the highway south, the morning sun rising in the eastern sky.

On the way, they come across a row of infected turtles walking along the side of the road, verifying that they are headed in the right direction. Up ahead, they come across an infected warthog. Then some infected raccoons. All of them headed in the same direction.

"They're headed for the Forbidden Zone," Bunny says to the group, yelling over their engines as they ride. "There's a southern coast down there. I'm sure a sea beast lives in that ocean just as there was a sea beast in the western ocean."

"Why's it called the Forbidden Zone?" Vermin asks, looking back at Bunny from Hyena's bike.

"I don't know," Bunny says. "It used to be called Texas in the old world. There's a community of people who live down there. The Meat who imprisoned me called them *Zoners*."

"Are they dangerous?"

"I have no idea," Bunny says. "The Meat knew practically nothing about them."

The wolf women stop every two hours for a ten minute rest. Every third stop they rest for an hour, where they eat and try to get some sleep, just enough to trick their bodies into believing that they've rested.

They are on their second hour-long rest stop now, hiding out in a long-abandoned train car that is warped and rusted into the track. As long as they stay out of sight, the infected animals traveling along the highway won't attack.

Hyena stares at a map of the old world in an ancient book, the last remaining copy in the Warriors' possession.

She says, "I don't know if we're going to have enough gas to get there, let alone get back."

"Where is it?" Slayer asks, trying to understand the map.

With her long black index claw, Hyena points at the highway they're on and where she believes they are at the moment. Then she shows Slayer where she thinks they need to go, down to the coast of the Gulf of Mexico.

"We're going to have a long walk if we don't get any gas by the time we reach the Forbidden Zone," Hyena says. "And there's nobody out here to raid."

"I'll figure something out," Slayer says.

"We should have stopped at the Outpost when we came to it," Hyena says. "There surely would have been plenty of gas. We could have gotten all we needed there."

"It was too much of a risk," Slayer says. "I can't afford to lose anyone on the way to the Forbidden Zone. It's going to be hard enough with just the eight of us."

"We can still go back," Hyena says. "I'm sure the infected Meat have already cleared out and started heading south with the animals."

Slayer shakes her head. "We keep moving forward."

"Yeah, we keep moving forward," say the three teenagers in unison, hovering behind Hyena's back.

The girls giggle.

When Hyena puts the atlas down and steps away, the three teenagers leap for the book. They gather around and flip through the pages, covering all the maps with muddy fingerprints. Hyena doesn't go back to stop them, but growls with annoyance. The girls don't even know how to read.

All three of the teenagers on the mission (as well as Vyra back at camp) were born in the wasteland. They were all conceived in the same way: between the joining of a werewolf mother and a male captive. They all had different mothers, each one eventually killed off in one battle or another. They never knew who their fathers were.

Wolf women born in the wasteland don't even understand the concept of what a father is. They understand that women mate with men to become pregnant, but other than that they see no significance to the men. The men are slaves, no more than cattle to the women.

Like cattle, their mothers most likely ate their fathers eventually. For all these girls know, they might have shared in eating their fathers as well. The wolf women often share their meals with the rest of the tribe. And all teenage girls in the wasteland grow up on the flesh of men. They do not see it as cannibalism. They are taught that men are not of the same species as wolf women.

Hyena has eaten quite a few men herself since she's joined the Warriors, yet she still thinks of it as unusual and barbaric. She finds it difficult to understand how easy young wolf women take to eating members of the opposite sex.

Most women who refuse to eat the flesh of men are usually ostracized in the tribe. So Hyena, who found the idea of being ostracized incredibly appealing, decided she wouldn't eat men for a while. But then something happened. The first time a man was slaughtered for a feast, the blood in the air made Hyena ferocious with hunger. The wolf in her craved to eat the meat of men, *needed* to. It was as if her brain had been rewired to think of human males as her primary food source. The more attractive a male was to her, the more delicious his meat would be. It was as if hunger and sexual desire had somehow gotten mixed up in her head and she couldn't tell them apart anymore, nor did she want to.

But deep down, she still knew how wrong it was. It still felt like cannibalism to her. It still confounded her how normal it was to the younger women, especially the pre-pubescent virgins who were still completely human. It disturbed her how much she actually enjoyed it. Still, she did it anyway. And the more of a wolf she became, the harder it was to resist.

Thirty hours of following ancient highways on the map. The further south they travel, the more infected animals they cross on the highway. It sometimes becomes difficult to get through them. Only once do the animals try to attack them on their bikes, but the women move too quickly for them.

It is also increasingly becoming hotter for the women the

further south they go. The bright sun beats down on them as they travel across the desert wasteland, causing them to sweat profusely through their fur, especially those who have not shed their winter coats yet. The less furry girls, like Nova, Zizzy, and Baretta, are doing okay, but the hairier women are really suffering in the heat. Vermin is collapsed against Hyena's back, panting loudly in her ear. Marrow looks like she's ready to fall off her bike. And Bunny has stripped down naked with her sweat-drenched underclothes wrapped around her head like a wet towel.

Slayer seems to be toughing it out, even though she has to be suffering worse than anyone. She has more hair on her body than any of them and her hair is black, which attracts the sun's light. She is also covered from head to toe in black leather, with only her face uncovered.

When they come to their next ten minute rest stop, Slayer unzips her leather jacket and a pool of sweat splashes onto the asphalt. She stands with her jacket open, facing the wind. A wide satisfied smile stretches across her black dog lips.

"I'm ready to shave all of this shit off," Marrow says, as she pulls globs of wet fur off of her body and slaps it to the ground. "I can't fucking stand the heat."

The knights begin to get low on fuel. Even their reserves are almost dry. At first, Hyena thought Slayer was just ignoring their fuel situation and hoped to make it to the Forbidden Zone on what they had. But Slayer has a plan.

"How much further do we have?" she asks Hyena.

"At least fifty miles to the border of the Zone," she says. "And there's still a long way to go before we reach the coast."

Slayer nods and turns to the rest of the group.

"We're going to separate," Slayer says. "Bunny, Marrow, I want you to empty your fuel tanks and put it in the other two bikes. We're leaving you here. Hyena and I will take Zizzy and Vermin up ahead. We'll get enough gas for our mission and bring it back to you."

"That's assuming you'll find gas there," Marrow says. By her tone, Hyena can tell she really doesn't like being among the women to be left behind.

"There's gas there alright," Bunny says. "All of our gas comes from the Forbidden Zone. The question is, will you be able to get some in time?"

"We'll get it," Slayer says. "While you wait, I want you four to hunt for food. There's got to be uninfected animals out here somewhere that we can eat. Get some food in your stomachs and dry the leftovers for the rest of the trip."

Bunny and Nova nod in agreement, but Marrow kicks an empty gas canister across the road.

"Is there a problem?" Slayer asks Marrow.

Marrow opens her mouth to complain, but holds her tongue. Something in Slayer's eyes causes her to stand down. Hyena is surprised to see the young leader already using her alpha wolf muscles, especially on a warrior twice her size.

No signs of life as they cross the border into what should be a part of the Forbidden Zone. The landscape remains the same. It is just as desolate and dead as anywhere else. They pull over into a parking lot of a collapsed mini-mall in the middle of the desert, which now looks more like a giant mound of soggy newspaper.

"We aren't going to last much longer," Hyena says.

Slayer responds, "We have to look for signs of life."

"Maybe you should take our gas and go on alone," Hyena says.

Slayer shakes her head. "Not yet. If we have to take the gas by force I need all four of us."

Hyena pointed at a nearby mountain. "I could climb up there and get a good look of the area. If there's any civilization within a twenty mile radius I'll be able to see it."

Slayer stares off at the mountain for a few moments.

"I'll go," she says.

She drops off Zizzy and heads for the mountain slope. Hyena doesn't enjoy being left alone with the two youngsters. Neither of them speak to her, but they do stare up at her as if expecting her to give them some kind of words of wisdom, which is almost just as bad.

When Slayer gets back twenty minutes later, she says, "Come with me. There's something on the other side."

Around the side of the mountain is a vast open desert filled with oil pumps that stretch as far as the eyes can see. They ride out and investigate, but none of the pumps are working. There are no people around.

"Are these from the old world?" Zizzy asks over Slayer's shoulder, as they pull up to one of the pumps.

Hyena gets off of her bike and goes to it.

"Some of them are," Hyena says. "But this one's more recent. Only three or four decades old."

"Can we get oil from them?" Slayer asks.

Hyena looks across the desert.

"No," Hyena says. "The wells are long dry. Even if they weren't it wouldn't be much use to us. We couldn't actually refine it into gasoline ourselves."

Slayer nods. "Let's keep following the pumps south. There's bound to be one still pumping out there somewhere. And once we find it, we'll also find a person responsible for it. And that person will surely have gasoline or know how to get some."

They follow the pumps for miles, but the pumps are all dead. Hundreds of them line the landscape, like a vast mechanical cemetery.

"It looks like they've pumped every drop of oil out of this land," Slayer says.

Hyena nods. "They've been pumping it for a hundred years. It had to run out eventually."

"There still has to be more somewhere else, right? It can't be all gone."

"There's probably more. Somewhere."

"There must be."

A roaring sound in the distance grabs their attention. The sound of an engine. A vehicle. All of their ears perk up at the same time.

"Let's go," Slayer yells, and races off in the direction of the engine.

They don't see anything ahead. Just more dead pumps and abandoned machinery. They rev the gas and fly through the desert, large dust clouds rising in their wake.

"Use my rifle," Hyena yells at Vermin. "I want you to aim for their tires."

"I've never fired a gun," Vermin yells in her ear.

"What?"

"I use my own weapons," the ratty girl says.

Hyena shakes her head. She's annoyed, but not surprised. There were only so many guns available in their tribe. The guns and ammunition would always go to the more experienced fighters. The smaller, weaker sisters would never even get to hold a rifle like the one Hyena uses, let alone practice firing one. They were stuck with weapons they constructed themselves, such as spears, slings, and in Vermin's case, blowguns.

"Do your best," Hyena says.

When Vermin takes the weapon, she raises it high above her head to try to get the strap off of Hyena's shoulder. She doesn't see the arm of the pump as they pass underneath it. The gun slams hard against the metal, bending the barrel in half, and it flies out of her hand.

"I dropped it," Vermin says, casually. As if it were actually a normal mistake for a warrior knight to make.

Hyena growls and speeds up.

A highway comes into view as they pass through a wall of thorny yellow bushes. And on it, they see a white truck-like vehicle driving west, away from them. It is some kind of construction vehicle that looks like something between a crane and a fire truck.

The second they get on the road, Slayer's bike gurgles to a stop. She tries to start it again, but it stalls. She's out of gas.

As Hyena passes her, Slayer yells out, "Keep going. Get that thing!"

Hyena and Vermin speed off toward the white vehicle. All they have is a blowgun with a handful of darts, a machete, and Hyena's spear. She wishes Slayer would have recognized their situation and tossed them a gun or something.

"Get your blowgun ready," Hyena says. "You're going to have to aim for the driver once we get close enough."

"Maybe we can just ask him for some gas?" Vermin says.

"We can't afford him saying no."

It takes four minutes to catch up to the vehicle, but it takes Vermin six minutes to screw her blowgun together and load it up.

171

"Are you ready yet?" Hyena barks.

"Just a minute," she says. "I've never done this on the back of a bike before."

"Well, don't drop it this time."

Hyena rides up to the driver's side window.

"Now," Hyena yells, as she passes the window.

"I can't," Vermin says.

Hyena is ready to shove her off the bike for saying that. "Why?"

Vermin points at the truck. "The window's rolled up. It won't go through."

The driver side window is coated in a greenish mud. Hyena can't see anything inside. Not the driver. Nothing. The wheels look pretty strong. Too strong for Vermin to pierce with her machete.

"What do we do?" Vermin asks.

"I'll handle it," Hyena says.

Hyena takes the spear from the side of the bike. Like a javelin, she throws it with all of her wolf strength. The blade of the spear breaks through the window, hitting the driver. The vehicle spins out of control. It goes off the road, slams into an oil pump, and flips up onto its side.

They slow the bike down.

"Keep your blowgun ready," Hyena says as she steps off the bike. "If anything moves in there you shoot it."

"No need," Vermin says.

She points at the bodies hanging out of the truck. The driver and the passenger are already dead.

When Slayer and Zizzy arrive to the vehicle, Hyena is already siphoning the gas from their tank.

"Great choice of warrior," Hyena says to Slayer.

Slayer squints her eyes at her. "What's the problem?"

"Vermin," Hyena says. "She was useless out there. She can't shoot a gun or even hold on to one. She's good with a dart gun, but has no idea how to use it on a bike. She's not knight material. You should have left her back at camp."

Vermin cowers at Hyena's words, reacting as if her own mother had just told her she hated her guts.

"She's new at this," Slayer says. "It's going to take her time to get used to fighting as a knight."

"We don't have time to get her used to fighting as a knight."

"That's why Vermin and Zizzy are with us now," Slayer says. "They need all the practice they can get before the real battle begins."

Hyena fills another gas canister.

"Why did you have Vermin ride with me?" she says.

Slayer rolls her bottom lip-piercing.

Then she says, "Because you two make a perfect team."

When Slayer turns to the truck, Hyena growls under her breath. She knows the bitch said that just to piss her off.

While Hyena finishes siphoning the gas, Slayer inspects the truck. The side of the vehicle has a number of storage compartments. When Slayer opens one, a strong fishy odor overtakes their senses. Inside the hold, there is a mass of green sludge. They are large round balls inside of some kind of syrupy goop.

"What is it?" Hyena asks.

Slayer closes up the container. "They smell like the yolk of rotten snake eggs."

"Do you think they eat that foul crap?"

Slayer shrugs.

"I would eat it," says Vermin.

Hyena bets she would.

Then Slayer gets a better look at the driver of the truck.

"Come take a look at this." Slayer waves Hyena over, not taking her eyes off of the corpse. "It's odd."

When Hyena gets up she knows exactly what Slayer is talking about. The man has scales growing down his neck, like the scales of a fish or reptile. The fingers on his right hand are fused together, webbed.

"Are they mutants?" Zizzy asks. "Like the Meat back home?"

"They could be," Hyena says. "They traded food and supplies with the Outlanders. It's possible they were infected with similar mutations."

"Do we get to eat them?" asks Vermin. "We shouldn't waste the meat."

"No." Slayer goes back to her bike, not taking her eyes off of the scaled men. "We need to get back to the others. We've still got a long way to go."

When they get back to the others, the four women are sitting around the fire, eating barbequed meat. Nova is a little further away from the others with her back turned, her pants are off and her bare butt is covered in dirt.

Slayer hands off canisters of gasoline to Bunny as she steps off of her bike. Marrow gorges herself on a large piece of pig fat. When Hyena drops off gas cans by Marrow's bike, she passes Nova and looks down at her. She's not masturbating, but she is staring down at her vagina and poking it with a fingernail.

"Something wrong?"

Nova looks up at her, then back at her vagina. "It's all swollen. It hurts."

Hyena looks at it. The inner part of her vagina is puffy and sticking out in such a way that it looks like a long dangling tongue.

"You must have rubbed it raw," Hyena says. "If there's no lubrication don't force it. You'll only hurt yourself."

"I didn't force it."

"Your fingers are too gritty then. It must be like sandpaper. You might have even given yourself an infection."

Nova winces and pokes at it some more.

When Hyena goes back to the others, they are being accosted by Slayer.

"What the hell is this?" Slayer yells at them.

She holds out a platter filled with the remains of dead metal worms. The platter was next to the remains of the wild pig they are eating.

"Are you eating infected meat?" Slayer yells.

"We couldn't find anything else," Marrow says. She doesn't stop eating.

"I told you to hunt down an animal that wasn't infected," Slayer says. "Did you all eat this?"

"All of us except for Nova," Baretta says, feeling ashamed rather than worried that she ate the meat.

Bunny steps in. "I told them not to eat it. I'm immune, so I had no problem eating an infected animal, but Marrow was tired of hunting and decided to take the risk."

"The meat's cooked," Marrow says. "Bunny took out the parasites. We'll be fine."

Slayer looks at Baretta, "I know Marrow's an idiot, but why'd you eat the meat? I thought you'd be smarter than that."

Baretta's face flashes with worry, pointing at Marrow. "She pressured me. She said a *real* warrior wouldn't be scared of eating it."

"I did not," Marrow says, spitting a piece of bone into the fire.

"You did!"

Slayer slaps the meat out of Marrow's hand. "You're Warriors. Start acting like it." She leans in close to Marrow's face. "Follow my orders next time." Then she leans in close to Baretta. "Have some backbone."

"I should abandon you both here," Slayer says. "If you're infected you're a danger to us all."

"We're not infected," Marrow says.

Slayer goes back to her bike and revs the engine. The girls start packing up their things, but Marrow still sits there, brooding.

Hyena looks down on the insubordinate wolf woman and tells her, "You better not be."

Chapter 6

Marrow

Hyena asks Nova to keep a sharp eye on Marrow while they ride. If she actually is infected, the bitch could go rabid at any minute.

Marrow has turned out to be quite a disappointment to Hyena. All of the new wolf women are turning out to be disappointments to Hyena. She knew there weren't many options left, but she thought at least Marrow would have been a good choice. She can now see why Talon has never considered her for the knights in the past.

The only thing Hyena really knows about Marrow is that she was loyal to her two younger sisters to the very end. When her youngest sister, Moon, was raped in McDonaldland as a teenager, Marrow decided to voluntarily go into exile herself so that she could protect her. She also convinced the middle sister, Lith, to exile herself so that the three of them could stick together.

And stick together, they did. The three were inseparable. They went on hunts together, ate Meat together, slept together in the same tent, and rode into battle together in the same vehicle.

Hyena saw it happen when Marrow's two sisters were killed during the battle of McDonaldland. Their car was crushed underfoot by the great beast Kroger in the center of the battlefield. The three women were okay, but they no longer had a vehicle. They went out on foot. Marrow was pissed that their vehicle had been crushed, and wanted to take revenge on whoever was responsible. She wanted to kill Mayor McCheese, lord of the Outlanders, who was controlling the monstrous wolf, Kroger.

The women attempted crawling up Kroger's leg to get to the Mayor, but they couldn't get very far. The first attempt nearly got Lith crushed, so they had to figure out another way to get the Mayor. Then they followed Kroger, hiding in its massive shadow, waiting for a moment to strike. When the beast broke through the wall into McDonaldland, the three sisters followed it. And when they saw Talon kicking the Mayor off of the great beast, they knew it was their chance to strike.

The Mayor was shooting random innocent McDonaldland citizens when the three wolf women showed up.

Marrow looked at him calmly with her shotgun leaning over her should. Then she said, "If you want a *real* fight we'll give you one."

Mayor McCheese pulled out his sledgehammer and eyeballed them with his bulbous cartoonish eyes.

"Come get some, bitches," said the Mayor. "Your furry asses are mine!"

The three girls went at him on all sides. Moon and Lith went in first. Lith attacked with her handmade broad sword and Moon with her trident. The two of them fought him well, or so it appeared. He couldn't seem to break through their defenses and they very nearly got through his. Marrow didn't rush into the fight right away because she was so proud of them. She admired what graceful warriors they had become.

But it all changed once Marrow got into the mix. She was more threatening to the Mayor by bringing a shotgun into the fight. He could no longer play around with them. When Marrow raised her shotgun at the Mayor, he slammed his sledgehammer down into Moon's knee, crushing her bone in two places, causing the girl to fall down directly into the line of fire. Moon acted as a human shield as Marrow fired, and the blast shredded half the flesh from her backside. She went down.

As the Mayor went for Lith, Marrow froze up. She looked down at her sister. Moon raised her hand up, begging for help. Then the Mayor whipped out his own shotgun and blew Lith's legs out from under her. As she fell, he a brought the sledgehammer down on her forehead and crushed her skull like a watermelon.

Before Marrow could react, the Fry Guy police force engaged him, shooting at him from multiple directions. When all the townspeople, Fry Guys, and other wolf women crowded around the Mayor to end his life, Marrow was in too much shock to join in the killing. Even after Moon died in front of her, Marrow couldn't bring herself to avenge them. The lord of the Outlanders was killed at her feet, but she did not take part. The only life she took in the entire battle was her younger sister's, the person she loved most in the world.

Hyena could see it from the distance as she entered the city. She is likely the only wolf woman alive who knows what happened, aside form Marrow. After the battle, Marrow was silent for several hours. Once she started speaking again, she acted as if nothing had happened. As if her sisters were still alive, off hunting in the woods somewhere. But whenever Marrow goes quiet, everyone knows she's thinking back to what happened that night, during the war. Her eyes begin to shake and her spine gets cold. She will be haunted by that memory until the day she dies.

The number of infected animals they cross paths with, as they go through the Forbidden Zone, increases dramatically. The further they go, the more they find. After a couple of hours, they come to an army of infected beings. Hundreds of them, stretching as far as the eyes can see.

Strangely, over half of the creatures are infected humans. Some are mutant Outlanders, most likely coming from the Outpost Bunny had described. But most of them were other humans. They were not Outlanders, nor Warriors, nor McDonaldland citizens. They were humans from some place else, from another civilization outside of both McDonaldland and the Forbidden Zone. Someplace to the east.

"Let's follow them the rest of the way," Slayer says.

Soon, more of the infected come in from behind them and they find themselves surrounded on all sides. They must now travel with the horde, rather than following behind it. After an hour, the crowd becomes so tightly packed that they have to get off of their motorcycles and walk their bikes the rest of the way.

The younger wolf girls have nervous looks on their faces as the infected squeeze in around them. Their vicinity to these creatures might get them all infected.

"Why aren't they attacking?" Slayer asks.

An infected woman with strange, foreign clothing gets too close to Baretta and the girl squeals.

As Bunny pushes the infected woman away from Baretta with her bare hand, she says, "They aren't in attack-mode right now. From what little I remember of being infected, the parasites have two commands they put into your mind. One: attack and infect every living being you can find. Two: return home. Right now, they are returning home."

Bunny moves around to the other side of Hyena and shoves three infected cows that are getting too close to her bike.

She continues, "The commands aren't in words, but emotions. I remember being infected with an emotion, which was similar to that of home sickness, but more intense. I had the uncontrollable urge to return home. But the parasites changed my definition of *home*. I thought of home as one thing, and that was the belly of that horrible sea creature. Its belly was like a warm, welcoming, familiar, comfortable place, the only place I truly belonged. Like being reunited with your true family that you never knew you had."

She looks around at the people with dead expressions on their faces. "That's what all these people are yearning for right now. They all want to go home. They have no idea that their minds are being warped, toyed with, to feed a monster."

Hyena looks at all of the animals and people surrounding them.

She says, "It looks like this monster is about to have a good-sized feast."

The wolf women and the horde of the infected pass through an abandoned village. The houses are all spiral-shaped, like seashells, with greenish-blue paint. The structures are crumbling. Some are collapsed. Many are coated in red weeds that crawl up the structures like vines.

"Are they from the old world?" Vermin asks, staring at the houses.

Hyena examines them. "No. They are much more recent. Thirty years old, maybe? Zoners must have lived here at one point. Perhaps the infected got them."

Vermin grabs Hyena by the arm and yanks her.

"Look, look!" Vermin says.

When Hyena looks, Vermin is pointing at a cracked window.

"What?" Hyena pulls the girl's greasy hands away from her.

"There was somebody in there," Vermin says. "A boy."

Hyena looks carefully. Through the window, the insides of the building are rotten, empty. "There's nobody there."

"There's somebody else!" Vermin says, pointing at another structure. "People live in these houses."

Hyena looks, but that house is empty as well.

"There's nothing there," Hyena says. "Nobody's lived here for a long time."

When they exit the village, they smell salt water in the air.

"We're here," Hyena says. The other girls don't recognize that ocean smell, but Hyena does. "The coast should be just ahead."

"What's the game plan?" Bunny says. "Are we just going to follow these infected until we see the creature, then kill it?"

Slayer squints her eyes at Hyena, as if asking for advice.

Hyena says, "Last time, as soon as we attacked the creature, all of the infected animals went back into rabid mode. This time, there's just too many of the infected. We can't fight them all. We need a plan."

Slayer looks away, bites on her lower lip ring.

Then she says, "We wait for the creature to eat all of these infected ones. Then we kill it."

Hyena says, "Last time, the creature puked all of the infected up so they could attack us."

"Then we go in hard and fast. Kill it before it has a chance to puke anything up."

Hyena looks around at the infected people surrounding them.

"You know, we can save all of these people if we kill that thing before it eats them. None of them have to die. They'll be cured."

Slayer looks at them briefly and shakes her head.

"They aren't our sisters," she says. "They don't matter."

As they go around a hill, they see a stretch of beach and the great blue ocean beyond it. Other than Hyena and Bunny, the wolf women pause, staring out at the enormous body of water. None of them have ever seen anything like it in their lives. The young girls had never even seen pictures of the ocean before, and Vermin had never even heard the word until a few days ago.

There are already hundreds of infected animals on the beach. Hundreds more come in. The wolf girls separate from the horde and push their bikes up the nearest hill, to get a good look at what they're dealing with.

In the center of the beach, twenty men in red robes stand in a circle. Around them, there are ten more men in blue robes, but these men are twice as large as the others, over ten feet high. In the center there is a man in a yellow robe, holding a pearl scepter. He appears to be their leader. None of them appear to be infected.

"Who are they?" Marrow asks.

"Must be the Zoners," Bunny says.

Although they can't see the Zoners' faces, they can see their hands sticking out of their robes as they raise them toward the sea. Their hands are greenish-blue, scaled with long reptilian claws. Some of them have tentacles for arms. Some of their robes are bulged in odd places, on their backs and shoulders.

"They're cultists," Hyena says. "They must worship the sea creature like a god."

"How come they're not infected?" Slayer asks.

"Perhaps they're immune, like Bunny," Hyena says.

"We might have to kill them as well," Slayer says.

"They're unarmed," Hyena says. "It shouldn't be a problem."

Baretta begins to feel sick and pukes over the side of the hill. She clutches her stomach and squeezes her fuzzy eyelids. Pieces of yellow slime dangle from her whiskers.

"Are you okay?" Slayer asks.

"I'm infected," Baretta whines. "You have to save me."

The girl pukes again. Marrow and Bunny are also looking sick. Slayer examines the puke. "There aren't any worms in it."

"Don't let me get eaten," Baretta says.

"You're not infected," Slayer tells her. "You just ate bad meat."

Baretta has an attack of diarrhea. She pushes her way to the back of the pack, just a few feet from Nova, and relieves herself.

"She's right," Bunny says. "I'm feeling kind of sick, too. Parasites wouldn't make me feel this way."

"You should have listened to me when I said not to eat the infected meat," Slayer says. "Even you, Bunny. The parasites can control an animal even after it's dead. The meat you ate was probably from a long dead animal. Its meat was already rotten."

Bunny looks down at her greasy fingernails.

"Are you going to be able to fight or are all of you useless to me now?"

"I can fight," Bunny says.

Slayer looks at Marrow.

"It's not that bad," Marrow says. "I'll be fine."

When Slayer asks Baretta, the young girl can't even respond as she continues to be violently ill. Her wolf tail is drenched in yellow diarrhea. Marrow and Bunny are not as sick because they are more wolf-like than Baretta. Their wolf stomachs are stronger than a human's. Bacteria doesn't affect them as much, they can digest raw or even some rotten meat.

"She's not going to be able to help us," Slayer says. "We'll have to leave her behind."

An electrical buzzing sound pulses out of the leader's scepter as he raises it over his head, then a red light beams out of it into the sky.

The ocean water bubbles and foams as the sound reverberates along the coast. When the sea creature emerges from the depths, it towers so high that it casts a wide shadow across the crowd of infected. Its tentacles whip in the breeze like medusa snakes as it makes its way up toward the beach, inching through the shallows.

The Zoners back away from the beach, making more room for the infected to step forward. As the creature opens its mouth, a mob of empty-eyed people step within the deep chasm. Thick black oils drip onto their heads from the roof of its mouth, covering them like fudge on a McDonald's sundae. When its mouth is full, it slides its rubbery folds closed and gulps them down. Then its lips widen for more.

"Here's the plan," Slayer tells her wolf sisters. "As soon as the last group of infected animals enter its mouth, we ride in. Half of us will go after the creature, the other half will take on the Zoners."

She points at Marrow and Nova. "You flank the Zoners on the right." She points at Bunny. "You go through the middle and try to get them to scatter."

Baretta is lying in the dirt behind them. Slayer looks back at her. "I want you to stay back and cover them from up here. Do you think you can handle that?"

Baretta nods.

"Your goal isn't to kill the Zoners. It would be best to just scare them into retreating. If you can get them to run away, then help us with the monster. Whatever you do, don't let them interfere with our attack."

Bunny and Marrow nod at her. Slayer turns to Hyena.

"The two of us will ride right down the middle." Slayer points at the creature as it feasts. "Do you see that soft spot on the side of its head? I want you to target that."

As Hyena examines the weak spot on the creature, she sees movement in the water behind it. The ocean is bubbling fiercely.

Giant waves crash against the beach as if an earthquake is breaking out beneath the surface.

Slayer's words drop off as she sees them emerge from the sea. The creature is not the only one of its kind. Dozens of them surface, some even larger than the first. Then, in the distance, even more surface. The wolf women stare in shock. There has to be nearly a hundred of the monsters out there.

"We'll never be able to kill all of those things," Hyena says. "Just one was going to be difficult enough."

"We don't necessarily have to kill them all," Bunny says. "We just have to kill the one that controls the parasites that infected Talon and the others."

"But how will we know which one it is?" Hyena says.

The girls watch the monsters as they come up to the beach and open their mouths wide. The thousands of infected animals march forward, feeding themselves to the sea beasts in an organized, casual fashion. It seems to be a daily occurrence for these creatures.

"Find the group of animals that attacked our camp," Slayer says. "Look for deer and elk. Look for claw marks or bullet wounds on their bodies. Whichever creature they go toward will be the one that we need to kill."

The women scan the beach, but they don't see any deer or elk among the animals out there.

"We rode faster than the deer," Hyena says. "They won't be here yet. It could even be days before we see them."

Slayer presses her tongue against one of her fangs and thinks.

"We'll have to hide out in this area and wait for them to come," Slayer says. "It's our only chance."

The other girls agree.

"We'll need to find some kind of shelter," Hyena says. "Maybe those shacks we passed earlier."

Slayer nods. "Let's pull out."

As the wolf women roll their bikes back down the hill, Marrow locks eyes with one of the creatures. Hyena glances back at her, wondering what she's looking at.

"It's staring at us," she says.

The creature out in the waves, waiting in line to feast, has all of its eyes on the wolf women. It opens its mouth, salivates at them. Then it lets out a gooey roar.

The infected humans surrounding the hill turn around and look up at them. With widening filmy eyes, they transform from their docile, submissive state into rabid-mode. They open their wormy mouths and snarl at the wolf women, then race up the hill to attack.

Baretta opens fire with her submachine gun.

"Don't shoot," Slayer says, but it's too late.

The Zoners on the beach turn to them and their leader points his scepter in their direction.

"Outsiders," cries the head cultist.

The twelve-foot-tall men in blue robes glare up at them with glowing green eyes. Then they charge.

"Let's get out of here," Slayer calls, getting on top of her bike and firing down at the rabid men.

The wolf women rev their motorcycle engines and ride into the horde. Slayer shoots open a hole in the crowd for them to get through. They ride east, away from the horde into a new region of the Forbidden Zone. Hyena slashes with her spear and decapitates a rabid woman as she crosses in front of her bike. Vermin hits one of them with a poison dart.

Once they reach a dirt road, the only infected animals they come across are in docile mode. They are able to ride around them without incident. Up ahead, a new village comes into view. This one is larger, with many blue cone shell towers. The structures are slightly less dilapidated, but still look abandoned. The streets are empty, coated in blood-red weeds. A quiet breeze rustles through ancient metal wind chimes.

Far behind, the giant blue-robed cultists are chasing after them. They move as if flying, their heads leaning forward.

"They're fast," Vermin says.

When Hyena looks back, she notices that these large Zoners are gaining on them quickly. They run even faster than their motorcycles. From beneath their robes, strong muscular scaly legs can be seen, pumping through the dirt, leaving dust clouds in their wake.

As the wolf women reach the village, the cultists catch up. Half of them spread out, running behind the shell-shaped buildings to flank them.

In the back, Marrow fires her shotgun behind her shoulder as they approach, the blast speckles their robes with tiny holes but does not slow them down. On her bike, Nova sits calmly, staring forward, off into the distance, thinking about something else.

One of the blue-robed men comes from the side, leaps from a rooftop and slams into Bunny's motorcycle. Baretta's sidecar breaks off as Bunny's bike rolls across the street. The rabbit girl finds herself pinned beneath the large man, her neck squeezed between his scaly claws.

"Fucking Meat . . ." Bunny wheezes at the creature, trying to breathe in his grasp, trying to reach her chainsaw weapon down by her feet.

Slayer lets Zizzy off of her bike, turns around, and rides directly at the attacker. When she opens fire, his robe shreds open. The Zoner releases Bunny from his grasp.

He turns to Slayer, throws open his shredded robe and reveals his mutant body. He is not human. His head is that of a shark's, with a wide jaw filled with rows of pointed teeth. His arms and back are covered in large muscled lumps. His flesh is scaled and covered in tiny metal spikes. His eyes glow green like radioactive waste.

He goes for Slayer. Bunny grabs her chainsaw-boomerang and flips it on. Slayer opens fire on the shark man as Bunny cuts into his leg. It slows the creature down, but he keeps going. When he punches Slayer in the chest, her body is tossed across the street and slams through the door of a nearby tower. Then the rest of the mutant Zoners attack.

Hyena, Vermin, Marrow, and Nova get down from their bikes and engage the enemy. As they approach, the creatures remove their robes and open their fleshy jaws wide. Dozens of rows of knife-sized teeth chew the air toward them.

Marrow aims for the legs of a shark man coming at her and blows off his foot. A pump of the shotgun and another shot, blows off his knee. The shark man goes down. As his head hits the dirt, she drops her gun to his forehead and blows his cartilage skull into a spiral of stripped fish skin. Marrow smiles wide at her sisters.

"They're easy," Marrow says. "We can take them."

Hyena backs off and points the head of her spear at their open mouths as they growl around them. She looks back at Slayer as she picks herself off the ground, retrieving her weapon. Bunny holds

out her chainsaw-boomerang at the creatures. Nova pulls out her sickle-shaped sword and rubs the blade down her thigh.

"Let's kill these ugly fuckers," Marrow says, then calmly raises her shotgun and opens fire.

Marrow's torso explodes and her insides shower the air in wet stringy chunks. It happens so fast, the other wolf women hardly know what's happening. One of the shark men lunged at Marrow as she fired, breaking the barrel of her gun in half with one hand and slashing at her with the other. His claw entered through her belly and ripped up her chest through her head, pulverizing the upper half of her body in one swipe.

As Marrow's body falls to the ground, Slayer yells, "Retreat."

All of them fall back except for Nova, who stares down the group of shark men with yellow violent eyes, growling under her breath.

"Nova," Slayer yells, but the girl doesn't listen. She's in her own world.

"She's trying to kill herself," Hyena says.

Slayer runs back for Nova as the creatures close in. Nova slices through a shark man's chest, but three of them slam into her, throw her to the ground. She goes unconscious as her head bangs into the dirt. Slayer charges in and opens fire at one, pointblank range in the mouth. His teeth shatter against the bullets and blood-bubbles pop in the back of his throat. Bunny tosses her chainsaw boomerang into one of them. It cuts off an arm and returns to her.

Slayer's gun bursts in her hands as a mutant claws it in half. She steps back.

"Get out of here," she tells the others.

When she opens her mouth to yell at them again, a shark man bites into her ribcage. It picks her up from the ground and thrashes her body in the air. Blood rains across the street, splashing onto Nova's coffee-colored skin. The smell of blood causes the other sharks to frenzy.

Before the wolf women can retreat, the sharks fly at them. Only Vermin gets away, dodging into the shadows and creeping into a small crack in the foundation of an old building. Baretta screams and breaks away from Zizzy, running for a motorcycle.

With no one watching her back, a shark comes up behind Zizzy and rips off one of her arms with its teeth. It's so fast that she doesn't even notice as it happens. Zizzy looks down at the stump where her arm used to be. A hollow, confused look spreads across her pale face as blood spurts across her white fur.

As Baretta runs off, two more shark men chase her down the street. She gets out of view by the time they catch up to her. All they hear are her screams echoing through the village.

Hyena looks at Zizzy as the young white wolf tries to find her missing severed arm. She's in too much shock to scream.

"Get her out of here," Hyena tells Bunny.

The rabbit girl nods and goes for the young wolf woman. She slashes a chainsaw blade at the shark with Zizzy's arm in its mouth. Its throat opens up and blood sprays across Bunny's face. Zizzy's breaths are frantic as Bunny grabs her, careful not to infect her with parasites, and pulls her out of the fight.

Hyena gets between them and an approaching shark, pointing her spearhead at it.

"I'm not leaving without Slayer," Hyena says.

Bunny nods as she gets on her bike. Then she rides off, with Zizzy on her back. The young girl is several inches away from the infected wolf girl, but looks ready to collapse onto her back and take in the parasites at any moment. When they ride off down the street, they pass Baretta's body as it is torn to shreds by two ravenous shark men. One of the shark men leaves the body and chases after the motorcycle. Hyena watches them as they leave. With one of them wounded, the two wolf women will be easy prey.

Hyena is now alone. With Nova out cold in the street and Slayer dangling from a shark's mouth, she's the only warrior left facing the beasts.

Before the war, Hyena was never considered one of the best fighters in the Warrior army. She was competent, loyal, brave, respected, and was even one of the fastest and most athletic. But nobody thought of her as in the same league with Talon, Slayer, Casper, Bunny, or even Pippi. She just wasn't anything special.

But she became one of the main knights of the tribe because Talon knew something about her that nobody else knew. Hyena was a very strong fighter when she fought alone.

When she's alone, her mind is clear and at ease. She's able to focus. She's able to use act on instincts. When others fight beside her they become distractions. They make her nervous and her brain becomes jumbled with too many thoughts. She fights at only a third of her abilities.

Now that she's all alone on the battlefield with these shark men, she's able to begin fighting for real.

Hyena charges the shark holding Slayer in its mouth, her spear guiding her as she runs. As another shark comes in to intercept her, she squats down, bending her ankles back. Then, like a grasshopper, she launches into the air. Using the force of her jump, the blade of her spear cuts the shark man's ribcage in half as she goes up. Her body soars above their heads, somersaulting through the blood of her victim. When she comes down, Hyena dives spear-first at the shark chewing on Slayer, driving it through his chest.

She lands with such force that Hyena's entire body goes through the shark man's torso. She slides out of his back and pulls her leader out of his limp jaw. Slayer is barely conscious, blood leaking from the teeth marks in her leather coat. Hyena puts Slayer down next to Nova, then stands between the two wounded wolf women and the oncoming sharks.

The four sharks come at her at once. She swings her spear at them and all four bend back, dodging the attack. One of them strikes quick and hard, jabbing a claw into her side. The taste of blood mixed with stomach acid fills her mouth. She wheezes and steps back. Then swings at her attacker, leaving her back open. A sound like fabric ripping echoes in her ear as a shark's claw tears through her flesh down her spine. She drops to one knee. The sharks hover over her.

Hyena acts more wounded than she is. She squats down, rolling her eyes back, shivering as if the pain is pulling her into unconsciousness.

When the shark men move closer to finisher her off, she lunges into the air, spinning her spear like a windmill at them. Blood gushes into the street as two fall back, not sure what has just happened to them, not aware their throats have just been cut.

As one of them comes up behind her she leans backward—her head nearly touching the back of her ankles—and drives the spear into the shark's chest. Then she flips over his corpse to get back on her feet.

As Hyena returns to her fighting stance, pointing her spear at the last of the shark men, she feels an intense and sudden pain in her stomach. She notices the shark man holding something in his claw. A red, dripping bundle of rope. She follows the rope with her eyes and notices that it's connected to her. It takes her a moment to notice her torn-open stomach.

Due to the adrenalin, she hadn't realized when it happened. The shark man ripped her intestines out while she was flipping through the air, and now holds them out in front of her.

Hyena suddenly goes weak and can no longer hold herself up, watching the shark man as he opens his jaws wide to eat her ropey guts. As she falls, Hyena puts all of her strength into one final attack. Like a javelin, she launches her spear at the mutant. It enters his mouth and explodes out the back of his head.

Their lifeless bodies hit the ground at the same time.

Chapter 6

Swaggat

When Hyena awakes, she is in a bed.

"You're going to be alright," says a gentle, whispering voice.

She opens her eyes to a young man's face, blue scales grow across his neck and chest. His face bobs slowly up and down in her vision.

"You'll survive," he says.

He's naked on top of her. They are pressed against each other between sealskin sheets. His penis moving tenderly inside of her.

Hyena sits up when she realizes the man is having sex with her. He's small, almost half her size. Like a thin child with the eyes of an adult.

"Don't worry," he says. "I'm a doctor."

Before she can react, the fish man wraps his tentacle arms around her voluptuous hips, presses his lips against her spotted fur, and ejaculates inside of her.

As he looks up into her yellow eyes, she snarls at him and throws him across the room. She jumps out of the bed, looking around for an exit. There is furniture made of coral and fish skin, but no sign of an exit.

"What's the matter?" asks the small man with the tentacle arms. "What did I do wrong?"

"You were fucking me," she says, upset but trying to remain calm. "I almost came, asshole."

His face is confused. He doesn't know what the problem is. "I saved your life," he says.

"And you thought that gave you the right to fuck me in my sleep?"

As Hyena growls downward at the tiny man, her fur standing up on her head and back, she has the sudden urge to jump on him and fuck him to death. At first she thinks the desire comes from wanting to get him back for what he did to her, but then she realizes it is something else. Her body craves the man. Something about him drives a strong urge through her flesh.

"You didn't want me to have sex with you?" the man asks.

"Of course not," she says, as she imagines pinning him to the ground and swallowing his dick deep inside of her.

"Hmmm…" He rubs his scaly chin with a tentacle. "Your culture must be different from ours. I know very little of your kind. You're the first Furry I've ever met. I assume sex isn't very common for you?"

Hyena ignores the question, rubbing at the fishy bandage wrapped tightly around her stomach. "What am I doing here? Where are my sisters?"

The man leans back in a casual way. Hyena can't keep her eyes off of the thing between his legs.

"I found you out in the street and rescued you," he says. "The Rashers won't be able to find you here."

"What about my friends?"

"I could only save two of them," he says. "The other two were beyond saving. The living ones are in the other room. You were in the worst shape so I had to heal you first. I was just about to get to them."

"Where?" Hyena says.

"Follow me."

Hyena rubs her wound as she walks. Her insides aren't in much pain, but she feels nauseous, as if her stomach is doing flips inside of her. The next room is filled with tables and work-benches. Nova and Slayer are sleeping on them. Slayer has been stripped naked. Lying on her back, she is just a blob of black fur with a fluffy tail. The only area that is not coated in fur is a spot on her front, just below her breasts.

"That one is fine," the man says while pointing at Nova. "But this one needs my help," pointing at Slayer.

He climbs up on the table and wraps his tentacles around Slayer's hips, lifts her tail, and then aims his erect wiggling worm-like penis at her the fluffy mound below her asshole. Hyena shoves him off of her, using the balls of her foot.

"What are you doing?" he asks. "I need to have sex with her."

"I thought you were going to help her."

"That's what I'm trying to do. There's a good chance that she's going to die. The only way to ensure her survival is to put the sea worms in her."

"Sea worms?"

"The males of my people have these metal worms that grow in our semen. If I ejaculate inside of her the worms will keep her body alive even after her heart stops beating. It is the only way."

"Metal worms? Like the parasites that cause animals to go rabid?"

"Yes," he says. "But—"

Hyena grabs him by the throat. "If you even try to put those in her I will break your neck."

His words choke out of him, "But it is how I saved you . . ."

Hyena drops him and looks down at her belly. She rips open the bandage to reveal an open hole. Her intestines have been scooped out and replaced with hundreds of metal worms, swimming around each other in her belly.

"The worms are dormant," the man says. "They will keep you alive, but they won't take over your mind. My worms are not connected to the sea mothers."

Hyena assumes *sea mothers* is their term for the giant creatures that live in the ocean.

As she wraps herself back up so that she doesn't have to look at the worms anymore, she says, "So I'll be okay? The worms will keep me alive?"

"You're not quite as alive as you were," he says. "Some parts of your body won't function properly. But you will live as long as the worms are in your body. Your mind will remain your own."

Hyena feels her flesh. Her body is still warm. She still feels alive. The only difference is the movement under her skin.

"So please," he says, "I need to have sex with your friend."

Hyena grabs his arm/tentacle. "No, you can't. You have to try to save her without having sex with her."

"There is only a small chance she will live without the worms," he says. "You're willing to risk her life for that?"

Hyena looks down at Slayer's body. "I don't want you to infect her until we have no other choice."

The small fish man groans.

"Very well," he says. "I'll need your help. We need to stop the bleeding."

Hyena nods and the two of them get right to work.

After the surgery, they carry Slayer into the bedroom and wrap her in sealskin sheets.

"She's going to need a lot of rest," the man says. "It's going to take her a long time to recover."

"But she'll live?" Hyena asks. "You won't have to put worms in her?"

"She seems strong enough to make it," says the doctor.

"Wolf women are always strong," Hyena says. "But she is one of the strongest. She'll heal quickly."

The doctor finally puts on some clothing. He wears a green robe, but stays completely naked beneath it. He offers her another green robe.

"You should wear it," he says.

"I don't like to wear clothes," she says. "Especially in this heat."

"It will cover all of your fur," he says. "Wearing this, you could walk around the village and nobody would suspect that you're an outsider."

She looks at the green robe, but she doesn't put it on. The tentacled man takes her up a blue coral spiral staircase to the next floor and sits her down at a table made of driftwood.

"Tea?" he asks.

Hyena nods. He returns a few minutes later with a tray of white rose-shaped porcelain glasses filled with a steaming green fluid. When Hyena takes a sip, her whiskers point upward at the salty flavor.

"What is this?" Hyena says, as she pulls a thin slimy green strip out of her tea.

"Seaweed," he says.

"More like a soup broth than tea," she says, drinking more of it. "It's sort of okay."

The man doesn't realize that this was Hyena's way of giving a compliment.

"So what's your name?" the man asks.

"They call me Hyena," she says, "for the obvious reason."

"And what reason is that?"

"Because I look like a hyena."

"Oh," the man says, as if he has no idea what a hyena is. "My name is Swaggat."

While they talk and drink tea, Hyena stares at the man's legs sticking out from under his robe. She wants to lick his ankle and bite his inner thigh.

"Why did you rescue me?" Hyena asks. "Do you know how many of your people I killed outside?"

The man spits angrily. "The Rashers are not my people. They are oppressive monsters. I rescued you *because* you killed so many of them."

He stands up and goes to the window, looking down at the

shark blood in the streets.

He continues, "My people don't stand up to the Rashers anymore. They used to, a long time ago. But the last group to resist them was massacred. There were fifty men against just three Rashers. Just three. My people don't stand a chance against them."

He turns to her. "But I saw you kill six of them all on your own. That's never been done before."

"It cost me too many of my friends," Hyena says. "I don't even know how many of them are still alive."

"It doesn't matter," he says. "You still beat them. Not just one, but six. You're a hero to our people. We need your help."

"My help?"

"I want you to lead our people against Vinson and the Rashers."

"I'm not interested."

"But my people are practically enslaved by Vinson and his clerics. You have the power to free us from his tyranny."

"I only care about freeing my sisters who are infected with your disgusting sea worms. I came here to kill the monster who controls them."

"I can help you free them," he says. "There are other ways to free them. I will help you if you help me defeat Vinson."

Hyena decides to hear him out. Swaggat tells her a little about his society. It is split into four classes; each class wears a different color robe representing their class. The working class, which Swaggat belongs to, wears green robes. They are called Green Fish. The military class, which consists exclusively of the mutant shark men, wears blue robes. They are called Blue Fish, or Big Fish. The religious class, which consists of the clerics who Hyena saw on the beach worshipping the sea monsters, wears the red robes. Vinson, and those of the ruling class, are the Yellow Fish.

Their culture revolves around the religious class. The Red Fish, as they are called, are served by the working class Green Fish. And they are protected by the militaristic Blue Fish.

"Why do you want to kill Vinson?" Hyena asks. "What will it solve?"

"It will allow us to create a new society out of the ashes of the old one," he says. "We don't need the other classes. The Red Fish spend their time praying to the sea mothers or they waste their time in the creative arts. They live in luxury while the rest of us are worked half to death to support them. My people are farmers and builders, yet we aren't allowed to keep what we produce. We grow their food and build their homes, yet we hardly get any of the food we grow, we have to live in dilapidated houses a tenth the size of the ones we build for them."

"I guess you would find that unfair," Hyena says.

"You don't sound like you find it unfair."

Hyena shrugs. "I agree that it isn't fair. It's just . . ." She finishes her tea. "Isn't that the way all societies work?"

Swaggat wraps a tentacle around his tea and drinks.

He says, "Who says societies have to be that way? If we can overthrow the Yellow Fish we can create a new society. A better one, where there is only one class. Where everyone is equal. Wouldn't you want that in a society?"

"It doesn't matter to me." Hyena holds her stomach, feeling the worms inside of her. "I'm not interested in any type of society."

"But you don't really mean that. You have to—"

Before the man can debate his point any further, Hyena cuts him off. "If you can save my infected sisters I'll help you kill whoever you want me to kill. That's all that matters to me."

The man pouts the suckers on his lips, then he nods. "Very well. We have a deal."

When they go downstairs, Nova has regained consciousness and appears to be getting ready to masturbate again. As the doctor goes into the next room to check on Slayer, Hyena confronts the dark-skinned wolf girl.

"You nearly got Slayer killed," she tells Nova.

"Where is she?" Nova asks.

"Recovering. She's really messed up. If you had followed orders she wouldn't be in the state she's in now."

Nova looks down at her moist fingers, but says nothing.

"She nearly got herself killed saving you, I nearly got killed saving the both of you, and without Slayer the others went into a panic." She walks around to Nova's face so the girl will look at her while she's talking. "Baretta was killed. Zizzy's arm was ripped off. She's probably dead now. I have no idea if Vermin or Bunny escaped. It could just be the three of us left for all I know. "

Nova has nothing to say for her actions.

"You fucked up the whole mission," Hyena says.

As Hyena storms out of the room to check on Slayer, Nova finally speaks.

She says, "You're the one who wanted me to come on this mission. I'm not the one at fault. You are."

As Hyena looks down at Slayer's black furry face, Nova's words ring through her mind.

Hyena realizes that it really was her own fault that all of this happened. Slayer didn't want to bring Nova. She knew her head wasn't in the right place. Slayer said the same thing about Marrow. Although she was obviously a strong warrior, Marrow was the first to get killed. And Slayer was also right that Baretta was the most cowardice of the young warriors. If Baretta didn't panic and run away she might not have been killed, Zizzy might not have been wounded.

Nova isn't the one responsible for fucking up the whole mission. Hyena is. She should have had more confidence in her leader. Talon had confidence in Slayer as a leader, so why didn't Hyena? Perhaps it would have been different had Vyra and Toy come instead of Nova and Marrow. Those two might not have been strong warriors, but they might not have gotten everyone killed.

"I promise I'll do better, Slayer," Hyena tells the unconscious woman. "I won't doubt you ever again."

There is a loud knocking at the door.

Swaggat runs to the window.

"It's the Rashers," he says. "You've got to hide."

When Hyena goes to the window, she sees the blue-robed shark men running frantically through the streets, going house to house, searching for the outsiders who killed their brethren. A Rasher had never been murdered before, and now at least eight of them lay dead in the street. Hyena can tell that this has caused a massive panic among the Blue Fish.

Swaggat tries to pick Slayer from the bed.

"What are you doing?" Hyena asks. "You'll rip open her stitches."

Swaggat doesn't stop. "If they find her you're all dead."

Hyena helps him carry Slayer to a storage closet.

"Wait here with her," Swaggat says, closing the closet door on her.

But Hyena has no intention of trapping herself in a small room. She looks down at her leader, folded up in the corner of the closet. Slayer is still in a deep sleep.

Hyena grabs her spear and goes into the front room, hiding behind a wall. She can see Nova across the room, hidden behind the spiral staircase.

When Swaggat opens the door, three Rashers shove him out of the way and enter the room, led by a man in a red robe.

"Where are they?" the Red Fish hisses.

Swaggat reacts calmly. "What's the problem?"

"There are outsiders here," says the Red Fish, his voice rough and whispery. "They've murdered ten of our Rashers. An eye witness has said the Outsiders had help from a Green Fish. We believe they are being hidden in one of the houses on this block."

"Communicating with Outsiders is forbidden," says Swaggat. "I find it hard to believe a Green Fish would help them."

The Red Fish ignores Swaggat's comment and turns to the Rashers. "Search the place. Look everywhere."

The Rashers spit up and investigate the room. One heads toward Hyena's direction, one toward Nova, and the third goes toward the bedroom Slayer's hidden in.

Hyena backs slowly away from them. She goes into another room, a second bedroom, likely the one where Swaggat sleeps. With her claws extended, Hyena climbs up the grooves in the seashell wall until she gets to the ceiling. Her spear points down as the shark man enters the room. He looks in the closet, throws blankets into the air, searches under the bed.

In the main room, the Red Fish says, "What is this?" as he picks up a wad of black hair from Slayer's back. "It's hair."

"It's not what you think," Swaggat says.

"They're here!" Red Fish tells the Rashers.

When the shark man in Swaggat's bedroom looks back at the doorway, he sees Hyena clinging to the wall. Hyena growls at him as she closes the door, trapping him inside.

As the Red Fish and another Rasher open the door to Swaggat's bedroom, they see a shark man's severed head rolling across the floor. Before they have a chance to react, Hyena drops into sight, hanging upside-down from the doorframe. Using her spear like a pool cue, she drives it through the other Rasher's eye and out the back of his head.

From behind, the third Rasher cries out as he stumbles through the room. Nova is on his back like a cat. Her claws sinking into his flesh, she bites into his throat.

Red Fish runs for the door. He yells out to the other Rashers in the street.

"They're here!" he cries. "The outsiders are in—"

As he gets to the front doorway, he stops in his tracks, his words cut short. A machete blade is sticking out of his back. When he hits the ground, Vermin pulls her machete out of him, hops over his corpse and pulls him inside. Then she closes the door.

Blood sprays across the seashell wall as Nova bites open

the Rasher's jugular. After he dies and hits the ground, Nova doesn't stop biting him. Her teeth thrash at his meat, ripping him apart like a ravenous wild animal. Hyena decides to let the girl enjoy her meal. She walks around her to Vermin.

"Where have you been?" Hyena asks the grubby wolf girl.

Vermin smiles wide with gritty teeth. "I've been near the whole time, watching out for you."

"This place isn't safe," Swaggat says. "There are too many of them outside. We need to go.

They go to Slayer. They pick her up out of the closet and carry her. Her head rolls from side to side, her eyes flickering. Hyena grabs Slayer's clothes and weapons on the way.

"Have you seen any of the others?" Hyena asks Vermin. "Bunny? Zizzy? Did they get out alive?"

Vermin shrugs as she helps carry Slayer out of the bedroom. "I saw them get chased away by those blue meanies. They never came back."

"Even if they survived, I don't think they would have. Not with Zizzy's wound."

Nova is still violently eating the shark man as they head toward the back door. She snarls and growls while she eats, blood coating the front of her body.

"Nova, come on," Hyena says.

The girl continues eating.

"Come on!"

With Hyena's words, Nova snaps out of it. She looks up with a piece of meat dangling from her lips.

There is knocking at the door and voices yelling outside, wondering what is taking the Red Fish so long. Nova jumps to her feet. She wipes the gore from her chin and follows after the others.

In the backyard, Swaggat loads Slayer into the back of a large truck. It is similar to the vehicle they came across out in the desert of the Forbidden Zone, but it is longer with seats for six more passengers. The wolf women get inside and Swaggat takes the driver's seat. He starts up the vehicle.

As several Rashers and Red Fish enter the backyard, the truck roars forward, plowing through a metal gate into the street. The Rashers follow after them.

Racing down the road at top speed, they go deeper into the Forbidden Zone rather than back the way they had come.

"You should go in the other direction," Hyena says. "That's where Bunny went. We need to find her."

Swaggat disagrees. "First we have to hide you four." He wraps his tentacle around the gear stick, shifts into a higher gear, and hits the gas. "I know the perfect place."

Behind them, a dozen shark men are running after them, their raggedy blue robes flapping in the air. Their muscled legs pump so quickly that they are almost a blur.

"They're gaining on us," Vermin says.

Hyena looks back. Even though the vehicle is going at top speed, two of the shark men catch up. They jump up and grab onto the back, standing on the rear bumper.

"We need to get up top," Hyena says.

Hyena grabs her spear and Slayer's machine gun, and climbs out the window onto the roof of the vehicle. Nova and Vermin follow her, climbing like furry wolf spiders up the side of the truck.

As the sharks get their claws into the roof, Hyena runs across the truck and swipes at their limbs with the blade of her spear. One of them dodges the attack by releasing his hands. But before he can grab another hold, Hyena spin-kicks him in the chest. Fishy fluids splash into the air as he falls from the truck. His face is torn apart against the dirt as he hits the ground at seventy miles per hour.

The other one makes it to the roof before Hyena can stop him. He opens his jaws to attack, but a dart hits him in the neck. He turns to Vermin pointing the blowgun at him. He charges toward the small wolf girl as she loads another dart. She fires before he can reach her, hitting him in the face. He moves in slow motion as he raises one claw up in the air to attack, but the poison hits him hard before he can swing. He drops off the roof of the truck and disappears beneath its back wheels.

"Hold them back," Hyena says, as the other shark men close in on the vehicle.

Nova grabs a wooden package from her ankle and hits a button. The package unfolds into a small crossbow that she straps to her wrist.

"Aim for their legs," Hyena says.

They open fire on the school of Rashers. Hyena fires Slayer's machine gun at them, blowing their legs out from under them. Three of them go down. It doesn't kill them, but they won't be able to run fast enough to catch them with those wounds.

Nova fires crossbow arrows at their legs. The bolts go through their thigh muscles, but it doesn't take them down. It slows them only a little bit. Vermin fires poison darts at the Rashers, but the shark men are so large that one dart takes several minutes to even slow them down.

Another vehicle roars into the street and slams into Swaggat's truck. It's a large jeep full of Red Fish.

"Pull over!" the Red Fish yell at Swaggat.

They slam into the truck again, slowing them down by 15 MPH.

Four shark men catch up. They go for the truck at different directions, two on the back, and the other two on each of the sides. With Vermin and Nova too close to her, Hyena knows she won't be able to fight at her full ability. She'll have to get rid of them before they get onto the roof.

"Knock them off," Hyena says.

She fires at the hands of the shark men. It fills the roof of the vehicle with bullet holes, close to where Slayer is sleeping. She stops firing. Two of the shark men get to the roof.

Hyena charges them and drop-kicks both of them in the chest. They fall off the back of the vehicle, but one of them grabs Hyena's legs, pulling her off her feet.

The Rasher is dragged along the ground, holding onto Hyena's leg, trying to take her with him. Blood erupts from his flesh as he's dragged. Hyena tosses her spear onto the vehicle and uses both of her hands to hold on. Vermin grabs the spear before it rolls off the roof.

Her legs bleed as the Rasher's claws dig into her calves. She barks and growls at the shark, wiggling to break free. Nova fires her crossbow into the face of a third Rasher as he climbs up the side of the truck. He continues climbing with the bolt in his face. She fires two more bolts, one in his eye, but he won't let go.

More of the Rashers come up from behind them. Vermin hits them with darts but they keeping coming, catching up to Hyena. The dragged Rasher starts climbing up Hyena's body, clawing into her thigh, then pulling himself up to her waist. It climbs all the way up to Hyena's face and slobbers onto her cleavage.

As he opens his jaws to bite into her throat, Hyena bites first. She bites into his jaw, just above the chin, holding his mouth in place. She growls and tugs on his jaw as his teeth clack together. The Rasher chomps and chomps at the air, but Hyena won't let go of him. Her teeth dig dipper into his gums, growling viciously. Blood drips down his chin. His lips tear against her teeth.

The car goes over a bump and Hyena is drenched with wetness. She bends the man's jaw to see what has happened. The car has gone over a large rock, which caught the shark man's crotch and ripped off his legs from the crotch down. His intestines spill from what was once his anus. The Rashers pursuing them slip on his insides and hit the ground so hard that they don't get up again.

The upper half of the shark man continues thrashing and chomping, but his muscles slowly relax. His chomps grow weaker, quieter. Eventually he is too weak to hold on. Hyena pushes his body off of her. It rolls beneath the wheels of the jeep chasing after them.

As Hyena turns to crawl back to the roof of the truck, she sees Slayer awake inside. The dark-haired wolf leader is fighting a shark man from inside the cab. The shark is on the side of the vehicle, its head through a window, biting at Slayer. In her weakened state, Slayer tries to fight him off. Kicking him in the face with her furry foot, clawing at him. She's naked and all of her secondary weapons were attached to her leather outfit, so she has to fight bare-fisted.

"Slayer," Hyena calls.

Slayer looks back at Hyena.

"Your stuff is on the seat in front of you."

Slayer leans over the back of the seat and grabs her leather pants. She pulls two pistols from the holsters, then fires them into the shark man's mouth repeatedly until he lets go and tumbles to the ground.

When Hyena gets back onto the roof, Nova is finishing off the last of the shark men. She has her sickle-sword inside of his belly, twisting it in a circle, spinning his intestines around like noodles on a fork. When Nova pulls her sword out, he falls off the truck. Nova bites through the intestines on the hook of her blade so that he doesn't take her sword with him. Then she chews the leftover meat on her fingernails.

The jeep slams into the truck, nearly knocking Nova off the side as she eats. Hyena looks at the Red Fish as they grind their vehicle against Swaggat's truck, trying to slow them down.

Hyena reloads another clip into Slayer's machine gun and fires it at them. She runs across the roof and jumps onto the hood of the jeep, firing through the windshield at the Red Fish. Their bodies are pulverized by the bullets. The passenger dies first. Then, as the driver dies, the jeep spins to a halt.

The two Red Fish in the back scramble to get out of the Jeep. Hyena shoots them in their backs as she hops into the driver's seat. Only one of them makes it out of the back alive, two holes in his guts. He falls to the ground, writhing in pain, as Hyena speeds off in the jeep after Swaggat.

The other Rashers are so far back, moving so slowly with their wounds, that Swaggat and Hyena are able to lose them in the wilds of the Forbidden Zone.

Chapter 7

Vermin

Swaggat brings them to a rundown outpost. They hide the vehicles in a rusted garage and take stairs down into a hidden underground shelter.

"This is where the resistance used to meet," Swaggat says. "Back when there was a resistance."

Slayer is able to walk on her own feet, but she needs Vermin to assist her.

"Where is everyone else?" Slayer asks. "Are we the only ones who made it?"

"We don't know," Hyena says. "Marrow and Baretta are dead. Zizzy was critically wounded, but she escaped with Bunny."

"We can't be hidden away like this," Slayer says, as she sits down on an old clay stool. "We have to watch for the animals who infected Talon. It's the only way to save them."

Hyena says, "We might have another way." She points at Swaggat. "This Zoner says he can cure Talon and the others."

"How?" Slayer asks him.

"We would have to remove all of the worms," Swaggat says. "It's difficult, because they reproduce so quickly. It'll take a lot of time and several operations. But I've been able to do it in the past. Without the worms, your friends will regain control of their minds."

"Then let's take you back to them right away," Slayer says.

Swaggat holds out his hands. "No, you have to help me take down our corrupt leader, Vinson. That's the deal. You help us kill him and the Rashers, and I'll save your friends."

"No deal," Slayer says.

Hyena steps forward. "But Slayer, I already—"

Slayer gives Hyena a look that shuts her up.

"If you really want us to help you then come with us back

to our camp. We have five infected wolf women that need to be cured. One of them is the strongest warrior of our tribe. If you heal them then we will help you. If you fight with Talon on your side you will not lose, no matter how strong the enemy."

Swaggat rubs his neck with a tentacle. "It's going to take weeks to heal them. We should really strike now, while the Rashers are in a panic."

Hyena says to Slayer. "I already told him I would do it. If you don't want to you can stay here."

"I'm ordering you not to go," Slayer says. "It would be a mistake to fight now. We aren't in any condition to take on an entire army."

"But we have to try."

Slayer stands up and charges him. "Trying could get more of my sisters killed."

As she finishes speaking, she falls to her knees, clutching her stomach. Blood dribbles from her mouth.

Swaggat examines her. "She's opened up her stitches." He looks up at Hyena. "Help me get her to the barracks."

The barracks are just a few rows of bunks with old handmade mattresses on them. No sheets or pillows. The doctor stitches Slayer up and asks her to take it easy. She breathes deeply but says nothing.

"Come on," Swaggat says. "We can't upset her like that again."

They go to the other corner of the barracks and sit down to talk in private.

"I know your friend thinks it would be wise to have more of your friends fighting alongside us," Swaggat says. "But it would be better to attack sooner. Just one of you would be enough."

The man's robe is wide open, revealing his chest and belly. Hyena grinds her claws into her knee at the sight of his flesh. Saliva builds inside her maw.

"Slayer isn't going to trust you," Hyena says, then she swallows a gulp of saliva. "If you were to save our sisters she would give her life for your cause. But otherwise she won't go with the plan. You're a man. The women in my tribe never trust men."

"But you trust me, don't you?"

Swaggat puts his tentacle on Hyena's thigh. The oily appendage curls around to her kneecap, wetting her spotted fur.

"I . . . I guess so." Hyena can hardly speak as sweat drips down the back of her fuzzy neck.

"We can do it together," he says.

As his tentacle inches higher up her thigh, Hyena can't take it anymore. She lunges at him so hard that he flies out of his seat and the wind gets knocked out of him as he hits the concrete floor. She rips his robe off with her teeth and digs her claws into his love handles, licking and biting at his shoulder and neck. The man nearly half Hyena's size is completely pinned down by the massive dog woman. He immediately gives in, wrapping his tentacles around her and sucking on her furry breasts that are smashed against his face.

As soon as they kiss, her black dog-lips wrapped around his gooey scaled fish-lips, she stops. She pushes off of him and stands back.

"What am I doing?" Hyena asks herself aloud. "I've always been able to control myself before."

"Just give in to it," Swaggat says, crawling on his tentacles toward her. "It's natural. It's nothing to be ashamed of."

Hyena shakes her head. "No, you don't understand."

He gives up and sits on one of the beds. "Why are your people so sexually repressed?"

"Sex turns us into beasts." She rubs her fuzzy chest. "Every time we have orgasms we become more wolf-like. If we have sex enough times we completely lose ourselves to the animal side."

"Interesting," he says, pulling his robe back on. "My people have sex with each other as often as we have conversations. We would go insane if we ever had to resist our sexual urges."

As he sits there, Hyena has to fight the urge to pounce on him again.

"My people sweat a strong aphrodisiac," the man says. "You're probably feeling the effects of it now."

Hyena smells the air, "Aphrodisiac?"

"Among my people, when two members of the opposite sex come in contact with each other it is nearly impossible to resist the urges. Until you actually go through with it it's all you'll be able to think about. The chemical released in our sweat is just far too powerful."

As Hyena recognizes the sweet fishy pear-like odor in the air, the aphrodisiac gets stronger. Her entire body feels like it will burst with hot moisture. She clenches her fists and moves several feet away from the man, trying to breathe in fresh air that doesn't contain the sweet scent.

"Let's go back to the others," she says.

Then she leaves.

When they return to the other wolf women, Hyena can immediately see the effect Swaggat's sweat has on her sisters. They begin to wiggle in their seats, crossing their legs, then uncrossing them. Vermin squirms her butt against the concrete floor. Nova wags her tail quickly until she can't take it anymore. She gets up and goes to another room to masturbate.

"So what's the plan?" Vermin asks.

Hyena and Swaggat look at each other.

Swaggat speaks for them. "You all will stay here for the night. When it's dark I'm going to go out and get some support amongst my people. We will attack Vinson and the Rashers in the morning."

Vermin looks at Hyena. "I thought we were going to kill the sea beast."

"The plan's changed," Hyena says.

"But Slayer said—"

Swaggat cuts her off. "I can't allow you to kill the sea mothers. They are important to my people."

"Those creatures are important to your people?" Vermin asks. "But why? They are responsible for so much death."

"You don't understand," Swaggat says. "The sea mothers and my people are the same."

Swaggat explains the evolution of his people.

"The sea mothers were once females of my people," Swaggat says. "As my people get older, we become more squid-like. But the males of my species stop changing once we reach puberty. Females, on the other hand, continue to become larger and more squid-like every year they are alive. Once a woman is in her late fifties, she usually has mutated so much that she is no longer able to survive on land and must go into the sea. There she grows into one of the large creatures who control the sea worms.

"Women try to have as many children as possible before their transformation. They especially try for as many sons as they can get. A sea mother's sons spread their seed into the world.

Everything they have sex with becomes infected with parasites that their sea mother controls. The females their sons infect will infect other animals which will infect other humans and other creatures. This is how our sea mothers obtain their prey.

"Before a female becomes a sea mother, the worms inside of her sons are dormant until she goes out to sea. They can infect people with their worms but the mother won't be able to control them until after she matures in the ocean. My sea worms are forever dormant, because my mother died when she was still young.

"Those infected with dormant sea worms, such as Hyena, are immune to all other worms. A brain can only be in tune with one sea mother. The brain will not be able to connect with other parasites, even if the original sea mother dies and loses connection."

"What about the Rashers?" Hyena asks. "Where do they fit in?"

"The Rashers are neither male nor female," Swaggat says. "They do not reproduce themselves. The Rashers are the children of the sea mothers. Before the women go out to sea, their husbands impregnate them one last time, which often costs the husbands their lives. Nine months later, once the sea mothers are fully matured, they crawl on land and lay dozens of eggs. These eggs hatch into small legged fish creatures that crawl back into the sea, grow to adulthood within a year, then return to dry land and join the ranks of the Rashers.

"The Rashers have only one purpose. They protect the sons of the sea mothers."

"Are they immune to the sea worms?" Hyena asks.

"No," he says. "None of my people are immune unless they carry dormant sea worms. But the Rashers are not in danger of being eaten by the sea mothers. A sea mother can inactivate sea worms in any creature if she wishes it. Sea mothers do not wish to eat the Rashers, so she will not control infected Rashers. Likewise, she will not eat any of my people who are infected with her sea worms. Unless she wants to."

"The sea mothers sometimes eat your people?"

"My people treat our women with respect. Not just because

they will one day become the sea mothers that keep our society alive, but because if you're not kind and respectful to a woman while she is a human she will eat you once she becomes a sea mother.

"Those who are in the most danger of being eaten are the wives of a sea mother's sons. Women in my culture are always very caring of their mothers-in-law. Because once a wife begins to have children with her husband, she becomes infected with his sea worms. They are dormant only until the mother-in-law goes into the ocean. If the sea mother doesn't like her daughter-in-law she will eat her with no remorse. A wife often becomes an obedient servant to her mother-in-law until the mother makes her transformation. However, those who are in the most danger are the ex-girlfriends. If a girl breaks a boy's heart and is infected with his worms she has to pray his mother dies before she becomes a sea mother. A sea mother's first meal is usually all the young women her sons have slept with, especially the ones she didn't like."

"I take it that not many of your women live long enough to become sea mothers?" Hyena asks.

"This is true. Only about ten percent of our females make it out to sea."

Hyena nods at Swaggat's story, mildly interested in his culture.

"My people are similar to your people," she says. "Our women also go through transformations, from woman to wolf. But when we become large hungry creatures like your sea mothers, we only eat men. We don't discriminate. We eat all men."

Swaggat leaves at nightfall. He drives without his truck lights, knowing that the Rashers are patrolling the area.

Vermin and Hyena sit in silence, wagging their tails, grinding their teeth, until Swaggat's aroma fades from the room.

"I like him," Vermin says, curling her lips around her bottom teeth.

Hyena wipes the moisture from her fur. "Are you going to be ready to fight tomorrow?"

"I'm always ready," Vermin says.

"We'll be fighting a lot more of those shark men," Hyena says. "Your darts aren't very effective against them."

"I've got lots of the venom," Vermin says. "I'll just triple dip the darts and aim for arteries. They should go down faster."

"You're going to have to learn how to fight on a motorcycle," Hyena says. "You are worthless as a knight otherwise."

"I'll get used to it. I've learned how to shoot while running, then while jumping. It shouldn't be hard to learn to shoot while riding."

Hyena nods. "Learn quickly."

Vermin was never known as a capable fighter or hunter. She was good at setting traps and hunting small animals like rabbits and squirrels, but she was rarely seen on the battlefield. This was because Vermin was always hidden. After the great battle of McDonaldland, people thought of her as merely a survivor of the battle, not one of the heroes who brought them to victory. But the truth is that Vermin killed more mutant soldiers than any of her sisters.

Vermin knew she couldn't stand up to many enemies in hand to hand combat, so she preferred to kill her victims before they even knew she was there. She crept through the shadows of the battlefield, going from crushed-car to crushed-car. She would fire a poison dart at a mutant, sprint toward him on all fours, cut his throat and disappear into the shadows before anyone saw her.

Although it was not yet night, the great hermaphrodite wolf, Kroger, and the large city wall around McDonaldland cast long shadows across the battlefield, giving Vermin plenty of places to hide. She went from mutant to mutant, picking off those who were fighting solo or had momentarily separated from their fighting squad. It didn't matter what they were armed with; machine guns, flame throwers, chainsaws. Once she hit them with her darts, they didn't stand a chance.

The only time she was in any real danger was the time she

decided to take on six mutants at once. They were in the back of a truck that had lost its engine in the jaws of the giant wolves Talon was commanding. The six mutants were in the center of the battlefield, protected by armor plating surrounding the truck, firing at all the wolf women who came near. Several of Vermin's wolf sisters were falling to these gunmen. Even though she was one of the youngest warriors on the battlefield, she knew it was up to her to take the men down.

The first one was easy. As a mutant stood up to shoot at Slayer riding by on her motorcycle, Vermin put a dart in the back of his chubby neck. It took a while for the other five to realize what was going on. They found the dart in his neck, then looked back in the direction Vermin had fired. But Vermin was not there anymore. As they put a spotlight on the shadows in that direction, Vermin scuttled like a wolf spider quickly around the other side of the vehicle. She hit the one manning the spotlight in his neck and he dropped out of the truck. She cut his throat before disappearing beneath the vehicle.

When the mutant's friends saw his blood gushing out of his neck as he choked on his last breath, they began to panic. They thought they were fighting a ghost. They aimed the light across the battlefield, but didn't see anything. By the way they shouted at each other, Vermin could tell they were beginning to get scared. This was part of Vermin's plan. The more they feared her, the more control she had over them.

But it all didn't go according to plan. The next time she fired at them, she missed. The dart hit the truck between two of the mutants. Before she could hide in the shadow of a nearby wrecked vehicle, they saw her black ratty tail. The mutants fired at her, shining the light on the vehicle she was using for cover. There was no way to sneak away. She was trapped. In a shootout, one blowgun was no match for four men with machine guns.

Vermin believes that there's always a way to win, no matter the odds. She just had to be clever enough to figure a way out of her situation. She couldn't outgun them. They were too close for her to run away. And with the spotlight on, she couldn't sneak away. As pressure built in her lower belly, she got an idea. She knew it wasn't a very good idea, but it was the only idea she had.

The ratty wolf girl had to take a shit, so that's what she did. She shit into her hand and tossed it at the mutants, hoping to hit the spotlight. Without breaking cover, she didn't aim well and the shit splattered on the bed of the truck. When they felt it hit their ankles, they recoiled in surprise. Then another handful of shit was thrown at them. It hit the edge of their barricade, splattering all four of them. The mutants wondered why the wolf

woman was tossing mud at them. But then one mutant tasted a droplet of the mud that had gotten into his mouth.

"It's shit," he cried.

As another splatter of her wet shit hit one of them in the face, the four men ducked for cover, whimpering at the rancid odor. Vermin made a break for it. With a handful of diarrhea, she charged around the side of the truck and covered two-thirds of the spotlight in the crap, rendering it useless. The second she was hidden, she shot a dart at one of them, through a crack in the barricade, in an ankle. Three were left standing.

One of them went to wipe the shit from the spotlight with his third hand. But he only spread it around more. Then a dart hit him in the forearm.

The other two fired into the shadows until their guns were empty. As they were reloading, Vermin held her blowgun in her teeth, climbed up the back of the truck and stabbed them with two poisoned darts. One of them didn't go down right way. He punched her in the face so hard that she fell down in the mud, dazed.

As she tried to get up, the mutant reloaded his clip and aimed it at Vermin. He shook his head and blinked his eyes as the poison spread through his system. He tried to aim down at Vermin but he couldn't keep his balance. Before he passed out, he slipped on a piece of Vermin's shit and broke his jaw against the edge of the truck's metal armor.

As Slayer rode by on her motorcycle, she saw Vermin cutting their throats and retrieving her darts. Slayer gave the girl a nod of approval and rode on. Even though it was just a quick nod, it made Vermin very happy. It was the first time she had ever been acknowledged as a warrior by one of her sisters. It was all the acknowledgement she needed.

She spent the rest of the battle fighting in the shadows, but not a single Outlander or wolf woman saw a trace of her again until the war was over.

Whimpering and growling noises come from the next room. Hyena goes to the barracks and finds Slayer, wriggling and turning in her sleep. She's having a wet dream. Swaggat's arousing fragrance is still in the room and is affecting the wounded wolf woman.

Slayer's thighs press together, rubbing her oversized clitoris. Her fur fluffs out as she reaches orgasm. Then her body mutates, turning her just a little bit more into a wolf. The only difference Hyena notices is the lengthening of her teeth and tail.

When she's done, Slayer wakes up panting. She looks down at her crotch, and says, "Damn it . . ."

Then she looks up to Hyena, "Where's my cup?"

Hyena gets her clothes. She hands over the cup first, which Slayer quickly straps to her crotch.

"I don't know how you manage with that thing," Hyena says, pointing at her oversized clitoris. It's so large that it's visible through her fur.

Slayer speaks with deep breaths. "It's been bothering me even more lately. Damn thing brings me nearly to orgasm just by walking around, even when wearing my cup."

"Ever think of cutting it off?" Hyena asks. "It's not like you need it for anything. You don't have sex."

Slayer looks down at it. She shakes her head.

"It's a part of me," she says. "It keeps me on my toes."

Hyena doesn't push it.

"Plus . . ." Slayer begins. "I'd like to have real sex someday. At least once before I turn."

"It's not really that big of a deal."

"Maybe," Slayer leans against the wall of her bunk. "But I'd rather see for myself."

After she recovers from her orgasm and transformation, Slayer puts her clothes back on.

"So how are you feeling?" Hyena asks.

"I'm okay," Slayer says. "I think my orgasm helped a little. The change added some muscle and sealed up my wounds. I should be ready to go in the morning."

"I'm sorry," Hyena says.

"For what?"

Hyena squats down, the weight of her furry butt on her feet, and looks up at Slayer.

"I'm sorry for fucking everything up," she says. "You were right about Nova and Marrow. We shouldn't have brought them. They nearly got us all killed."

"We made it through okay," Slayer says. "We had no idea it was going to be this difficult to accomplish the mission. We're lucky any of us made it out alive."

"Still," Hyena says. "Talon made you the leader because she knew you were best for the job. I had no right questioning your decision. I bullied you into doing things my way and this is what happened. I'm a horrible second in command."

Slayer squints her eyes at Hyena.

"No," she says. "You're doing great."

"How can you possibly believe that?"

"You're supposed to challenge my decisions. That's your job. If my decisions are strong enough then I won't crumble beneath the challenge. You didn't decide to take Nova and Marrow with us. I did. I was not confident enough in my choices. You did what you were supposed to do. Not only that, but you were able to take command when I fell. You saved our lives. I couldn't have asked for a better right hand."

"Are you sure about that?" Hyena asks. "I also disobeyed your orders and took Swaggat's deal against your wishes. I'm leading his people in the revolution tomorrow."

Slayer closes her eyes for a moment.

"I guess we have no choice then," she says. "We'll do it. But you're not leading. I am."

"Are you able to fight?"

"I told you I'll be fine in the morning."

"Okay then. You lead."

"Do you trust him?"

"Swaggat? Of course not. He's a man. But he saved my life, and yours. We owe him. And if there's a chance he can cure Talon and the others, I think we've got to take it."

"He better not fuck us over. I'm not risking any more of my sisters' lives for nothing."

Hyena nods.

Slayer rolls onto her back. "I'd like to be alone now. I need to think and rest."

Hyena gets to her feet.

As she leaves, Slayer says, "One more thing."

Hyena turns to her.

Slayer says, "If you ever disobey my commands again I'll break your legs."

Hyena snickers at her words, but quickly realizes that Slayer isn't joking.

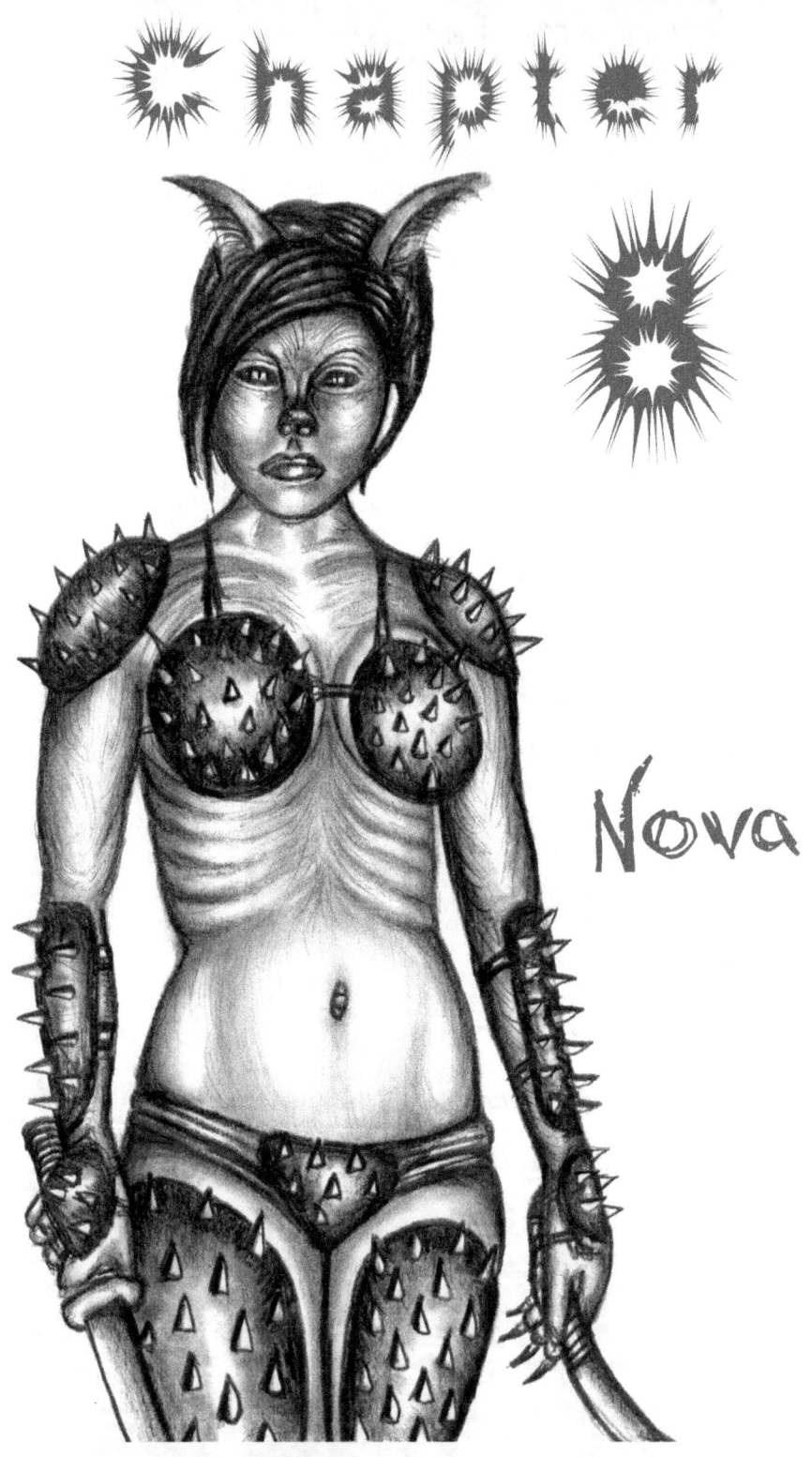

Chapter 8

Nova

In the morning, Hyena wakes to a room full of Zoners. There are about ten of them in green robes. Swaggat isn't with them. They sit in a circle around the room with solemn expressions on their faces. Slayer and Nova are awake, sitting amongst them. Vermin is in the corner chasing her own tail.

"Where is he?" she asks them.

They look up at her through their hoods. Their eyes glossy and fish-like.

"He'll be here shortly," one of them says.

Then they continue their silence. It has always been forbidden for them to speak to outsiders. Even though they are the revolutionaries of their people, they still want to stick to their traditions. They don't feel comfortable speaking with the wolf women.

The air is so thick with the fish men sweat that all four of the wolf women squirm in their seats. Vermin's tail wags rapidly. Saliva builds in Hyena's mouth. Nova doesn't last long before she goes into another room to masturbate. Even Slayer has to adjust the cup in her pants every few minutes. The fish men don't know what is wrong with them. The group sweats and whimpers, impatiently waiting for Swaggat's return.

By the time Swaggat arrives, Hyena's jaw aches from grinding her teeth. Her muscles are sore from keeping them so tense. The sight of Swaggat relieves her of some of the tension, because she knows she'll be getting out of there soon. But she's slightly annoyed that the squid man only brought six people with him.

"This is it?" Hyena asks him, pointing at his six friends.

"There are more in the villages," Swaggat says. "We will spearhead the attack. Then they will join us later."

"Are you sure they will fight?" Slayer asks.

"They are afraid of the Rashers," Swaggat says. "They'll need to see some of them fall before they will fight."

"Then let's make sure to kill them as quickly as we can," Hyena says.

Swaggat wets his lips. "There's on more thing."

Hyena is worried by the tone of his voice. "What's wrong?"

"Two of your friends have been taken prisoner," Swaggat says.

"Bunny and Zizzy?" Slayer asks.

"They're going to be fed to the sea mothers within the hour," he says.

Slayer jumps to her feet and grabs her machine gun.

"Then we're going now," she says. "Where are they?"

"On the beach," Swaggat says. "I don't think we'll reach them in time."

"We'll reach them," Slayer says.

"We're leaving," Hyena tells Nova.

Nova is masturbating furiously. She looks up at Hyena and growls, jerking her entire body in a frenzy. Hyena hardly recognizes her. Nova now has so much hair on her body that very little naked human skin can be seen. She looks more like a taller, bony version of Slayer. Her eyes are wild. It's as if she's already about to turn.

"We don't have time for this," Hyena says. "We need to go. They're going to kill Bunny and Zizzy."

Nova can't hear her. She howls. It is more animal than human.

"Come on!"

The aphrodisiac in the air hits Hyena hard. Watching Nova masturbate, Hyena's muscles quiver, dying to join Nova in a masturbation frenzy. The sexual frustration becomes too much for her and she explodes. But she releases the sexual tension into anger.

Hyena kicks Nova over, tosses her in the air, and slams her back against the wall. The bricks crumble into Nova's fur as Hyena pins her arms above her head and growls in her face.

Nova thrashes and barks, biting the air at her. She wraps herself around Hyena and humps her leg.

"Snap out of it." Hyena head butts Nova, but she doesn't stop snarling and barking.

Hyena head butts her again and Nova's eyes roll to the ground. She calms and breathes heavily. When Slayer enters the room, Hyena drops her. Nova shakes and twitches on the floor.

Slayer goes to the wild girl. Nova's gone through so many changes in such a short period of time that it's beginning to affect her mind.

"Cut this out," Slayer says, locking eyes with her.

Nova cowers beneath the alpha wolf.

"We need you today," she continues. "You just have to last long enough to complete the mission. Then I'll let you turn."

"I can't take it anymore," Nova says.

Hyena can hardly believe she's still able to speak after going through such a big change. With longer teeth and a new dog tongue in her mouth, her words are like muffled growls. Nova begins to cry.

She says, "Why couldn't I be with him? Why did I have to fuck it up?"

Hyena isn't sure who she's talking about.

"I forgot him after the first few changes," she says. "Why can't I forget him now? No matter how many times I change he's all I can think about."

"Who?" Slayer asks. "The Meat you took from Pippi?"

Nova nods.

"With every change I feel a section of my memory disappear," she says. "But he stays. He refuses to leave my head."

Nova feels the fur on her face. "What if I can't ever forget him? Even if I completely turn, what if his face is still in my mind? I'd roam the wilderness as a giant wolf, with no recollection of my humanity, except for my love of that fucking worthless asshole."

"Then here's what you do," Slayer says, grabbing Nova by the jaw. "If you still have him in your head after you become a big sister, you find his scent. You track him down and you eat him. Then you'll be able to get him out of your head."

Nova says, "I don't want to eat him. I just want to forget him."

"You're a predator," Slayer says. "Start acting like one."

Slayer steps away from her and turns to Hyena. "We leave in three minutes. Make sure she's ready to fight." Then she leaves the room.

Hyena watches Nova as she scratches her new furry parts. Hair always itches when it first comes in. Nova tries to put on her spiked metal bikini, but it doesn't fit anymore. Her body has grown too much. She tosses it aside and grabs her weapons.

"One more battle," Nova says. "Then I'm done."

Hyena rides with Nova, Swaggat, and four other Zoners in Swaggat's truck. They head for the beach where Bunny and Zizzy will be sacrificed to the sea mothers.

In the back seat, Nova is drunk on the Zoners' scent. She sniffs the robe of one of the Zoners sitting next to her. She smells his shoulders and head, taking quick dog-sniffs. She opens his robe and presses her nose up and down his chest. Her hands grab him, pulling him closer as she inhales the scent deeply.

Nova crawls on top of the man's lap and wraps her fur around his small body. Then she pulls him inside of her. The man politely gives in to Nova's advances. As she fucks him, he expresses awkwardness and discomfort, but he tolerates the act. He reacts as if he's stuck in a boring conversation with a stranger who insists on making small talk. He's just nodding his head politely, hoping it's over soon.

"Is it safe for my friend to have sex with him?" Hyena asks Swaggat. "Won't she get infected with his worms?"

Swaggat shakes his head. "His worms are dormant like mine. Very few Green Fish are connected to the sea mothers."

Hyena looks down at her stomach and feels the worms crawling through her abdomen. "Nova, you should stop. You don't know what you're doing."

Swaggat puts his tentacle hand on Hyena's shoulder. "Don't worry. The sea worms will make her stronger. She won't fall so easily in battle."

Nova orgasms twice against the man, digging her claws into his neck. When he goes limp, she crawls across the seat to the next man. She's drunk on the drug they release. She can't get enough.

"Don't go too far," Hyena tells her.

Nova licks her plump black nose at the hyena woman, but doesn't stop.

They drive into a village, down a street lined with purple and blue cone shell buildings. The place looks deserted.

"Where is everyone?" Hyena asks Swaggat.

Swaggat looks around, scanning through the windows.

"They must be on the beach," Swaggat says.

Just outside of the village, they pull over and open the backs of their trucks. Inside there is an assortment of weapons. All of them are from the old world. Lots of ancient rusted pistols and rifles.

"We don't know how to use them," Swaggat says. "We were hoping you could show us."

Hyena pulls out an old shotgun. When she pumps it, the barrel breaks off.

"These are worthless," Hyena says.

"What do you mean?" Swaggat says. "We've been saving them for generations, just for this day. They *have* to work."

Slayer comes over to their vehicle.

"None of them work?" Slayer asks.

Hyena digs through the old guns. "I don't think so."

Out of the dozens of guns in the truck, only four seem like they could possibly work. And even those are most likely too dangerous to operate. There is very little ammo and most of it is the wrong caliber.

"I don't think you should bother using these," Slayer says.

"But four of them work," Swaggat says.

"They're just going to blow up in your face. What else have you got?"

Swaggat frowns at her and goes to the back of the next truck. "We've got plenty of spear guns and flame-saws."

Hyena examines a flame-saw. It is some kind of strange mix of chainsaw and flame-thrower. The chainsaw blade stretches about five feet, like a long sword. Swaggat takes one of them and straps it on.

"We invented these flame-saws in secret," he says. "But

we've never actually used them in battle before."

"It looks deadly," Hyena says.

"Hopefully it's as deadly as it looks," Swaggat says.

Slayer pulls a blanket off of a large machine behind the spear guns. It is an enormous double-barreled Gatling gun.

"What is this?" she asks.

Swaggat says, "We have no idea. Some kind of weapon that was built by revolutionaries long ago. They died before it was ever put to use."

Hyena examines it. "It's not that old. I think it'll still work."

She inspects the ammunition. There is plenty of it. The bullets are enormous. Just one could barely fit inside a tin can. They must be 180 caliber. The thing wasn't designed to shoot people. It was designed to shoot tanks.

"The thing must weigh a ton," Hyena says. "I don't know how we'll be able to carry it. Maybe if we had three wolf women holding it as one fired."

"We can fire it from the back of the truck," Slayer says.

"We can't take the trucks on the beach," Swaggat says. "The wheels will get stuck in the sand."

"And they'll hear us coming," Vermin says, peeking over Hyena's shoulder.

"We'll leave it for now," Slayer says. "If we run into trouble we'll retreat here. We can use it for defense."

The others agree. The Zoners take spear guns, axes, flame-saws, and pitchforks. Then they head up the hills toward the beach.

When they arrive, the beach is empty. They see no one for miles, not even infected animals coming to feed themselves to the sea beasts.

"Where are they?" Slayer asks Swaggat. "You said they'd be here."

Hyena squints her eyes at something down the beach, near the water. It looks a bit like a large dead animal that has washed up on the shore.

"What's that?" she asks them.

After staring for a while, they discover that it is two women, tied back to back. Bunny and Zizzy. They are still alive. There is also a group of eight Red Fish coming down the beach toward their prisoners.

"Let's go," Slayer says.

Slayer leads the charge, sprinting down the beach. She fires her machine gun, taking three Red Fish down. Spear guns are fired. The Zoner cultists go down without a fight. None of them even try to run away. Once the last of them falls, Slayer goes to Bunny and Zizzy. Bunny has a bloody nose and black eye showing through her fur, but otherwise she's fine. Zizzy, on the other had, snarls and snaps at Slayer as she approaches her. Worms crawl in and out of her face.

"She's infected," Bunny says to Slayer. "Stay back."

Swaggat examines the bodies of the dead Zoners. He says, "These aren't Red Fish." He points to the bonds around their wrists. "They're *my* people, in disguise."

"It's a trap," Slayer says, as an army of shark men emerges from the sea.

At the sight of the massive army of shark men, many of the Zoners panic and flee for their lives. Even Nova and Vermin flee. Those who remain to fight against the Rashers only do so because it is too late for them to get away.

"One of your friends sold you out," Slayer tells Swaggat.

The fish man ignores her, fidgeting with his flame-saw in a panic. It doesn't seem to be working.

Hyena cuts Bunny free of her ropes, but leaves Zizzy tied up. The young girl thrashes on the ground with her ankles tied to her one remaining arm.

As Bunny gets to her feet, Slayer tosses her a pistol from her side holster. Then they all stand back to back as the Rashers surround them. Just three wolf women and five Zoners against the horde of shark soldiers.

As Hyena spins her spear at them, Bunny speaks over her shoulder. "Some rescue."

"We just need to kill some of them," Hyena says. "Once the other villagers see that they can be killed, they will join the fight." Then she looks at Swaggat. "Right?"

Swaggat looks at her. His panicked face shows more than just doubt. His followers are probably so far gone that they won't be able to see any of the Rashers fall. Without answering, he returns to his weapon. The chainsaw motor isn't working. The machine slides around in his sweaty tentacles.

They open fire on the Rashers. Bunny and Slayer focus their fire on one of them at a time. They aim for the face and neck. Red bubbles pop from fishy flesh as the bullets hit. It takes twelve rounds to the head before the first one goes down. The Zoners shoot them with their spear guns, but the spears don't go very deep and it takes them several minutes to reload between shots. Swaggat still tries to get his weapon to work.

Hyena isn't able to fight at her full potential with the others around, but she does her best. She runs at one of the Rashers spear-first. As he swings a claw at her, she drops to the ground and drives the blade of her spear through his crotch. It cuts into his pelvis. But it doesn't kill him. The Rasher stomps down on Hyena's chest so hard she hears a crack in her ribs and all of the air is crushed out of her lungs. She twists the spear inside of his pelvis, digging it deeper into his abdomen, cutting through his entrails. The Rasher only puts more weight on his foot, grinding her body into the sand.

Three Rashers charge the main group, trampling Bunny down. They grab two Green Fish and rip their chests open, biting through bones like french fries. One of the Green Fish is picked up over a Rasher's head and then torn in half.

Swaggat gets his flame-saw going and revs the engine. The five-foot chainsaw blade roars as fire shoots out below the chain. He swings his flaming chainsaw at a rasher like a sword. The flame-saw only burns the Rasher, but it makes him recoil. Then Swaggat drives it into the shark man's stomach and holds it there, cutting and burning at the same time.

Hyena can't stab the spear any further into the shark man's abdomen. It's caught on a bone somewhere inside of his body, and for some reason the shark is still fully alive. He stomps down on Hyena's chest again and blood erupts from her throat into the air. He stomps again and several sea worms rise up into her mouth.

As the spear slips from Hyena's grasp, the shark man's head explodes and he drops to the sand next to her.

Nova and Vermin walk down the shore toward them. Hyena hardly recognizes Nova anymore. Her muscles are incredibly large, with a full wolf snout and blood in her eyes. She carries the massive double-Gatling gun over her head, like it's only as heavy as a cinderblock. The gun probably weighs 800 pounds, but Nova has enough mass on her body now that she can lift it. She has the strength of ten werewolf women.

She drops to her knees, holding the gun over one shoulder, and Vermin takes the controls. They fire the 180 caliber rounds at the crowd of Rashers. The thunderous, booming sounds of the bullets hammering out of the Gatling barrels are closer to that of an earthquake than a machine gun.

Hyena stays on the ground, covering her head, as the shark men explode all around her. The bullets don't pierce their flesh, they pulverize it. Like grenades going off beneath their skin, the Rashers' torsos her blown in half. Their heads are blown from their necks. Their stomachs are split down the middle. Their limbs are shredded into confetti. Hyena looks up at the sky as blood rains down, chunks of meat splash into the water, and intestines spray across the beach like washed up seaweed.

Then hundreds of villagers come over the hills with axes and pitchforks, to join Swaggat and the wolf women in the battle. They cry in hissing fish-like voices as they gang up on the Rashers and drive them back into the sea.

As Swaggat drives his flaming chainsaw deeper into the Rasher, he hits a trigger that releases a spurt of gasoline which covers the shark. As he goes up in flames, Swaggat cuts him in half, and stands victorious over the mutant three times his size.

The Green Fish cheer as the Rashers retreat. Only a handful of the shark men make it back into the water. The others splatter into messy pieces as they flee across the sand, not quick enough to get away from Nova's colossal machine gun.

When it is over, Nova drops the gun in the sand and walks away, over the hill, toward the village.

When Vermin meets up with the others, Slayer asks her, "Where's Nova going?"

Vermin has no idea.

As Hyena pulls her spear out of the Rasher corpse, she says, "She said she would leave as soon as the battle was over. That's probably what she's doing."

"But the battle isn't over yet," Slayer says.

Chapter 9

Bunny

Swaggat brings them to a dock down the beach. Several motor boats are tied here.

"We still need to take down Vinson," he says.

He points out to the sea.

He says, "The ruling class lives on an island out there. He'll be there."

The Green Fish load several spear guns into the motor boats.

"We can only take you," Swaggat says to Hyena. "The other women must stay."

"Why?" Slayer asks.

He points to the waves. "The sea mothers will attack our boats if we have wormless humans on board. You have dormant worms, so we can only take you."

Bunny steps forward. "I'm immune. I can go as well."

Swaggat examines her. "Your worms aren't dormant. Why are you able to control your own mind?"

"I told you I'm immune," she says.

Swaggat shakes his head. "That's impossible."

Hyena steps in. "Two years ago she was infected with the parasites, but we killed the sea creature that controlled her. She's been immune ever since."

The Zoners are shocked by her words.

"You killed a sea mother?" Swaggat asks. "Impossible."

He looks at Bunny. Bunny shrugs. The Zoners are disturbed and offended by this. These revolutionaries might be enemies of the Rashers, but the sea mothers are still sacred to them.

"Fine, both of you will go," Swaggat says, his eyes angry and suspicious at Bunny.

"I'll be right back," Bunny says.

She runs over the hill and several minutes later she returns on her motorcycle, holding her chainsaw-boomerang over her shoulder.

She hops off the bike and gives it to Vermin.

"Take care of it for me," she says.

Vermin smiles.

"Let's go," Bunny says. "I'm ready to kill shit."

Swaggat fumes in silence as he takes a gas can out of a boat's storage hold and fuels up the engine.

Before they leave, Slayer looks at Hyena and says, "It's up to you now. Finish the mission. Save Talon and the others. Don't get yourself killed."

Hyena nods. "I won't fail you."

"I know you won't," Slayer says.

Even though she might not be coming back, they don't say good-bye. Only Vermin waves as Hyena, Bunny, and twenty-six Zoners head off in their motor boats toward the island of the ruling class.

As they speed toward the island, Hyena stares into the water, watching for shark men. She wouldn't want to have to fight them in the water. They already have the upper hand on dry land; she couldn't even imagine how deadly they would be in the sea. Swaggat can tell what she's thinking.

"Don't worry about the Rashers," he says. "We killed most of them. The survivors will regroup to protect Vinson."

"How many do you think are left?"

"Ten Rashers at most," he says. "But Rashers aren't the only soldiers we have to worry about. There's also Vinson's royal guard. The Red Knights."

"Do we have enough men to defeat them all?"

"No," Swaggat says. "Not at all."

Hyena's whiskers point up. "Then why didn't we bring a larger force?"

"We don't have to kill all of them. Only Vinson. If he dies, the fight will be over. Avoid combat with everyone else. Just go straight for the man carrying the scepter."

Hyena nods.

"That shouldn't be a problem," she says. "The second I see him, he'll be dead in less than a minute."

Swaggat sees a fin in the water up ahead. It's a wounded Rasher, struggling to get back to the island. Swaggat hits the gas and aims for the shark man's head. When the boat runs over his head, Hyena can feel a loud thud rumble through the boat. Swaggat smiles and speeds up even faster toward the island.

When they arrive, Hyena realizes that it's not actually an island. It's an ancient oil rig. The sides of the structure are covered with barnacles that have grown out so far that the oil rig looks like a metal building on top of a large white rocky mountain. It is almost like a small island, covered in moss and blood-red vines. The vines grow out of the tops of the platform and mushroom into brain-shaped trees.

The Zoners pull their boats up along the craggy sides and tie them to metal hooks sticking out of the barnacle cake.

"Let's go," Swaggat says.

The Green Fish grab their spear guns and charge up the white mound to the platform.

"He'll be in the tower," Swaggat tells the two wolf women.

Hyena looks at a tall metal structure that's shaped like a clamshell propped up on its side, with giant whale bone bridges and balconies.

"I'll lead the charge," Hyena says.

As soon as they cross the platform, several Red Fish and a few Yellow Fish retreat into the metal buildings around them. The Green Fish let them go.

Before they get to the entrance of the clamshell tower, four Rashers step forward and block their path. They don't engage the Green Fish, just stand guard. A living barricade of muscle and teeth.

"The Red Knights," Swaggat says, pointing in the air.

From the top of the tower, figures are jumping from a balcony and gliding through the air, circling the platform. Hyena doesn't realize they are human until they dive for her.

Hyena drops to the ground and turns back to see a Green Fish's head hanging from his neck, connected by a string of meat. Blood sprays at Hyena as he drops to the ground. Then she gets a good look at the Red Knight as he flies back up into the sky.

The Red Knights are riding on top of flying stingrays, their cloaks flapping in the wind. They look like any of the other Zoners, but have two extra pairs of tentacles. And attached to the sides of each tentacle there are three razor sharp blades.

Another Red Knight swoops down at Hyena, swinging his bladed tentacles around like a blender. There is a sound of scraping steel, as she rolls out of the way. One of the blades catches her by the shoulder and cuts through a spot on her fur. Hyena growls at the pain.

The Green Fish fire spear guns at the Red Knights, but the stingrays move so quickly through the air, they dodge the attack.

Hyena can't even count how many there are. Maybe seven.

Another Knight swoops in, swings his tentacles out and cuts the bellies out of three Green Fish in one swoop. Only Bunny dodges his attack, flipping backward over the stingray. Bunny throws her chainsaw boomerang at his back as he passes. It cuts him through the side and he slumps forward, but the stingray flies him away from the platform before Bunny can retrieve her weapon and finish him off.

"Forget about them," Swaggat tells them. "We need to get into the tower. The knights won't be airborne inside."

The turn their attention to the four Rashers.

"Bunny," Hyena says to her wolf sister. "Cut a path."

Bunny smiles and throws her chainsaw boomerang into the Rashers guarding the entrance. The Rashers jump out of the way and the boomerang breaks open the metal door. When the Rashers get back into place, the chainsaw weapon returns and cuts through two of them. They each lose an arm at the elbow and a faucet of gore rains from their hips. Within seconds they hit the ground.

Bunny and Hyena charge the door. The other two Rashers close together, but Hyena springs over them, pushing off of their bulbous fishy backs with her paws. They turn around to attack Hyena, but Bunny comes up behind. Their ankles are cut out from under them as Bunny runs between their legs on all fours, holding the chainsaw boomerang in her mouth. Swaggat and some of the Green Fish follow after. The others keep the Red Knights busy.

Inside, it is a great church with stained glass windows and rows of benches facing a podium. A few Yellow Fish hide in the aisles.

"Upstairs," Swaggat says.

As they head for the stairs, the cowering Yellow Fish scream as Swaggat's men fire spear guns at them. Red blood spreads across the yellow cloth.

They climb the stairs up to the top floor, to Vinson's throne room. Vinson doesn't just think of himself as the religious leader of the Zoners. He is also their overlord. Hyena runs spear-first onto the red carpeting in the center of the room, then faces the overlord seated on the throne. Swaggat, Bunny, and the other Green Fish gather behind her. The man stares at them calmly.

"We're finally going to end your reign, Vinson," Swaggat says. "I'm taking you down."

Vinson stands from his throne and removes his yellow hood. His bald scaly head and wide white fish eyes glimmer in the sunlight pouring in from the stained glass windows.

"You're such a child, Swaggat," says the overlord, pointing with his scepter. "Like all other revolutionaries, you are just a child throwing a tantrum. You want more toys. You are angry because I said you can't have more toys."

"I want justice," Swaggat says.

"Justice?" Vinson snickers until he gags on his laugh and coughs. "You don't want justice. You just want to be the one on top. You want power. You want to wear a yellow robe."

"Kill him," Swaggat tells Hyena.

Hyena hesitates. The man is unarmed.

"Ordering your furry little pet to kill for you, Swaggat?" Vinson says. "You know it's forbidden to play with our mothers' food."

Four men step out from the shadows and get in front of the overlord. They drop their red robes to reveal six bladed tentacle limbs, spiked metal armor, and metal face masks shaped like the heads of barracudas.

"Kill them," Vinson orders his guard.

The Red Knights raise their bladed limbs and attack, spinning their tentacles in circles like razor tornadoes.

"Go for Vinson," Swaggat yells.

The Green Fish fire their spear guns at Vinson, but the Red Knights cut the spears out of the air.

Bunny throws her chainsaw boomerang at the overlord. The Red Knights try to block with their tentacles, but the chainsaw cuts off their bladed limbs. The weapon continues through the air at Vinson.

A red light shines out of the overlord's scepter at the chainsaw boomerang. The weapon freezes in midair as Vinson catches it with the light. He smiles as the chainsaw blades roar in his eyes, then he swings his scepter and the light drives the chainsaw weapon back, sending it spinning toward Bunny.

The rabbit girl ducks and grabs the handle of the boomerang, but the force of the red light is too strong. Her body is pulled with it, thrown across the room. She slams against the back wall and the boomerang ricochets through the knees of a cowering Green Fish.

Hyena charges with her spear, but Vinson catches her spear with his light, freezing her weapon in place. A Red Knight comes at her. With one side of her body paralyzed in the beam of light, she catches one of the knight's tentacles with her teeth and bites it off. As the man looks in shock at his severed limb, Hyena swings the bladed tentacle back at him. It slices through his barracuda mask and cuts the front of his face off.

But the second Hyena slices through the man's face, another knight attacks. Hyena's arm disappears from her sight, replaced with a cloud of blood, as the Red Knight severs her arm. She falls to the ground, staring at her lost limb as it twitches in front of her like a lizard tail.

As the knight swings down on Hyena with bladed tentacles, his body goes up in flames. Swaggat drives his flame-saw through his chest and the knight crumples into a ball of fire as gasoline pours down on him from Swaggat's weapon.

Vinson turns his scepter's red beam on the rebellion leader. He catches Swaggat by the throat, choking him with the light. Swaggat gags as his feet lift off of the floor.

"It's time for your punishment, child," Vinson says, raising Swaggat higher. "You've been a naughty, naughty boy."

Hyena stares at the worms crawling out of the bloody stump on her shoulder. As the other two Red Knights come toward her, she grabs her severed arm and examines the worms crawling out of the wound. The knights swing their blender tentacles at her. The sound of clashing metal reverberates loudly in her ears.

Several more Red Knights pour into the room from the stairwell. They attack the other Green Fish, slicing them down. Hyena looks at Bunny unconscious on the floor, then up at Swaggat's face turning blue as he's being strangled to death with the beam of red light.

As the last of the Green Fish fall to the ground in a pile of shredded fish flesh, Hyena rolls into a squatting position. She puts her severed arm back on the bloody stump where it should be. The sea worms from each of the wounds curl around each other, pulling Hyena's arm back into place. She regains feeling in her fingers as the worms seal the wound and reattach the nerves and blood vessels. She squeezes a fist. It's as good as new.

When the Red Knights come down on her, Hyena rolls out of the way, grabs her spear, and jumps over the knights' heads. As they turn around, she cuts their throats. Vinson sees her at his feet, drops Swaggat and turns his scepter on Hyena.

She flips backward over the beam, catches the wall with her back feet, then jumps to the next wall as the beam chases her around the room. Dozens of bladed tentacles slash over her head as she runs on all fours across the wall. Then she pushes off the ceiling and soars over the heads of the Red Knights, their blades sing in a chorus of metal clangs as they miss her spotted fur, just inches out of reach.

Just as Hyena comes down on the overlord like demon monkey, Vinson catches her with the light, suspending her in the air. His lips curl into a smile at the sight of his captured prey. She growls and thrashes above him. Then his smile falls away as Hyena stretches her spear out over her head.

She drives the blade of her weapon down into the overlord's

face, through his left fish eye and out the back of his head. As he dies, the red light dissipates and Hyena falls to the ground. The remaining Red Knights back away.

When Swaggat gets to his feet, rubbing his neck, he takes the scepter from Vinson's corpse and raises it over his head.

"I have defeated Vinson," he tells them. "I am your ruler now."

All of the Red Knights in the room bow to him. Swaggat removes his green robe and asks them to bring him a yellow one.

The Red Knights and the Rashers are now under Swaggat's command, so they move aside as Hyena and Bunny leave the clamshell tower. There's something about the look in Swaggat's eyes that makes Hyena want to stay far away from him.

As they stroll across the platform, Bunny picks up a flame-saw from a dead Green Fish and examines it.

"I wonder how this works," Bunny says. "It would be pretty fierce if I could apply this technology to my boomerang."

"A flaming chainsaw boomerang?" Hyena asks.

Bunny chuckles as she straps the gas tank to her back and holds the chainsaw blade out like a sword.

"I would be invincible," she says.

"You're already invincible," Hyena says.

They continue walking across the platform. They pass Yellow Fish and Red Fish, taking care of their wounded and their dead. All of them have worried looks on their faces.

Hyena makes sure none of them hear her as she says, "I've got a bad feeling about Swaggat."

"You think he'll back out of the deal?" Bunny asks.

"I'm not sure yet," Hyena says. "It's just a feeling. I don't think he's really the freedom fighter he made himself out to be."

They go to the center of the platform and lean against a guard-rail overlooking a pit at the rig's core. The smell of crude oil fills their nostrils.

"What is that stuff?" Bunny asks, swinging her chainsaw blade in mock combat.

"Oil," Hyena says. "Tons of it."

The pit is split into two pools. One is full of crude oil. The other is full of sea water.

"Where did it all come from?" Bunny asks.

As she says that, something moves inside of the pit. Hyena squints her eyes. The movement comes from the side with the sea water. Judging by its depth, the pool must connect with the ocean outside of the rig.

Colossal tentacles emerge from the water and curl around the walls of the pit. A large sea beast crawls out of the water into the oil pool. Bunny and Hyena step back as it blinks its eyes up at them.

"What the . . ." Bunny says, holding out the flame-saw, as if in defense.

As Bunny tries to figure out how to work the weapon, Hyena says, "What's it doing?"

The creature doesn't attack them. It turns itself around and spews a black substance out of its rear.

"It's taking a shit," Bunny says.

The goop coming out of it isn't shit. It's oil. Crude oil. Several gallons of the sludge oozes out into the oil pit. When the sea mother is finished evacuating her bowels, she climbs back into the sea and submerges into the depths.

"I guess you've stumbled upon our little secret," Swaggat says from behind.

Hyena turns to him. "Your sea mothers shit oil?"

Swaggat nods. "That's where we get our oil from."

"What about all of the oil pumps out in the wasteland? I saw hundreds of them on the way here."

"There hasn't been oil out there for decades," Swaggat says. "Our ancestors sucked out every last drop until the land was dry. We don't pump oil anymore. We get it from the sea mothers."

"How?"

"It's how we evolved," Swaggat says, leaning against the railing, staring into the pool of black. "Our culture has always revolved around oil. Our lives depend on it. From powering our homes, our vehicles, our farming tools. Everything runs on it. When the land was dry of oil, my people went through rapid evolution. We were dependent on the fuel. We wouldn't have survived without it. So our bodies went through this change. Our women began mutating into the sea mothers."

Hyena watches as another sea creature crawls out of the water and excretes black liquids.

"Oil was once a limited resource," Swaggat continues. "It comes from living material, the remains of ancient animals. It takes hundreds of millions of years for carbon matter to transform into fuel. But not with the sea mothers. All of the beings a sea mother consumes are digested, compressed, and transformed into oil. The process that once took hundreds of millions of years now only takes a matter of days inside of the sea mother's belly."

He smiles at Hyena, but she isn't smiling back.

Hyena says, "So all of those animals, all of those people, including my sisters, they all die just so that they can become fuel for your trucks and farming equipment?"

Swaggat nods without remorse. "The fuel is the lifeblood of our society. If some must die so that we may live then so be it."

"But you don't have to use oil for fuel," Hyena says. "Humans can survive without it."

"It's not just my society," he says. "Your people use the same fuel as we do. Where do you think your gasoline comes from? It comes from our refineries. Your machines are powered by the blood of your people, just as much as ours are."

Hyena looks away from him and grinds a fist.

Swaggat chuckles to himself and turns to walk away.

"Hold on," Hyena says, grabbing him by the wrist. "When are you going to heal my sisters?"

Swaggat takes her hand from his wrist.

"I'm sorry," he says. "I wasn't honest with you. There isn't a way to neutralize the parasites. They can't be cured."

"What?" Hyena yells, getting into his face.

As Bunny steps forward with a snarl on her face, the Red Knights surround them. They point their bladed tentacles at the women until they back down.

"I am in debt to you for all of your help," Swaggat tells them. "But I had to lie. It was the only way to convince you to help me."

Hyena growls at him.

"You've wasted my time," she says.

She pushes him out of her way.

"Where do you think you're going?" he asks.

"I'm going to save my sisters the only way I know how," Hyena says. Then she looks back at Swaggat. "I'm going to kill the creature that's controlling them."

Before she continues forward, several bladed tentacles block her path.

"I'm afraid I can't let you do that," Swaggat tells her. "The sea mothers are vital to our society. I can't allow you to kill any of them."

"Then you're going to have to stop me," Hyena says.

Swaggat raises his hands. "You don't have to do this. Forget about those infected bitches. You should stay here and become the general of my new army. You brought me to power. You deserve to rule this land at my side."

"Like a faithful guard dog?" Hyena asks. "Fuck you."

Swaggat sighs. "Fine. If you're going to act like a child we'll punish you like a child."

Hyena shoves the Zoners back with her spear and spins the blade around her head.

"Kill her!" Swaggat says, falling back behind his soldiers.

As the soldiers close in, Bunny yells out, "Stop!"

When Swaggat turns to the wolf girl and sees what she is doing, he agrees with her.

"Stop," Swaggat tells his men. "Don't move."

Bunny is holding the flame-saw to her side. The chainsaw blades are on fire. She dangles it over the railing, above the pit.

"If anyone moves I'm dropping it," Bunny says, "and we'll all go *boom*."

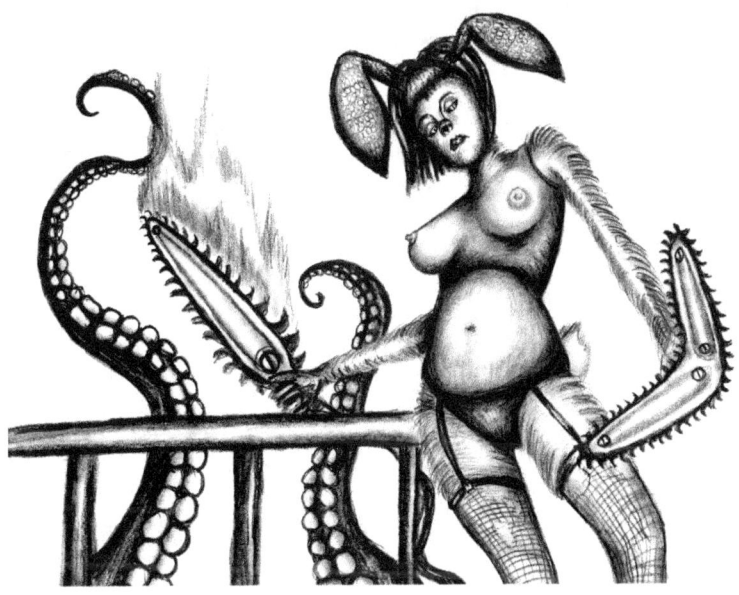

"Nobody move," Swaggat says, waving at his men to lower their arms.

"Hyena," Bunny says. "Take a boat and get back to Slayer. Let her know what has to be done. I'll hold the Meat here."

"You can't kill the sea mother," Swaggat tells Hyena. "Both of our peoples need them to survive. Isn't it worth sacrificing a few women's lives in order to keep your entire civilization running?"

"Isn't it worth sacrificing one of your sea mothers in order to keep your life?" Hyena says. "It would be a shame for you to die the same day you finally rose to power."

He doesn't respond.

She looks at Bunny, "Are you sure you'll be okay?"

"You know me," Bunny says. "I'm invincible."

Hyena's whiskers tickle her temple as she curls one side of her mouth into a smirk. Then she turns to leave. None of the Zoners get in her way as she crosses the platform and takes one of the motor boats out to sea.

As she drives the boat back to the beach, an explosion rumbles the water around her. She turns back to see a cloud of flames where the oil rig once stood. Her eyes quiver and turn back to the beach, keeping her sight on task. She doesn't want to think about what could have happened. She guesses the Zoners probably tried to grab the flame-saw away from Bunny and it was fumbled into the oil. Or, more likely, Bunny tossed it into the oil pit just to see the look on Swaggat's face before they all went up in flames. Either way, they're all likely dead.

When Hyena gets back to the beach, the Green Fish are staring out at the flaming island on the sea with confused and scared expressions peeking out from their shadowy hoods. Slayer and Vermin are standing amongst them. They don't realize the Green Fish are now their enemies.

Hyena hops out of her boat and takes Slayer and Vermin aside.

"Where's Bunny?" Slayer asks.

Hyena shakes her head. Then she tells them what happened. She tells them about Bunny, Swaggat's betrayal, and the truth behind the sea mothers.

"So we're back where we started," Hyena says. "We have to figure out which sea creature is the one that has control of Talon and the others. Then kill it."

"What if we can't figure out which one we need to kill?"

"Then we kill all of them," Slayer says.

Feeding time is coming and infected animals are beginning to arrive at the shore. The wolf women keep an eye out for elk and deer, but the infected animals are mostly small: wild cats, squirrels, snakes, quail, coyotes.

A buzzing engine sound grows in the distance. It's coming from over the hills, heading toward them. Hyena recognizes that sound. It's not a truck engine. It is a Warrior motorcycle.

Vyra zooms over the hill, leaping into the air at top speed. She nearly drives right into the water as she brakes her bike and skids across the sand. Toy must have gotten the fifth motorcycle up and running and sent Vyra out with it.

"Something's wrong," Hyena says to Slayer, as Vyra frantically jumps from the bike and rushes over to them.

"I've been looking for you all day," she says.

She leans over, catching her breath.

"What is it?" Slayer asks.

"It's Talon," she says. "Soon after you left, she turned and immediately broke out of the cage. We were able to stop Kimmy and Celia, but Talon, Likki, and Hunter got away. They're on their way here."

"How long do we have?" Slayer asks.

Vyra says, "They could be here any minute."

Slayer nods and turns to Hyena. "Then we've got to kill the creature before she gets here."

Slayer has a plan. She wants them to fight off every sea creature that comes near the shore. As soon as they see Talon, they will all focus their attacks on whichever creature she goes toward.

"What about Zizzy?" Hyena asks, pointing at their infected sister tied up across the beach.

"We'll save her as well," Slayer says, "but the creature that controls Talon is more important."

As the beach fills with infected animals, it also fills with Zoners. Green Fish and Red Fish have banded together and seem to be planning a way to get out to the island to help any survivors who might be trapped out there. But they also seem hesitant to go out on the sea. It must be dangerous to be in the water during the sea mothers' feeding time.

The fire seems to be dying down in the distance. Hyena wonders if some of the surviving Yellow Fish were able to get it under control. Or if the entire rig burned up and fell into the ocean.

Slayer has Vermin and Vyra retrieve their motorcycles from the nearby Village. The bikes still lay in the streets where they had fought the Rashers. She collects spear guns and a couple of flame-saws from dead Zoners and passes them out to her sisters. When the two girls return with the bikes, all four women carry the enormous double-barreled Gatling gun to the center of the beach. Even though Nova was able to carry the thing over her head all by herself, these four women together can hardly get it three inches off the ground.

The sea mothers surface in the distance, swimming to shore. One creature leads the way. It is an enormous one. Twice the size of the one Hyena fought years ago with Talon and Apple.

"Wait until it gets closer," Slayer says, standing behind Hyena and Vermin as they aim the giant machine gun at the waves.

The animals gather close to the shore, waiting patiently to sacrifice themselves. When the creature crawls up out of the waves onto the beach, its tentacles spread out, weaving through the infected. Zizzy goes nuts behind them. She thrashes at her ropes, rolling in the dirt to get free.

"That's the one controlling Zizzy," Slayer says, pointing up at the creature as it casts an enormous shadow down the beach.

The monster leans in, its eyes widening, as if it is more interested in the wolf women than it is its food. Its goopy mouth drops open and coughs a splatter of black oily mucus across the beach at them.

"Now?" Hyena asks.

"Not yet," Slayer says.

The creature crawls out of the water more, its tentacles pulling it up the beach as it towers over them, investigating them.

"Now?" Hyena asks.

The creature leans in. Its many eyes blinking slowly at them, examining them. It must not be used to seeing wolf women in these parts.

"Now," Slayer says.

When Hyena pulls the trigger, the sea mother shrieks and recoils as the enormous bullets rip through her flesh. Blood and eyeball jelly explode her face. Her tentacles flap around the beach, oil splashes across the infected animals standing motionless beneath its chin. They continue firing the weapon into the sea creature until the bullets run out.

When the gun goes silent, so does the sea beast. Hyena lets go of the trigger and stands up to get a better look. The creature is hunched over. Blood leaks out of its crater-sized wounds and fills the sea water. Then the creature snaps back into life and swings a tentacle at them. Hyena leaps into the air as the tentacle smashes the gun across the sand. She looks back at the other wolf girls. Two of them are still on their feet. Vermin is lying face down in the sand, as if she ducked under the tentacle attack rather than jumping over it.

"Now what?" Vyra says in a high-pitched squeal.

"Run," Slayer says.

They back away from their position as the sea beast's tentacles swing at them. As a tentacle hits the sand next to Vyra, it sounds as if a bomb had gone off. A cloud of sand explodes off of the beach and covers their fur.

Hyena doesn't run. She jumps over a tentacle and dashes toward the sea mother, grabbing a spear gun and a flame-saw along the way. She gets close up to its face and drops to the ground. A tentacle swoops over her head. She douses a spear head with gas from the flame-saw. Sand and salt water explode into her face. She sparks up the flame-saw and catches the spear head on fire.

A smack to her side and she splashes into a wave. The taste of blood and sand in her mouth, she finds herself being picked up into the air, upside-down. A tentacle squeezes tightly around her ankle. Facing the wrong way, she looks at an upside-down Vermin down the beach. The scraggly girl desperately shoots poison darts at the mammoth creature to no effect.

Hot breath on Hyena's back as she feels the sea mother's mouth widening, pulling her closer. Hyena bends backward to see the black hole coming toward her. She aims the flaming spear gun forward and fires into the depths of its gullet.

First there is a spark of fire in the sludgy dark. Then a great ball of flame. Hyena flies across the beach as the sea mother explodes. Tentacles and large chunks of gray squid meat scatter into the air and land with loud plops against the sand. Hyena rolls over, squishing her singed ass-fur into the wet sand. When she looks back at the sea mother, all that is left is a pile of blackened strips of flesh and a small fire.

The other wolf girls go to her.

"How did you do that?" Vyra asks.

"Their bellies are full of crude oil," Hyena says. "Highly flammable stuff."

"Now we know how to kill them," Slayer says.

Hyena nods, then hands her the spear gun and a few extra spears.

Zizzy awakes confused and stunned, as parasites crawl out of her flesh and die in the sand.

"You'll be okay," Slayer tells her.

As they untie the girl and get her to her feet, a crowd of angry Zoners surround them. After killing one of their sacred sea mothers, the wolf women have made enemies of all Zoners. Green Fish and Red Fish unite against them.

The Zoners circle around them, pointing spear guns at their heads. The wolf women go back to back. They don't surrender and drop their weapons, but they are horribly outnumbered.

Just as the Zoners are about to fire, a loud howl echoes across the beach. The Zoners turn their attention on something else. Hyena smells her on the air before she comes into view. It's Nova. She appears at the top of the hill.

"She did it," Hyena says. "She turned."

Standing on four legs, Nova is now a massive bear-sized black werewolf. There is no humanity left in her eyes. There is only the beast. There is only a carnal hunger. The great wolf charges down the hill toward the Zoners. The robed fish men scatter. Some of them hold their ground and fire their spears at her, but they've only got one shot each. Nova weaves in and out as projectiles come at her. When she barrels into the crowd, several fish men are thrown to the ground.

Throats are slashed open. Stomachs are torn out. A face is bitten off. Nova growls viciously as she rips through their flesh, going from man to man. But it isn't her stomach that she aims to feed. She pins one of the men to the ground with his throat in her enormous jaws. Then she rapes him. She violently shoves her crotch into his pelvis, slamming his body into the sand. When he doesn't get an erection, Nova rips out his throat and chases down another one.

With wolf-Nova handling the Zoners, Slayer gets her women back on track, "Let's move."

They remove the lighting mechanisms from the flame-saws, strap several spear guns to their backs with extra spears, all of them tipped with gasoline. Then they go to their motorcycles. Vermin and Slayer take a bike. Vyra takes her own bike. And because Zizzy is immune to the worms, she rides with Hyena.

"Think you can ride with one arm?" Hyena asks the young wolf woman.

"Hell yeah," Zizzy says. "It's just a fucking arm anyway."

"Good," Hyena says. "I want you to ride while I shoot."

The women tear across the sand as the army of sea creatures pull themselves onto the shore. They weave through hundreds of tentacles and infected creatures as the sea monsters roar at them. Large slimy heads with gaping mouths tower over them, swiping at their bikes. Sand clouds explode around them as the tentacles attack, barely missing them.

Then the wolf women attack back. They launch flaming spears into the mouths as they ride. Three of the sea creatures explode and litter the beach with their oily flesh.

They pass Nova on her rampage of rape and slaughter. She ravages the men, fucking them and eating them at the same time. She no longer understands the difference. All she wants is to feed her hunger. She wants to grow larger and wilder.

Two more sea mothers explode. The wolf women are now so coated in gore and fishy meat that they hardly recognize one another. Their fur is wet and flat to their bodies. The smell of blood electrifies the animals in them.

There are several red dots in the sky, heading toward them. They are Red Knights riding flying stingrays, coming to protect their sacred mothers of the sea. And emerging from the water, the last five Rashers step onto the beach, their flesh charred from the rig fire. Their eyes wild with anger.

The Rashers charge first, leaping over tentacles, their teeth chomping at the air as they run. On the back of Slayer's motorcycle, Vermin blows a dart at a Rasher's leg. It does nothing at first but then the shark man cries out. As he runs, the flesh from his leg melts like acid. At his speed, the fleshless bone breaks in half and he tumbles into the sand, rolling in agony.

Vermin winks back at Hyena as she loads another dart. The ratty wolf girl said she was going to make her poison more potent. But Hyena had no idea she was able to make them *that* potent.

The Red Knights soar across the beach and dive down at the wolf women. One of them goes straight for Slayer. The wolf woman pays him no mind. She lets off a quick burst of machine gun fire, aiming for the stingray. The Red Knight falls into the sand, but flips back onto his feet the second he hits.

Slayer's bike flies into the air, as the knight slashes her back tire in half with his bladed tentacle. Vermin and Slayer hit the mud. A wave comes in, splashing them off balance, keeping them off their feet. Vermin's blow gun is carried on the wave up the beach.

As Hyena and Zizzy ride by, they see Slayer falling back into the water as her machine gun is chopped in half by a tentacle blade.

A Red Knight flies after Hyena and Zizzy. It swoops in, following behind them as they weave through the tentacles. Hyena stands up on the back of the bike and swings her spear in circles. As the Red Knight flies at their bike, Hyena drives her spear into the knight's belly.

She falls from the bike, pulled up into the air. The knight is still alive. His tentacles coil around the spear, holding it in place as his stingray flies higher into the air. Hyena climbs up her spear onto the stingray. The knight slashes her with a tentacle blade, grazing her chest. The man is too weak to cause more than a small cut across her nipple.

Balancing on the stingray, she lets go of the spear. Her claws dig into his temples. Then she snaps his neck. The spear slides easily out of his limp body. She kicks him over the side, into the ocean of massive beasts.

Her feet on top of the stingray, she tries to figure out how to control the flying creature. Like a surfboard, she puts one foot in front and one in back. A puffy section of flesh near the back of animal's neck seems to be the key to controlling it. She places her foot on this section of its body. The flesh is cool and soft against the bottom of Hyena's foot. If she pushes down on it with the ball of her foot it dives toward the ocean. If she curls her toes around the puffy flesh it slows down. If she arches her foot to the right it goes right, arches left it goes left.

As Hyena surfs through the sky, circling the beach, she sees Vermin down there, firing poison darts into Rasher throats.

The necks of the shark men melt down their chests before they can attack her.

Nearby, Slayer is shooting at the Red Knight with her sidearm, but the knight can block the bullets with his spinning tentacle blades. Her pistol runs out of bullets. She drops the gun and charges the man. He charges her as well, spinning his bladed tentacles in a circle. As they are about to collide, Slayer pulls back. Instead of striking him, she swipes his leg outs out from under him. With his bladed tentacles swinging in circles, he gets knocked off balance and decapitates himself.

Hyena raises her spear at Slayer in a salute, as she soars overhead. The hyena girl turns her attention back at the sea, toward the sea mothers.

Riding the stingray, Hyena swoops down toward the water. Tentacles splash out of the waves, curling in the air, as she flies through. She pulls the spear guns off of her back and lights their tips. The sea creatures explode around her as she fires into their mouths.

She flies from one sea mother to the next, firing flaming spears down their throats as they open wide to devour her.

Two Red Knights fly after her. They are much more proficient at riding the stingrays than she is. They catch up to her quickly.

On each side of her, they whip their blades at her. She dodges as they strike. Their tentacles clink together. Her stingray nearly knocks her off when her foot goes out of position. She fires a spear at one of them and the knight knocks it away.

She goes down low to the water, between the sea mothers, in hopes that the knights won't dare to follow. The knights hesitate only for a moment, then they follow her.

They catch up to her again. A sharp pain up her back as a blade catches a patch of her spotted fur, cutting a deep gash. She focuses her attention on one of them, giving the knight behind her another free swipe at her back. She tries to slash at the knight's stingray, but he catches her spear with all six of his tentacles and pulls her spear up, away from his mount. With her other hand she aims the spear gun at him and fires. The flaming spear goes through his foot and through the stingray. He goes down.

Hyena pushes her foot down on the stingray and speeds up, dodging another attack from the second knight. She turns around and heads back toward the beach, leading him down through the maze of tentacles and hungry gaping mouths.

She loads her three spear guns and fires one of them back at the knight. He cuts the spear in half. She fires again. He catches it in midair and drops it into the sea. No matter how much she weaves through the army of sea beasts, he stays locked on her trail.

With the last spear, Hyena lights it on fire. She points it back at the knight. He swings his tentacles around, ready for her. As she flies past a sea mother, opening her mouth wide to swallow the wolf girl, Hyena changes her aim. She points the spear gun into the sea mother's mouth and fires as she passes it by.

When the Red Knight crosses the sea mother's face, the creature explodes. The knight is caught in the blast. When Hyena looks back, she sees his body falling into the sea in three flaming pieces.

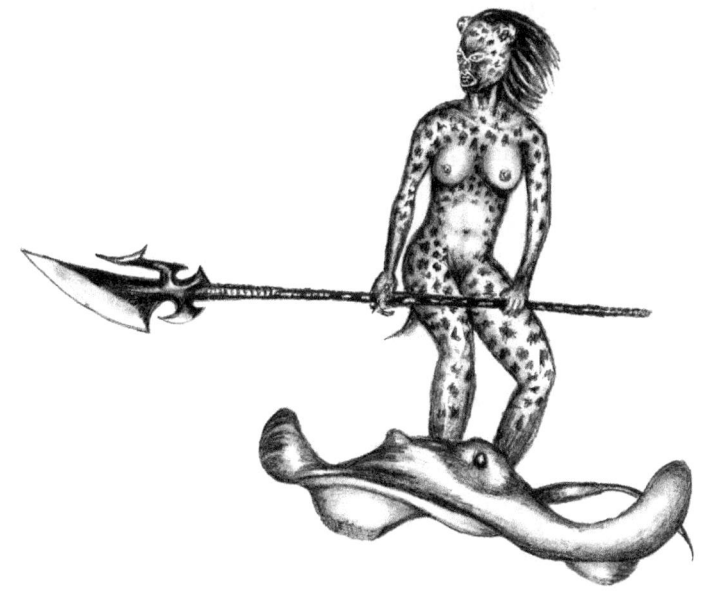

Up ahead, she sees Swaggat on the beach. The man's robe is black and parts of his body are burned, but he has survived the explosion on the oil rig. The fact that he's still alive means that Bunny probably wasn't so lucky. She wouldn't have let him leave the rig unless she was dead.

Swaggat is facing off against Nova. His flame-saw is on, revving it up, ready to cut the werewolf down to defend his people. Hyena flies toward him, coming at him from behind. Wolf-Nova charges him.

He holds his ground as the two wolf women close in on him from two directions. As Nova roars and leaps into the air at him, Swaggat whips out Vinson's scepter. A blast of red light sends the werewolf flying across the beach.

As Hyena dives toward him, her spear pointed at him like a jousting knight, Swaggat turns around and hits her with light. Her body is ripped from the stingray, tossed through the air, then she slams down hard into the sand.

With the wind knocked out of her, she has a hard time getting up. Swaggat steps up to her and points the scepter at her face. The red light pushes her head back into the sand.

"You don't understand the damage you've caused," Swaggat says. A tear slips down his eye. "Our mothers are precious to us. More precious than our own children."

Hyena tries to pull herself up. She resists the light's power and gets three inches off the ground. Swaggat steps closer, points the scepter two feet away from her face. The strength of the beam increases and Hyena is forced back into the sand with twice as much pressure.

"Now you will die," Swaggat says. "All of you will die."

A noise distracts both Swaggat and Hyena. It is a loud booming sound. Hyena shifts her eyes to the shore and sees a dozen sea mothers with their mouths wide open. They are regurgitating animals onto the beach. Hyena remembers back to when they originally fought one of the sea mothers. The creature spit up several half-digested rabid animals, wolves, and mutant men that attacked them. This is happening again. But this time there is a dozen of those creatures, which means they'll be attacked by twelve times as many creatures.

The bodies pile out of the mouths of the creatures. Hundreds of them in large bloody stacks along the shore. The melting figures stand up and stretch out their limbs. They search for the wolf women with rabid eyes. Then attack.

"See," Swaggat says. "You don't stand a chance. You will all die here today."

But Hyena isn't listening to him. Something else has grabbed her attention. Standing up out of the pile of regurgitated animals, Hyena recognizes one of the figures. Her eyes shake and water as she sees Talon. Her wolf sister was partially digested. Half of her face is melted off, revealing part of her wolf skull, including the bones in her snout. One eyeball is hanging from her head. Her knuckle bones are sticking out of her bloody hands. Behind her, two other wolf sisters stand there with crazed looks in their eyes.

Hyena chokes on her tears, cursing herself. They were too late. Talon had made it to the beach before them, probably during the night when Hyena was planning a revolution with that traitor, Swaggat. Her beloved leader had already been eaten and has now joined the ranks of their enemy.

Swaggat was right, Hyena thinks. They are going to die this day.

Just as Hyena is about to give up and allow Swaggat his victory, something happens. She sees the other wolf women. None of them are giving up. Vyra and Zizzy ride their motorcycles, shooting flaming spears at the wolf mothers. Vermin blows darts into infected animals. Nova continues her rampage of raping and devouring everything in her path. And most of all, Slayer doesn't give up, even as she sees her leader in the half-digested rabid state.

Slayer and Talon stand face-to-face on the beach. Slayer pants rapidly, holding two bladed tentacles she severed from a Red Knight. Talon glares at her, breathing deeply. Her melted chest expanding as she breathes, pieces of flesh dripping from her body. Slayer growls at her. A challenge to the alpha wolf. When Talon growls back, her dangling eyeball falls off and rolls down her breast.

Talon pulls her two axes from her back. Slayer swings the bladed tentacles in a circle. Then they charge each other.

As her two leaders battle each other on the beach, Hyena realizes that she can't give up. Even with the odds stacked against them, she knows there's always a way. Just as Slayer knows. Just as the younger, more optimistic wolf women know. The one positive side to Talon already being eaten is that they have now seen which creature controls her parasites.

She realizes what Slayer is doing. She is keeping Talon distracted so that Hyena can attack the sea beast and free her from the sea worms. Even though she is partially digested, she might still be able to pull through. Hyena realizes that it's all up to her to save them.

When Swaggat squeezes the light tighter around Hyena's throat, the wolf woman gives him a smile.

"What?" he says. "What are you smiling at?"

When she speaks, her words trickle out in muffled wheezes. "I thought of something funny."

"Oh yeah?"

A chaos of bloody infected creatures run wild on the beach around them as they speak.

"I imaged what I will do to you once I get out of this thing."

Swaggat laughs. "You're not getting out of anything. The power of the scepter will crush the life out of you. There's nothing you can do to—"

Before he finishes his sentence, Hyena breaks the scepter in half between the toes of her foot. The top of the scepter flies over her head, the red light spinning across the beach. Swaggat's shocked to see her leg bent at such an inhuman angle, surprised that she was able to put so much power into her lower body while her upper body was frozen in place. With just half a stick left in his hand, he tosses it aside. His mouth wide open, he pulls out the blade of his flame-saw and tries to turn it on.

As he backs away, he can't seem to get it to work. He tries to rev it. Nothing happens. He revs it again. The thing sparks for a second and burns his finger.

"Not very well constructed, is it?" Hyena says.

She smirks and looks over at the fight between Slayer and Talon. The younger wolf is holding her own against the mighty Talon. She whips the tentacles at Talon, slapping the axes away. Talon leaps into the air and sends an axe straight down toward Slayer's head, but Slayer rolls out of the way. She hooks Talon's leg with a tentacle and throws her down face-first into the sand.

As Swaggat gets the flame-saw going, Hyena attacks. She knocks the flame-saw blade out of her way and stabs him in the stomach. Swaggat steps back and coughs blood down his charred lips.

Hyena glances over at Slayer for a moment to see her stumbling backward. Talon has chopped one of her tentacles in half. There's a freshly opened gash running down her thigh.

While she's distracted, Swaggat swings his flame-saw at Hyena. She smells burnt hair first, then feels the pain as she looks down at her chest. One of her breasts has been cut in half, down the middle. Sea worms crawl out of the wound, down her stomach.

When he strikes again, she holds up her spear to defend. The chainsaw cuts through the staff and tears open her belly. Worms spill out onto the beach. With her spear broken in half she uses the bottom half like a wooden stake and drives it through his shoulder. He stumbles back. She slaps out the flames on her wound.

As Swaggat falls to one knee, Hyena points the blade half of her spear at him.

"I win," Swaggat says.

Hyena cocks her head at him.

"Even if you kill me here now," Swaggat says. "You'll still die."

He points at the worms coming out of her belly.

"I didn't tell you the full truth about your worms," he says. "They are dormant, yes, but they will awaken one day soon. I lied about my mother. She's not dead. She is alive and well and only a few months away from becoming one of the sea mothers."

Hyena pulls a handful of worms out of her belly and stares at them.

"And as soon as she becomes one of them she will have control of your parasites and control of you," he says. "You will become her first meal."

Hyena crushes the worms. "Then I will kill your mother after I kill you."

Swaggat wags a finger at her. "Ah, but that too would mean your death. If my mother dies then so do the sea worms. And those worms inside of you are the only things keeping you alive right now."

Hyena growls. She doesn't know what else to do. If he's telling the truth then she's dead no matter what she does.

"You see," he says. "I defeat you no matter what you do."

She growls again. Then her growl becomes a smile. Her whiskers stand up high against her cheeks.

"Well, if I'm going to die either way," she says. "Why *not* kill your mother? Sounds like a good last act before I die."

The thought enrages Swaggat. He jumps to his feet and charges her. He raises his chainsaw and she drives the head of her spear into his stomach. By the time she realizes he let her stab him on purpose, it's already too late. He saws her arm off at the elbow, then cuts her in half.

She falls back into the sand and looks up at him. Her severed hand is still holding the spear in his stomach. Her body from her breasts down is lying at his feet. Even though she's no longer connected to most of her body, she still lives. The worms keep her alive.

With only one arm left, she pulls herself up the beach. Swaggat steps after her, chuckling.

"You won't touch my mother," he says. "She will become a beautiful goddess of the sea."

As Hyena pulls herself away from him, using only five fingers, she loses hope again. The worms falling out of her flesh make her weak. There aren't enough of them to keep her going.

She looks over at Slayer and Talon. Both of Slayer's weapons are gone and it looks like she has several axe wounds covering her body. She staggers through the waves. Talon drops her axes and grabs her, picks her up into a bear hug. As she squeezes the wind out of Slayer, parasites crawl out of her fur. Slayer cries out as the worms burrow into her flesh.

Swaggat revs his flame-saw and fire shoots out of the blade like a dragon.

"Maybe I'll let you live," Swaggat says. "Maybe I'll keep you alive until mother goes out to the sea. I'd love to watch you crawl across the beach to her mouth, using your one remaining arm."

He looks down at her other arm.

"Or maybe I'll cut this one off as well," he says. "And let you roll your way down the beach."

Hyena screams as he brings the chainsaw down on her last limb. She can smell her flesh burning against the flame as it saws through her shoulder bone.

As he leans in close enough, Hyena reaches out with the stump of her other arm and presses it against the other half still attached to the spear in Swaggat's stomach. The worms fuse together and her arm becomes whole again. She feels her fingers wrapped around the top half of her spear.

When Swaggat cuts all the way through her limb, he looks back at her and laughs. Then she twists the spear inside of his belly and tears it out of him sideways. His shredded insides spill out of the hole.

Hyena releases her grip on the spear. As Swaggat staggers back, she pulls herself a couple feet further up the beach, digs her claw into the sand and pulls out the top half of Vinson's scepter.

Swaggat gurgles blood at her as she puts all of her anger into the staff. The energy flows out of her, into the rod, and emerges as a beam of light that hits Swaggat in the chest. He is thrown across the beach, waving his flame-saw at his sides.

She pushes him all the way into the mouth of a sea mother that instinctively gulps him down. Once the flame-saw hits the oil in her belly, the sea mother explodes. Chunks of goo and squid flesh rain down on the beach.

Talon and Slayer fall into each others arms as the worms inside of them die. The other two infected wolf women also fall. Slayer regains consciousness and hugs Talon's limp body to hers. Hyena watches without blinking. Slayer shakes Talon, trying to wake her up. Hyena shakes her head.

"We were too late," she says. "Too late."

Then Talon coughs out dead worms from her throat. She shakes the gore from her body and stands to her feet. Although much of her muscle tissue has been severely damaged and she'll be horribly scarred for the rest of her life, she'll survive. The other two infected wolf women stand, clutching their wounds.

Talon grabs her axes and hands one to Slayer. She nods at her two half-melted sisters. Then the four of them enter the battle.

As the worms slide out of her body, Hyena feels her consciousness fading. She knows she's dying, but she's at peace with that. They have accomplished their mission. Even though the women are now horribly deformed, they have been saved.

She watches Nova running off down the beach with half a man in her mouth. The girl got her wish. She has turned and left her old human life behind her. Now she can forget and join the big sisters in the wild.

She watches Vermin, Zizzy and Vyra. The three young warriors cut down infected mutants left and right. As she watches them, Hyena realizes Slayer was right about them. They truly are great warriors. In them is the future of their tribe.

Then, with the last of her energy, she rests her eyes on Slayer. Without any spears or fire left, the black wolf girl runs straight up to a sea beast and takes it on with only an axe. She climbs up a tentacle and chops out its eyes, then goes for the soft spot on the side of its head.

As Slayer chops up the creature two hundred times her size, Hyena smiles at her. She knows Slayer will make a great leader. She knows Slayer doesn't need her as her right hand. She'll do just fine on her own.

Hyena is the old guard. It's time for the new. As she watches all of her sisters fighting in the battle, she knows they'll do fine without her. She's ready to die.

She smiles and closes her eyes.

Then she opens them again.

She scoops the worms back into her chest, grabs her severed arm and fuses it back to her stump, then crawls down the beach to the lower half of her body. Once the worms have fused her two halves together, she stands up.

"Maybe I'm not ready to die just yet," Hyena says, brushing the blood from her spotted fur.

Then she picks up the head of her spear, raises it over her head, and charges into battle, to fight alongside her sisters one last time.

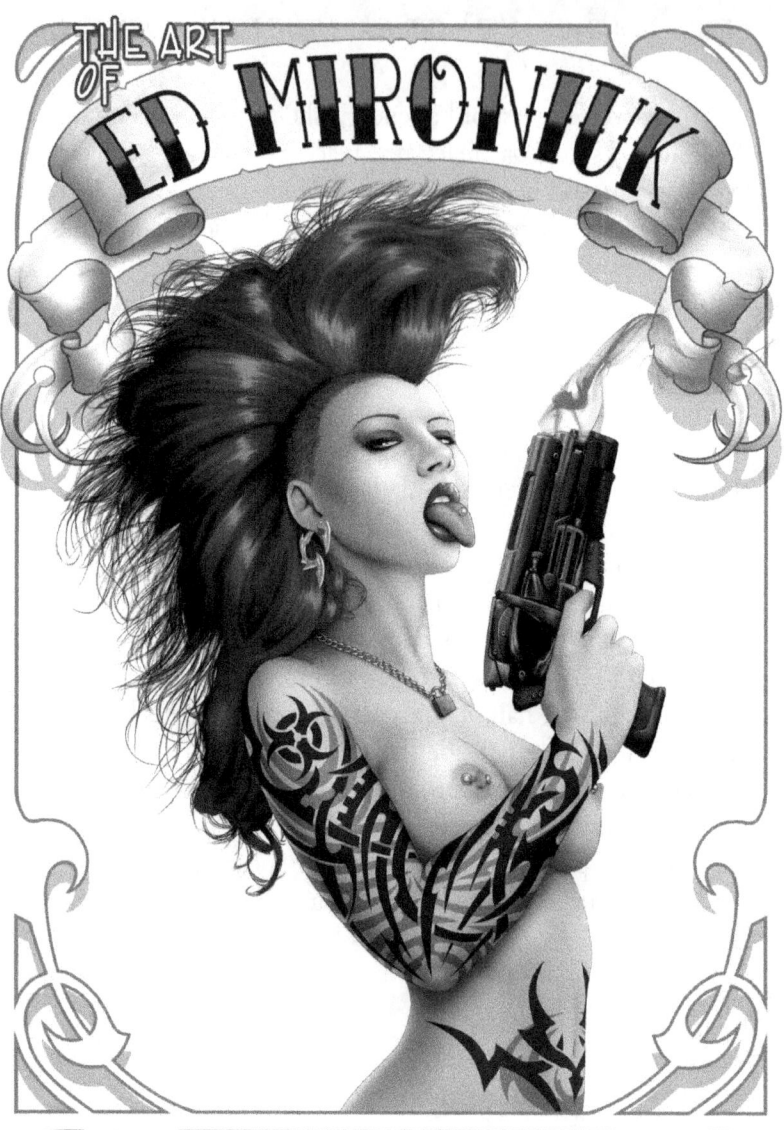

ABOUT THE AUTHOR

Carlton Mellick III is one of the leading authors of the bizarro fiction subgenre. Since 2001, his books have drawn an international cult following despite the fact that they have been shunned by most libraries and chain bookstores.

He won the Wonderland Book Award for his novel, *Warrior Wolf Women of the Wasteland*, in 2009. His short fiction has appeared in *Vice Magazine, The Year's Best Fantasy and Horror #16, The Magazine of Bizarro Fiction,* and *Zombies: Encounters with the Hungry Dead*, among others. He is also a graduate of Clarion West, where he studied under the likes of Chuck Palahniuk, Connie Willis, and Cory Doctorow.

He lives in Portland, OR, the bizarro fiction mecca.

Visit him online at **www.carltonmellick.com**

Bizarro books

CATALOG   SPRING 2011

Bizarro Books publishes under the following imprints:

www.rawdogscreamingpress.com

www.eraserheadpress.com

www.afterbirthbooks.com

www.swallowdownpress.com

For all your Bizarro needs visit:

WWW.BIZARROCENTRAL.COM

Introduce yourselves to the bizarro fiction genre and all of its authors with the Bizarro Starter Kit series. Each volume features short novels and short stories by ten of the leading bizarro authors, designed to give you a perfect sampling of the genre for only $10.

BB-0X1
"The Bizarro Starter Kit" (Orange)

Featuring D. Harlan Wilson, Carlton Mellick III, Jeremy Robert Johnson, Kevin L Donihe, Gina Ranalli, Andre Duza, Vincent W. Sakowski, Steve Beard, John Edward Lawson, and Bruce Taylor. **236 pages $10**

BB-0X2
"The Bizarro Starter Kit" (Blue)

Featuring Ray Fracalossy, Jeremy C. Shipp, Jordan Krall, Mykle Hansen, Andersen Prunty, Eckhard Gerdes, Bradley Sands, Steve Aylett, Christian TeBordo, and Tony Rauch. **244 pages $10**

BB-0X2
"The Bizarro Starter Kit" (Purple)

Featuring Russell Edson, Athena Villaverde, David Agranoff, Matthew Revert, Andrew Goldfarb, Jeff Burk, Garrett Cook, Kris Saknussemm, Cody Goodfellow, and Cameron Pierce **264 pages $10**

BB-001 **"The Kafka Effekt" D. Harlan Wilson** - A collection of forty-four irreal short stories loosely written in the vein of Franz Kafka, with more than a pinch of William S. Burroughs sprinkled on top. **211 pages $14**

BB-002 **"Satan Burger" Carlton Mellick III** - The cult novel that put Carlton Mellick III on the map ... Six punks get jobs at a fast food restaurant owned by the devil in a city violently overpopulated by surreal alien cultures. **236 pages $14**

BB-003 **"Some Things Are Better Left Unplugged" Vincent Sakwoski** - Join The Man and his Nemesis, the obese tabby, for a nightmare roller coaster ride into this postmodern fantasy. **152 pages $10**

BB-004 **"Shall We Gather At the Garden?" Kevin L Donihe** - Donihe's Debut novel. Midgets take over the world, The Church of Lionel Richie vs. The Church of the Byrds, plant porn and more! **244 pages $14**

BB-005 **"Razor Wire Pubic Hair" Carlton Mellick III** - A genderless humandildo is purchased by a razor dominatrix and brought into her nightmarish world of bizarre sex and mutilation. **176 pages $11**

BB-006 **"Stranger on the Loose" D. Harlan Wilson** - The fiction of Wilson's 2nd collection is planted in the soil of normalcy, but what grows out of that soil is a dark, witty, otherworldly jungle... **228 pages $14**

BB-007 **"The Baby Jesus Butt Plug" Carlton Mellick III** - Using clones of the Baby Jesus for anal sex will be the hip sex fetish of the future. **92 pages $10**

BB-008 **"Fishyfleshed" Carlton Mellick III** - The world of the past is an illogical flatland lacking in dimension and color, a sick-scape of crispy squid people wandering the desert for no apparent reason. **260 pages $14**

BB-009 **"Dead Bitch Army" Andre Duza** - Step into a world filled with racist teenagers, cannibals, 100 warped Uncle Sams, automobiles with razor-sharp teeth, living graffiti, and a pissed-off zombie bitch out for revenge. **344 pages $16**

BB-010 **"The Menstruating Mall" Carlton Mellick III** - "The Breakfast Club meets Chopping Mall as directed by David Lynch." - Brian Keene **212 pages $12**

BB-011 **"Angel Dust Apocalypse" Jeremy Robert Johnson** - Meth-heads, man-made monsters, and murderous Neo-Nazis. "Seriously amazing short stories..." - Chuck Palahniuk, author of Fight Club **184 pages $11**

BB-012 **"Ocean of Lard" Kevin L Donihe / Carlton Mellick III** - A parody of those old Choose Your Own Adventure kid's books about some very odd pirates sailing on a sea made of animal fat. **176 pages $12**

BB-015 **"Foop!" Chris Genoa** - Strange happenings are going on at Dactyl, Inc, the world's first and only time travel tourism company.
"A surreal pie in the face!" - Christopher Moore **300 pages $14**

BB-020 **"Punk Land" Carlton Mellick III** - In the punk version of Heaven, the anarchist utopia is threatened by corporate fascism and only Goblin, Mortician's sperm, and a blue-mohawked female assassin named Shark Girl can stop them. **284 pages $15**

BB-021**"Pseudo-City" D. Harlan Wilson** - Pseudo-City exposes what waits in the bathroom stall, under the manhole cover and in the corporate boardroom, all in a way that can only be described as mind-bogglingly irreal. **220 pages $16**

BB-023 **"Sex and Death In Television Town" Carlton Mellick III** - In the old west, a gang of hermaphrodite gunslingers take refuge from a demon plague in Telos: a town where its citizens have televisions instead of heads. **184 pages $12**

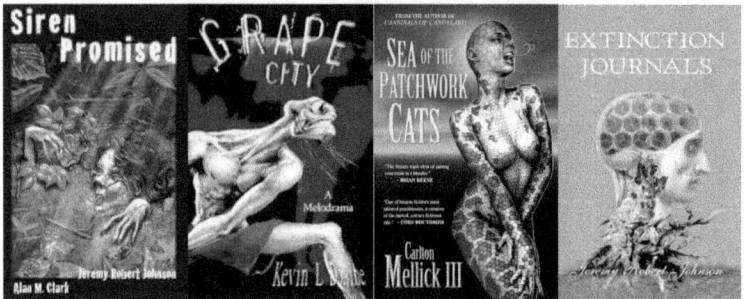

BB-027 "Siren Promised" Jeremy Robert Johnson & Alan M Clark
- Nominated for the Bram Stoker Award. A potent mix of bad drugs, bad dreams, brutal bad guys, and surreal/incredible art by Alan M. Clark. **190 pages $13**

BB-030 "Grape City" Kevin L. Donihe - More Donihe-style comedic bizarro about a demon named Charles who is forced to work a minimum wage job on Earth after Hell goes out of business. **108 pages $10**

BB-031"Sea of the Patchwork Cats" Carlton Mellick III - A quiet dreamlike tale set in the ashes of the human race. For Mellick enthusiasts who also adore The Twilight Zone. **112 pages $10**

BB-032 "Extinction Journals" Jeremy Robert Johnson - An uncanny voyage across a newly nuclear America where one man must confront the problems associated with loneliness, insane dieties, radiation, love, and an ever-evolving cockroach suit with a mind of its own. **104 pages $10**

BB-034 "The Greatest Fucking Moment in Sports" Kevin L. Donihe
- In the tradition of the surreal anti-sitcom Get A Life comes a tale of triumph and agape love from the master of comedic bizarro. **108 pages $10**

BB-035 "The Troublesome Amputee" John Edward Lawson - Disturbing verse from a man who truly believes nothing is sacred and intends to prove it. **104 pages $9**

BB-037 "The Haunted Vagina" Carlton Mellick III - It's difficult to love a woman whose vagina is a gateway to the world of the dead. **132 pages $10**

BB-042 "Teeth and Tongue Landscape" Carlton Mellick III - On a planet made out of meat, a socially-obsessive monophobic man tries to find his place amongst the strange creatures and communities that he comes across. **110 pages $10**

BB-043 **"War Slut" Carlton Mellick III** - Part "1984," part "Waiting for Godot," and part action horror video game adaptation of John Carpenter's "The Thing." **116 pages $10**

BB-045 **"Dr. Identity" D. Harlan Wilson** - Follow the Dystopian Duo on a killing spree of epic proportions through the irreal postcapitalist city of Bliptown where time ticks sideways, artificial Bug-Eyed Monsters punish citizens for consumer-capitalist lethargy, and ultraviolence is as essential as a daily multivitamin. **208 pages $15**

BB-047 **"Sausagey Santa" Carlton Mellick III** - A bizarro Christmas tale featuring Santa as a piratey mutant with a body made of sausages. 124 pages $10

BB-048 **"Misadventures in a Thumbnail Universe" Vincent Sakowski** - Dive deep into the surreal and satirical realms of neo-classical Blender Fiction, filled with television shoes and flesh-filled skies. **120 pages $10**

BB-049 **"Vacation" Jeremy C. Shipp** - Blueblood Bernard Johnson leaved his boring life behind to go on The Vacation, a year-long corporate sponsored odyssey. But instead of seeing the world, Bernard is captured by terrorists, becomes a key figure in secret drug wars, and, worse, doesn't once miss his secure American Dream. **160 pages $14**

BB-053 **"Ballad of a Slow Poisoner" Andrew Goldfarb** Millford Mutterwurst sat down on a Tuesday to take his afternoon tea, and made the unpleasant discovery that his elbows were becoming flatter. **128 pages $10**

BB-055 **"Help! A Bear is Eating Me" Mykle Hansen** - The bizarro, heartwarming, magical tale of poor planning, hubris and severe blood loss... **150 pages $11**

BB-056 **"Piecemeal June" Jordan Krall** - A man falls in love with a living sex doll, but with love comes danger when her creator comes after her with crab-squid assassins. **90 pages $9**

BB-058 **"The Overwhelming Urge" Andersen Prunty** - A collection of bizarro tales by Andersen Prunty. **150 pages $11**

BB-059 **"Adolf in Wonderland" Carlton Mellick III** - A dreamlike adventure that takes a young descendant of Adolf Hitler's design and sends him down the rabbit hole into a world of imperfection and disorder. **180 pages $11**

BB-061 **"Ultra Fuckers" Carlton Mellick III** - Absurdist suburban horror about a couple who enter an upper middle class gated community but can't find their way out. **108 pages $9**

BB-062 **"House of Houses" Kevin L. Donihe** - An odd man wants to marry his house. Unfortunately, all of the houses in the world collapse at the same time in the Great House Holocaust. Now he must travel to House Heaven to find his departed fiancee. **172 pages $11**

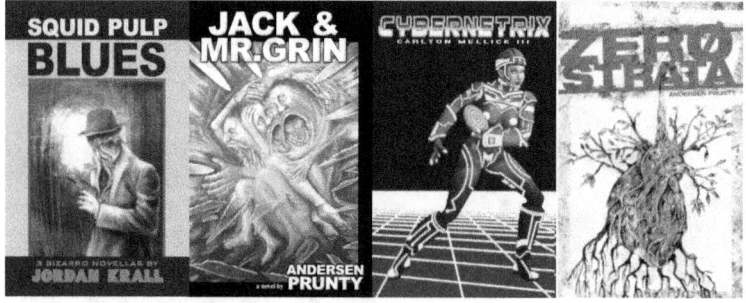

BB-064 **"Squid Pulp Blues" Jordan Krall** - In these three bizarro-noir novellas, the reader is thrown into a world of murderers, drugs made from squid parts, deformed gun-toting veterans, and a mischievous apocalyptic donkey. **204 pages $12**

BB-065 **"Jack and Mr. Grin" Andersen Prunty** - "When Mr. Grin calls you can hear a smile in his voice. Not a warm and friendly smile, but the kind that seizes your spine in fear. You don't need to pay your phone bill to hear it. That smile is in every line of Prunty's prose." - Tom Bradley. **208 pages $12**

BB-066 **"Cybernetrix" Carlton Mellick III** - What would you do if your normal everyday world was slowly mutating into the video game world from Tron? **212 pages $12**

BB-072 **"Zerostrata" Andersen Prunty** - Hansel Nothing lives in a tree house, suffers from memory loss, has a very eccentric family, and falls in love with a woman who runs naked through the woods every night. **144 pages $11**

BB-073 "The Egg Man" Carlton Mellick III - It is a world where humans reproduce like insects. Children are the property of corporations, and having an enormous ten-foot brain implanted into your skull is a grotesque sexual fetish. Mellick's industrial urban dystopia is one of his darkest and grittiest to date. 184 pages $11

BB-074 "Shark Hunting in Paradise Garden" Cameron Pierce - A group of strange humanoid religious fanatics travel back in time to the Garden of Eden to discover it is invested with hundreds of giant flying maneating sharks. 150 pages $10

BB-075 "Apeshit" Carlton Mellick III - Friday the 13th meets Visitor Q. Six hipster teens go to a cabin in the woods inhabited by a deformed killer. An incredibly fucked-up parody of B-horror movies with a bizarro slant. 192 pages $12

BB-076 "Fuckers of Everything on the Crazy Shitting Planet of the Vomit At mosphere" Mykle Hansen - Three bizarro satires. Monster Cocks, Journey to the Center of Agnes Cuddlebottom, and Crazy Shitting Planet. 228 pages $12

BB-077 "The Kissing Bug" Daniel Scott Buck - In the tradition of Roald Dahl, Tim Burton, and Edward Gorey, comes this bizarro anti-war children's story about a bohemian conenose kissing bug who falls in love with a human woman. 116 pages $10

BB-078 "MachoPoni" Lotus Rose - It's My Little Pony... *Bizarro* style! A long time ago Poniworld was split in two. On one side of the Jagged Line is the Pastel Kingdom, a magical land of music, parties, and positivity. On the other side of the Jagged Line is Dark Kingdom inhabited by an army of undead ponies. 148 pages $11

BB-079 "The Faggiest Vampire" Carlton Mellick III - A Roald Dahl-esque children's story about two faggy vampires who partake in a mustache competition to find out which one is truly the faggiest. 104 pages $10

BB-080 "Sky Tongues" Gina Ranalli - The autobiography of Sky Tongues, the biracial hermaphrodite actress with tongues for fingers. Follow her strange life story as she rises from freak to fame. 204 pages $12

BB-081 **"Washer Mouth" Kevin L. Donihe** - A washing machine becomes human and pursues his dream of meeting his favorite soap opera star. **244 pages $11**

BB-082 **"Shatnerquake" Jeff Burk** - All of the characters ever played by William Shatner are suddenly sucked into our world. Their mission: hunt down and destroy the real William Shatner. **100 pages $10**

BB-083 **"The Cannibals of Candyland" Carlton Mellick III** - There exists a race of cannibals that are made of candy. They live in an underground world made out of candy. One man has dedicated his life to killing them all. **170 pages $11**

BB-084 **"Slub Glub in the Weird World of the Weeping Willows" Andrew Goldfarb** - The charming tale of a blue glob named Slub Glub who helps the weeping willows whose tears are flooding the earth. There are also hyenas, ghosts, and a voodoo priest **100 pages $10**

BB-085 **"Super Fetus" Adam Pepper** - Try to abort this fetus and he'll kick your ass! **104 pages $10**

BB-086 **"Fistful of Feet" Jordan Krall** - A bizarro tribute to spaghetti westerns, featuring Cthulhu-worshipping Indians, a woman with four feet, a crazed gunman who is obsessed with sucking on candy, Syphilis-ridden mutants, sexually transmitted tattoos, and a house devoted to the freakiest fetishes. **228 pages $12**

BB-087 **"Ass Goblins of Auschwitz" Cameron Pierce** - It's Monty Python meets Nazi exploitation in a surreal nightmare as can only be imagined by Bizarro author Cameron Pierce. **104 pages $10**

BB-088 **"Silent Weapons for Quiet Wars" Cody Goodfellow** - "This is high-end psychological surrealist horror meets bottom-feeding low-life crime in a techno-thrilling science fiction world full of Lovecraft and magic..." -John Skipp **212 pages $12**

BB-089 **"Warrior Wolf Women of the Wasteland" Carlton Mellick III**
Road Warrior Werewolves versus McDonaldland Mutants...post-apocalyptic fiction has never been quite like this. **316 pages $13**

BB-090 **"Cursed" Jeremy C Shipp** - The story of a group of characters who believe they are cursed and attempt to figure out who cursed them and why. A tale of stylish absurdism and suspenseful horror. **218 pages $15**

BB-091 **"Super Giant Monster Time" Jeff Burk** - A tribute to choose your own adventures and Godzilla movies. Will you escape the giant monsters that are rampaging the fuck out of your city and shit? Or will you join the mob of alien-controlled punk rockers causing chaos in the streets? What happens next depends on you. **188 pages $12**

BB-092 **"Perfect Union" Cody Goodfellow** - "Cronenberg's THE FLY on a grand scale: human/insect gene-spliced body horror, where the human hive politics are as shocking as the gore." -John Skipp. **272 pages $13**

BB-093 **"Sunset with a Beard" Carlton Mellick III** - 14 stories of surreal science fiction. **200 pages $12**

BB-094 **"My Fake War" Andersen Prunty** - The absurd tale of an unlikely soldier forced to fight a war that, quite possibly, does not exist. It's Rambo meets Waiting for Godot in this subversive satire of American values and the scope of the human imagination. **128 pages $11**

BB-095 **"Lost in Cat Brain Land" Cameron Pierce** - Sad stories from a sur-real world. A fascist mustache, the ghost of Franz Kafka, a desert inside a dead cat. Primor-dial entities mourn the death of their child. The desperate serve tea to mysterious creatures.
A hopeless romantic falls in love with a pterodactyl. And much more. **152 pages $11**

BB-096 **"The Kobold Wizard's Dildo of Enlightenment +2" Carlton Mellick III** - A Dungeons and Dragons parody about a group of people who learn they are only made up characters in an AD&D campaign and must find a way to resist their nerdy teenaged players and retarded dungeon master in order to survive. 232 **pages $12**

BB-097 **"My Heart Said No, but the Camera Crew Said Yes!" Bradley Sands** - A collection of short stories that are crammed with the delightfully odd and the scurrilously silly. **140 pages $13**

BB-098 **"A Hundred Horrible Sorrows of Ogner Stump" Andrew Goldfarb** - Goldfarb's acclaimed comic series. A magical and weird journey into the horrors of everyday life. **164 pages $11**

BB-099 **"Pickled Apocalypse of Pancake Island" Cameron Pierce** A demented fairy tale about a pickle, a pancake, and the apocalypse. **102 pages $8**

BB-100 **"Slag Attack" Andersen Prunty** - Slag Attack features four visceral, noir stories about the living, crawling apocalypse.A slag is what survivors are calling the slug-like maggots raining from the sky, burrowing inside people, and hollowing out their flesh and their sanity. **148 pages $11**

BB-101 **"Slaughterhouse High" Robert Devereaux** - A place where schools are built with secret passageways, rebellious teens get zippers installed in their mouths and genitals, and once a year, on that special night, one couple is slaughtered and the bits of their bodies are kept as souvenirs. **304 pages $13**

BB-102 **"The Emerald Burrito of Oz" John Skipp & Marc Levinthal** OZ IS REAL! Magic is real! The gate is really in Kansas! And America is finally allowing Earth tourists to visit this weird-ass, mysterious land. But when Gene of Los Angeles heads off for summer vacation in the Emerald City, little does he know that a war is brewing...a war that could destroy both worlds. **280 pages $13**

BB-103 **"The Vegan Revolution... with Zombies" David Agranoff** When there's no more meat in hell, the vegans will walk the earth. **160 pages $11**

BB-104 **"The Flappy Parts" Kevin L Donihe** - Poems about bunnies, LSD, and police abuse. You know, things that matter. 132 **pages $11**

BB-105 **"Sorry I Ruined Your Orgy" Bradley Sands** - Bizarro humorist Bradley Sands returns with one of the strangest, most hilarious collections of the year. **130 pages $11**

BB-106 **"Mr. Magic Realism" Bruce Taylor** - Like Golden Age science fiction comics written by Freud, *Mr. Magic Realism* is a strange, insightful adventure that spans the furthest reaches of the galaxy, exploring the hidden caverns in the hearts and minds of men, women, aliens, and biomechanical cats. **152 pages $11**

BB-107 **"Zombies and Shit" Carlton Mellick III** - "Battle Royale" meets "Return of the Living Dead." Mellick's bizarro tribute to the zombie genre. **308 pages $13**

BB-108 **"The Cannibal's Guide to Ethical Living" Mykle Hansen** - Over a five star French meal of fine wine, organic vegetables and human flesh, a lunatic delivers a witty, chilling, disturbingly sane argument in favor of eating the rich.. **184 pages $11**

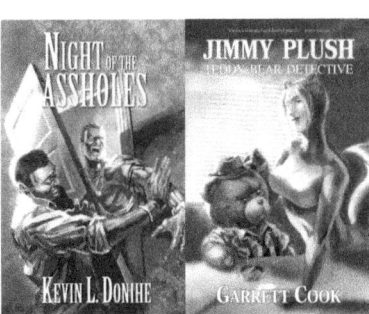

BB-109 **"Starfish Girl" Athena Villaverde** - In a post-apocalyptic underwater dome society, a girl with a starfish growing from her head and an assassin with sea anenome hair are on the run from a gang of mutant fish men. **160 pages $11**

BB-110 **"Lick Your Neighbor" Chris Genoa** - Mutant ninjas, a talking whale, kung fu masters, maniacal pilgrims, and an alcoholic clown populate Chris Genoa's surreal, darkly comical and unnerving reimagining of the first Thanksgiving. **303 pages $13**

BB-111 **"Night of the Assholes" Kevin L. Donihe** - A plague of assholes is infecting the countryside. Normal everyday people are transforming into jerks, snobs, dicks, and douchebags. And they all have only one purpose: to make your life a living hell.. **192 pages $11**

BB-112 **"Jimmy Plush, Teddy Bear Detective" Garrett Cook** - Hardboiled cases of a private detective trapped within a teddy bear body. **180 pages $11**

www.ingramcontent.com/pod-product-compliance
Lightning Source LLC
Chambersburg PA
CBHW052020020726
47501CB00004B/1149